THE BOY WHO TOOK
MARILYN
TO THE PROM

A NOVEL

HENRY MASSIE

◩ ARCHWAY
PUBLISHING

Archway Publishing books may be ordered through booksellers or by contacting:

Archway Publishing
1663 Liberty Drive
Bloomington, IN 47403
www.archwaypublishing.com
844-669-3957

ISBN: 978-1-6657-0364-2 (sc)
ISBN: 978-1-6657-0365-9 (hc)
ISBN: 978-1-6657-0363-5 (e)

Library of Congress Control Number: 2021904123

Printed in the United States of America.

Archway Publishing rev. date: 7/12/2021

For Bridget, Kate and Felice, my true experts, with love.

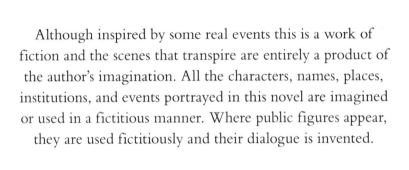

But if I could step outside myself and contemplate the person that I am …
—Anna Akhmatova

CONTENTS

PART 1   FIRST CONFESSION

One 1

Two 14

Three 24

Four 57

Five 76

PART 2   PROM NIGHT

Six 87

Seven 108

PART 3   AFTERMATH

Eight 127

Nine 141

Ten 147

Eleven 158

Twelve 170

PART 4   THE TRIAL

Thirteen 191

Fourteen 202

Fifteen 224

Sixteen 237

Seventeen..249
Eighteen...263
Epilogue..275

Acknowledgments...287
About the Author...289

PART 1
FIRST CONFESSION

CHAPTER
ONE

"I've slept with a patient." I stared at the phone in my hand as if it were lying to me. Robbie Carosso, noted psychotherapist, educator, and my best friend since childhood, was telling me the unfathomable. He stammered, "She thought we were going to get married."

"You had sex with a patient?"

"Yes, Eli. That's what I said. You've got to help me." Robbie was gasping for breath now, hyperventilating.

"I can't believe it." Robbie was one of the most eminent psychiatrists in the San Francisco Bay Area. He lived and practiced in Palo Alto, just off the Stanford campus. "Was it consensual?" I threw back at him, trying to get the lay of the land, to break through his panic.

"Yes, it was consensual. Do you think I'd rape someone?"

"Shrinks are supposed to know better."

Still panting, he stammered, "I knew better. It didn't help."

I stood up from my desk and started pacing slowly with the phone in my hand. It was a trick I used to calm clients—gather my thoughts while walking and ease their desperation at the same time. Outside the bay window of my law office, the late-afternoon sun was catching the golden dome of San Francisco's City Hall. I turned to the wall of legal books behind my desk, all bound with gold on red lettering, marching across the room, an army of legal precedents. I was already wondering which volumes I'd consult to defend Robbie—if it came to that.

"Robbie, take some slow breaths."

Still struggling for air, Robbie managed to say, "It ended a year ago. It was all in my office. Not like an affair."

"Then what do you call it?"

"A mistake."

"How could you be so stupid?" I hissed.

"It's never happened before. It was an aberration. I've never done anything like that with any other patient. It has nothing to do with Madeleine. I love her." Madeleine was Robbie Carosso's wife, a Palo Alto pediatrician. "The patient looked like Marilyn." Robbie's voice caught. He couldn't go on.

Gently I urged him on. "Surely you've had pretty women in your office before, on your couch. Why this one? Why now? I assume she was pretty."

"She wasn't even pretty when she came to see me. She was dowdy, really sad, and depressed. Kind of mousy, fair hair. Not even blonde."

"Okay. We have to talk. Can you come to my office tomorrow?

"Can't we meet today? The woman is suing me for more than you can imagine. She wants a million dollars for each time we fucked, which as it happened was about twice a week for two months. She's got me by the balls. If she wins, I'm going to lose everything. I will never be whole again. I will be *totally screwed*." His last words came out in an agonized sigh.

"Okay. I have one more client to see in the office. Come

to the house this evening. We'll have it to ourselves tonight. Get some dinner and start talking. Wait until the traffic dies down." Even then it would take him forty-five minutes to drive up from the Peninsula.

But who was Marilyn? He hung up, and I started putting the pieces together. Then it came to me: of course, Marilyn Monroe. But that was forty-six years ago, when Robbie and I were seniors at Hollywood High School in Los Angeles. And this was 2007. He and I were in our early sixties now. Suddenly like a film rewinding at high speed, I saw it all again, Robbie with Marilyn on his arm at our senior prom in 1961, a year before her death. He was seventeen, and she was thirty-five, looking no older than a college coed.

That spring, Marilyn had practically moved into Robbie's house because his father, Abel Carosso, a distinguished Hollywood psychiatrist and psychoanalyst, and Marilyn's last psychotherapist, was trying to give the actress a family life she never had. It was his unconventional attempt to save her from a downward spiral of anxiety, drinking, and tranquilizers. That spring the actress had therapy sessions with Dr. Carosso five times a week in his home office. She could stay overnight in the studio by the pool whenever she wanted, and she often took meals with the family.

Robbie had told me that one night over dinner, his dad said to Robbie and Marilyn, "Why don't the two of you go together to Robbie's senior prom? Marilyn has never had such an experience."

In fact, Marilyn had never graduated from high school. The actress smiled in her special pleasure-giving way and said, "I'd like that." Robbie was elated. He liked standing out. He was class valedictorian, princely handsome, and poised beyond his years, yet in an oddly stiff way that was both winning and made me feel protective of him. Marilyn on his arm would be another medal on his chest.

Robbie's mother, Anna, a still photographer on movie sets and a charity fundraiser, squeezed her eyes closed for a second. Then she asked her husband, "Are you sure it's okay?"

But Abel, who had steadied the lives of many people in the film industry, reassured her, "They will both get something out of it."

Anna deferred to her husband.

I started thinking about things I hadn't thought about for a long time. We were just teenagers back when Robbie's dad started treating Marilyn, and there should have been no reason to try to understand most of what happened around us. We were expected to just go with the flow. Except the whole Marilyn thing, the prom and the mystery of what actually transpired had bothered me then, and I still vaguely wondered about it in a once-in-a-while absentminded way.

I needed to sort out my memories to try to make sense of Robbie's legal dilemma.

After minutes of hard thinking, I understood that there must have been more to Robbie's father inviting Marilyn to join the family. There was more behind his trying to rescue her with his unorthodox treatment. There must have been an erotic attraction to her that was driving him. Abel Carosso was probably besotted by her, probably captivated by her beauty as so many others before him, though he had likely never admitted it to himself. He lived in a world of celebrity; we all did back then, buffeted by it each in our own way. Had Robbie's father been more aware of fame's effect on him, he probably would have kept better professional boundaries.

I remembered Dr. Carosso as a very nice person who always stopped to chat with us when we were at Robbie's house. He was tall and handsome like Robbie. He had a gentle manner, deep eyes, and strong, dark eyebrows. Even though we were kids, he took us seriously as people. He cared about people and probably was a damn good doctor. Robbie's dad served on the faculty of Los Angeles University Medical School, training other psychiatrists and psychoanalysts, and he'd authored several books and articles. Robbie told me his father had written about how therapists are tempted to relax professional boundaries with wealthy, famous, and important patients who are used to having their own way and special privileges. In one article, Abel described how doctors were tempted to rub shoulders with famous patients in real life. Away from the office, they wished that some of their glamour would rub off on them. Robbie's dad warned psychiatrists against thinking they could rescue a patient in deep trouble. It was okay to *try* to rescue a patient, he wrote, but not to believe one is so skilled or gifted that he or she were going to succeed. That would be grandiosity, which is dangerous to a therapist's integrity and more than useless to the patient. I remembered that advice and pinched myself with it when I took on a hard legal defense. I can't always rescue a client.

Abel's patient, Marilyn, touched our worlds for a time. She had ascended from virtual orphanhood to the pinnacle of success. At the time of her young death in 1962, she was the most famous woman in the world. She had been the wife of America's most famous athlete, Joe DiMaggio. After their divorce, she became the wife of America's most famous intellectual, the writer Arthur Miller. It was the rubbing shoulders motif again. Miller wrote in his autobiography that he hoped that some of Marilyn's youth and public effervescence would rub off on him, and she hoped some of Arthur's wisdom would become hers. It didn't work. And if that weren't enough, after Marilyn and Arthur separated, she became the consort of Bobby and Jack Kennedy. Now, five decades after her death and in a new millennium, Marilyn's pictures still adorn the walls of bars, boutiques, restaurants, airport concourses, magazine covers, books, and museums. Her image is still used to peddle liquor, food, clothes, publications, and art. Her life has become a symbol of how—even a person completely bereft of family— can attain success, the perils of achieving it, and how easily it can all become lost.

Marilyn's eyes—their vulnerability—must have ensnared Robbie's dad. They ensnared all of us when we were in high school. I figured there weren't too many psychiatrists out there who were immune to the silent appeal of a beautiful woman with sad eyes. Trying to make her smile was probably what a lot of shrinks lived for.

Now it had become Robbie's turn to fall for such a woman, and he was looking for me to save him. If the lawsuit against him came down to a jury trial, maybe I could convince the jurors that Robbie was innocent because he was a minor when his father thrust him into the actress's life. The real guilty parties were his parents who let Marilyn into their home with the teenage boy, and that caused him to go astray with the patient suing him. That, or some other argument I'd come up with when a trial got closer. There's a legal truism that it is not the truth that counts; it's what the jury believes is the truth. I've convinced juries of more preposterous arguments than Robbie's innocence.

My last client of the day wasn't going to need anything quite as preposterous to save his skin; his case was going to take work rather than creativity. Aaron Aldenbrand was an anthropology professor at Berkeley whom a student had charged with harassing him and interfering with his progression toward graduation. The professor had developed a new computer-assisted method to predict the future of a relationship between two people— lovers, coworkers, and even adversaries, for example. Based on an analysis of films of two people talking together on a park bench, the professor could accurately predict what their relationship would be like in five years. He and his computer looked at the pattern of the eye movements of two people sitting together to and away from each other, how close were they sitting, their hand movements, and how their bodies inclined to and away from each other. His research also registered the tone of their voices and who frowned, smiled, angered, or showed no expression from moment to moment. He called his instrument the Signs of Love Scale, and it was making a big splash academically, in business, and in the military.

As Aldenbrand described it to me, he had mentored the grad student and even invited him to his home where they had worked over the kitchen table a few times. He now chaired the grad student's doctoral dissertation committee, the dissertation itself being an application of Aldenbrand's Signs of Life Scale. It was the last hurdle the student had to pass before receiving his doctorate.

According to our professor, he read a draft of the dissertation and found that the student hadn't given references to the professor's publications. In a meeting in his office, Aldenbrand harshly told the student that he was plagiarizing because he hadn't cited Aldenbrand as the originator of the scale.

Completely caught by surprise, feeling shamed and

misunderstood, the student struck back. He said that he hadn't completed the reference section of the dissertation and filed a complaint with the dean that the professor was harassing him and blocking his advancement toward a PhD. He wanted to remove the professor from his dissertation committee. Ordinarily there were procedures for handling this kind of conflict, but they didn't take into consideration that the professor was being evaluated for tenure at the same time, a great honor and lifetime position with the university. Getting tenure should have been a slam-dunk approval given the professor's fine record, but a harassment charge could derail the tenure promotion and his future completely. The professor was afraid the university wouldn't take his side in the conflict, and he wanted me to protect him.

I had my investigator, Julia, sit in with me and the professor. She was three years out of law school and not ready to closet herself with books for six months to study for the Bar exam, so she had chosen to learn the underside of law by working as the firm's detective, so to speak. Some investigators were tough guys; Julia was a pretty, young woman, lean and fit as could be. Sometimes she worked in jeans, a hoodie, and running shoes when her detective-type chores took her there; sometimes in tailored clothes. Today her costume was the skirt, blazer, and low heels of a graduate student.

"Where do things stand with the harassment accusation?" I asked Aldenbrand.

The poor man, about forty, soft-bodied, bespectacled, and balding too soon in life, was almost trembling. He couldn't stop his leg from moving, and his foot kept knocking against our conference table and making it vibrate. His future was in the balance. He could hardly get his words out. He beat around the bush before finally answering my question. "The dean of social sciences has appointed a professor to act as an investigator and look into the charges. They are taking it seriously when all I was doing was trying to maintain academic standards. That is what I'm supposed to do, isn't it, maintain standards?" Aldenbrand's voice started to rise in an angry whine. He would make a terrible witness in his own behalf if I had to put him on the stand.

"Calm down. What kind of person is the investigator?"

"She is a professor of Renaissance art, from the humanities. She has a reputation for being meticulous in everything she does, whether in her scholarship or chairing faculty committees."

"Tell me how she thinks." Again Aldenbrand beat around the bush, defining thinking. "Please answer the question."

"Actually, she's a conformist and follows the rules. That's all I've heard about her; we've never met. Maybe that's why the dean chose her to investigate the harassment charge."

"We need the names of some of your other students and some of your colleagues. Julia will pretend she is a student who is thinking about taking your courses and studying with you; she will talk with the people whose names you give us. We need to get an idea of what the university investigator is going to find out. Julia will also talk with the graduate student who has filed charges with you and get his side of the story."

Julia was nodding, eager to get started. The professor's foot stopped tapping; he had some hope. It was curious to have a case similar to Robbie's in the sense that they were both about hurt feelings: a therapist getting too intimate with a patient and a teacher getting too close to a student. In each case, the older person had put distance between himself and the younger person—the professor by questioning his student about references and Robbie by disappointing his lover. Hurt feelings had erupted.

In cases like this, sometimes the younger person starts feeling too big for his or her britches, too self-important, and forgets that the mentor also has feelings. Either way, all hell breaks loose. It's about narcissism, self-esteem, people with too much self-regard, and others with too little self-esteem. The anger unleashed when feelings get hurt and the damage it causes have brought a lot of clients to my office over the years. Whether the accused is innocent or guilty, he or she still needs help. Maybe two cases like this at the same time would shed light on something new.

It was 6 p.m. and I locked up. I descended the long flight of stairs from the second-floor flat that was my law office. It was in an old Victorian house that had been built in late nineteenth century as a family home, spared in the 1906 earthquake, and had become three flats of very fine offices. Sometimes the brightly painted wooden sunburst in the gable smiled at the end of the day. Today when I glanced at it, it frowned back. I walked down Hayes Street, across Van Ness, past City Hall to the Civic Center Plaza, and retrieved my car from the garage beneath it. Dusk had already arrived this October evening, lights were coming on, and traffic eased as I crossed to south of Market Street, the great dividing line in San Francisco. Glittering department stores, expensive hotels, and high-rise glass and steel office buildings straddled Market as the street descended gradually from hills to the bay. Most San Franciscans lived in the neighborhoods of homes and apartments that stretched northwest to the Pacific Ocean.

Just south of Market spread skid row with people huddling alone or in small groups to escape their single-room occupancy flophouses, wondering where their next meal or drink would come from. I continued south on Fifth Street under the freeway coming off the Bay Bridge. This is where people lived who were even worse off than the folks on skid row. They were squirreled under blankets and tarps. They couldn't take care of themselves now, and most never would be able to, let alone afford to rent a room.

My wife and I lived on Twenty-Fifth Street facing Garfield Square, a plot of children's playgrounds deep in the Mission District, San Francisco's oldest neighborhood untouched by the earthquake and fire. It was a mix of ancient wooden homes divided into inexpensive apartments, warehouses, and light industry. Our home was a former printing company driven out of business by the internet and digital printing. We had put in wooden floors and turned the front reception area and business office into our living room and kitchen area, the stock rooms into bedrooms and a study, and a vaulted space in the rear into my wife's workshop.

I parked my old sedan, the kind of car that doesn't get tampered with, at the loading dock. Since my wife was away on a business trip, I walked to the Pacific Mambo Club on the corner and picked up a takeout dinner of grilled fish, rice, and beans. Just as I returned, Robbie arrived and pulled his Mustang up next to my car. Robbie had changed, not gently. The last time I had seen him a month earlier, he was still fair-haired at sixty-three, tall, tanned, and patrician, but now his skin was ashen with apprehension, his hair graying, and his shoulders sagged. Instead of the usual trim sport coat, slacks, and shirt he wore when he came to San Francisco, he wore oil-smudged, torn jeans and an ancient Stanford fraternity sweatshirt with holes in it.

He saw me taking stock of him. "I've been living on my fucking boat in Half Moon Bay for two weeks. It's not as if

Madeleine kicked me out, but she and I can't talk; we can't even look at each other. I told her what happened with the patient and it's there every second we are in each other's space, so I packed some clothes and left. I drive over the hills from the harbor to Palo Alto a couple of days each week to see patients in my office. Patients, ha!" he spat out self-derisively. "I'm not a doctor anymore. They suspended my license so they're not patients. They're clients. I can still do something called lifestyle coaching—no meds, no license needed. It means giving advice; anybody can do it. Free speech, you know."

I made a stab at lightening his self-derogation. "You're not anybody. Your advice is backed by college, four years of med school, and three years of psychiatry residency. Right?"

"And more. You got it," he answered sardonically. "Who cares? Sometimes even people with no education do lifestyle coaching, have talent, and give great advice. Mostly it means the blind leading the blind, like me. I came clean with Maddie. I came clean with my patients about what happened, and some must have felt I was helping them enough to stick with me. Or maybe they felt too sorry for me to quit."

I brought out a bottle of Scotch, glasses, ice, and water and laid out the dinner cartons on the battered, stained, low, oak table that sat between two leather couches. Robbie took his Scotch neat, water on the side, and I liked mine in a tumbler filled with ice. With our first sips, tension eased a bit more. Even though some color came back to his face, the room was still morose with regret.

Robbie explained that he'd received a notice from the California Medical Regulatory Board two weeks earlier telling him that a patient had reported him for a credible, severe boundary violation and he was under investigation. Pending the outcome of the investigation, they had suspended his license to practice medicine. He had been too ashamed to tell me until he'd received the letter yesterday from his former patient's lawyer notifying him that he was being sued for a huge amount of money.

"Will you come with me to the regulatory board hearing in Sacramento?"

"Of course, man. Tell me everything. Take your time."

"Here it is. Here's the whole story." Robbie slammed a manila folder down so hard on the table that sheets of yellow paper with his handwritten notes spilled out. "It's yours."

"No, tell me everything that happened, slowly, as long as it takes; I want to hear your voice." I wanted to get a sense of what kind of impression he'd make if he testified in court. "I'll interrupt sometimes as you go. If we don't finish tonight, we'll continue here, in my office, on your boat, or wherever. Don't hold anything back."

CHAPTER
TWO

Robbie and I had never held anything back when we were together, from the time we met in sixth grade in Franklin Middle School on Franklin Avenue in Hollywood. What drew us together was that we were both smart—Robbie whiplash so—and could bounce facts off each for fun and competition. And we were both good athletes.

My mother fueled competition between us by saying to me now and then, "Why can't you be more like Robbie?" it was more a demand than a question. She meant why couldn't I dress like him with my shirt always tucked in and my hair combed—as if I could comb my stiff, curly, red hair and make it look proper like his, which was always well-trimmed. She wanted me to always speak politely to my teachers and give them just the right words of appreciation, the way Robbie did in his kind of formal, practiced way when there were special occasions at school. Dr. Carosso also fueled our competition when he told Robbie to be rougher on the soccer field, "Hey, son, use your elbows like Eli does. A penalty here and there isn't going to hurt you."

We studied each other—gait, dress, speech, mannerisms—
me thinking that I would be perfect if I was as self-assured as
he was and had his patience and poise, and Robbie wishing
he could be more unbuttoned and blunt as me. We traded
encouragement like "Hey Robbie, go for it" and "Eli, cool it."

Robbie lived in a large, mock Tudor-style house a few blocks
up from the bottom of Beachwood Canyon in Hollywood,
and I lived nearby before my family moved to Beverly Hills,
where it was flatter and seemingly more settled. Beachwood
was one of the first Los Angeles canyons to be tamed with
home building, if one doesn't count summer grass fires in
the hills above and winter rain torrents cascading down the
street. Movie stars, producers, and directors started building
on Beachwood in the 1920s when movies became big, and so
far, the neighborhood had escaped major calamities. In middle
school, I often went home with Robbie after school to indulge
in one of our favorite pastimes: racing our bikes from the top
of Beachwood Drive to Robbie's house at the bottom. We'd
push our bicycles uphill past other Tudor houses then up past
modern, misshapen homes made from glass, steel, and concrete
on stilts and cantilevering out from the sides of the canyon, then
past vacant lots waiting to be built upon. After more than an
hour of sweaty work, we'd reach the place where Beachwood
Drive petered out at a falling down chain-link fence. Above
was the summit of Mt. Lee at the southern end of the Santa
Monica Hills.

We left our bikes at the fence and hiked up a long hill of
golden, waving grass that gave way to stubble and scree. After
a couple of hundred yards, we'd reached our goal—the great,
huge letters spelling "HOLLYWOOD."

One time as we took the last few steps, we saw a shadow on the hillside moving back and forth beneath the Y. I yelled, "See that!"

"Something swinging from the sign," Robbie answered.

"A body," I blurted out.

"Dead body my butt. It's a shadow."

"I'll throw a stone. See what happens." I picked up a fist-size rock and nailed the shadow with my throw. Nothing happened.

"It's Peg's ghost. That's what it is!" Robbie exclaimed.

"You're seeing things. There's nothing there."

However we weren't sure. We knew the Peg Entwistle story about the actress who hanged herself from the Hollywood sign way back in 1932 when it said, "HOLLYWOODLAND." People said her ghost visited this place. Maybe it was visiting this day. We pretended to quail with fear for a moment then raced the last ten yards to the top.

As usual the place was barren, silent except for the sign and moan of the wind coursing through the huge Hollywoodland letters. Nothing had changed since last time. Each letter, large as a car, was cut from a great big sheet of corrugated steel and bolted to rusted metal girders fixed into the ground. Some of the girders were working loose, their concrete bases cracking into pieces. You could kick at them and the letters they were tethering shook. It seemed like the next big wind or little earthquake might bring them down, yet there they were casting their spell over everything below.

Sweating, we sat down with our backs against a letter, took swigs of water from our Boy Scout canteens, and munched candy bars. "How do you think Peg did it?" Robbie murmured.

"I bet from one of the trusses in back. She climbed up the braces and threw a rope over a higher one, climbed back to a lower brace, put the noose around her neck, and stepped off into space. Only way. Logic," I announced.

"Or maybe she climbed to the top of a letter to jump off. Maybe she didn't really want to die, got up there, and changed her mind but lost her balance, fell off, and broke her neck. My dad says a lot of people start to kill themselves then change their mind when it's too late."

"Which letter?"

"D for death."

"H for hell," I said.

"Maybe she didn't use a rope. She could have had a long scarf or something like that in her car and used that for a noose. I bet she drove to the top of Griffith Park, walked down to the sign, or slipped and broke her neck falling down the hill."

"No. She was visiting her uncle who lived on Beachwood and walked up just like us. Her uncle was a talent agent."

"Why do you think she did it?" I asked Robbie out of deference to all the things he already knew about psychology because of his father.

"She was sad."

"About what?"

"Her life sucked. My dad told me. Her mother died when she was younger than we are. Then her stepmother died. Then her father was hit by a car and killed when she was fourteen. Her uncle raised her after that. She was in a play in LA called *Mad Hopes* that got bad reviews and didn't last very long. It closed three months before she killed herself."

"Did she leave a suicide note?"

"Yeah. My dad showed me a copy from the newspaper article." Robbie recited it from memory. 'I'm a coward. I'm sorry for everything. If I had done this a long time ago, it would have saved everybody a lot of pain.'"

"Wow. Downer."

"A woman out hiking found her body and took her shoes and purse to the door of the police station and left them there. Then she called the cops from a pay phone and told them where the body was."

"I wonder what *her* story was," I offered, ready to jump into a new mystery.

"Nobody ever found out. She disappeared."

I continued to wonder about Peg Entwistle. "Lots of people have bad things happen and they bounce back. My father does legal work with lots of people who think they are getting screwed this way or that. He says he leaves no stone unturned and gets all the facts. If you know more than the other side, you can win almost any case."

"My dad says it's about feelings. Facts and feelings don't always fit together. He says the actress's life is a cautionary tale."

"What's a cautionary tale?"

"I'm not sure," Robbie answered. We stared at our shoes for a time then shifted our gaze to our realm of golden grass below. And beyond that, big homes, swimming pools, people lounging by them tiny as play figures, a gardener mowing or clipping here and there, and the hot tubs like blue dots. Past Beachwood were the flats—an endless stretch of stucco bungalows, cars like crawling insects, and tall apartments and office buildings poking up occasionally from the flatness. Off in the distance to the right were the large lawns and big, white houses of Beverly Hills. We were looking down on and through the layer of smog that often hung like a sepia blanket over the LA basin in those years. Where the smog left off in the far distance, I saw a strip of milky-white and blue Pacific Ocean on the horizon. In the distance, I imagined seeing my name in a bold newspaper headline that said, "Famed Lawyer Wins Case."

Robbie said, "Someday I'm going to have my own boat and sail across the ocean like Sterling Hayden."

Hayden, an actor, was one of Anna Carosso's frequent guests at their swimming pool. He had an unshaven face that looked like chisels had cut it from a block of wood and scraped it with coarse sandpaper. He walked with long, loose strides and chatted Robbie up with an open invitation. "Hey, kid, come and crew with me sometime."

We sat for awhile and the breeze picked up. The big sign sighed.

"Peg's ghost?" Warning us?" I said.

"Of what?" Robbie answered, pretending to quail.

"Who knows," I said. Neither of us were really scared; we were grinning.

Suddenly I gave the signal. "No fear, man." We leaped up and charged down the hill to the chain-link fence and our bikes. Then we were flying as free as could be, in and out of the curves, tapping our coaster brakes lightly as we approached the curves, then leaning our bikes way over so that our knees were almost scraping the macadam, and pedaling furiously to regain speed and balance coming out of the bend. Some moments I was a length ahead, and some moments Robbie pulled into the lead up and down the rises. Twice we hit patches of gravel on the road and our wheels started to slide out from under us, but we attacked the pedals even harder and righted ourselves.

We screeched our fat balloon tires to a halt at Robbie's house. It looked like it had been transported from England with leaded windows, a slate roof with twin peaks and gables, and walls of half timbers and stone. Actually the stone was plaster, a good Los Angeles copy. We'd loop around the house through the side garden to the backyard and duck into a dressing room to put on our swimming suits. The pool itself was circled by a paved walk with grass beyond that, and on the sides of the yard, plantings completely covered the fences so no other homes were visible. There was a cabana or studio at the rear of the yard, which abutted the steep, ivy-covered wall of Beachwood Canyon, sealing off the yard from neighbors. As soon as we emerged from the dressing room, Mrs. Carosso would greet us as gaily as Doris Day doing a television commercial for Chevrolet—fair, smiling, gracious, and slim. Her words rolled smoothly off her tongue. "Would you boys like anything? There's iced tea, lemonade, root beer, chips. The refrigerator is so full I can hardly get in to get anything out. If there's something you want, help yourselves."

Another actor often visiting at the Carosso pool who made a lasting impression on us was Janice Rule. She was in her thirties, tall and willowy, self-possessed, and successful. She had left home to start out in show business when she was seventeen as a dancer in a nightclub show. After swimming, Janice put her hair up in white-towel turban and liked to talk seriously with us. One day she asked me what my father did. When I told her that he was a lawyer at Paramount, she said, "That's good. He has a real job. We actors are different, you know; we're like chameleons. We change with our roles and change who we are.

"We start thinking we are the people we pretend to be for the cameras. We forget who we've been and where we came from. If a writer hasn't given us a person to be, if a director hasn't told us how to act, if a costume designer hasn't given us clothes to wear, a lot of us feel like we're going to turn into dust and blow away. We need an audience or we're nothing."

"Why nothing?" Robbie asked.

"The audience lets us know we exist. Where there is no audience, we need to look into a mirror to know we're really here."

"What do you mean?"

"When we're alone, we spend too much time looking at ourselves in the mirror. After we finish doing a role, do you know what can happen?"

"You get to keep your costumes," I offered, half joking.

"Sometimes we think we are still the people we were playing." To Robbie, she said, "Your dad's a damn good psychiatrist. I'm taking courses with him." Abel Carosso was one of Janice Rule's teachers, not her therapist, but other visitors at the Carosso home did become Abel's patients and then they stopped coming to the home as guests.

After her acting career, Janice Rule became a psychoanalyst like Abel, and Robbie too later. She published articles in professional journals. The director Robert Altman may have had the same feeling about Janice's intuitiveness and empathy that we felt with her as kids for he lured her out of retirement to play a shaman-like mother figure in one of his later movies, *Three Women*.

Sometimes there were starlets at the pool, new young faces in Hollywood that either Robbie's mother wanted to meet and photograph or Abel wanted to meet. Beverly Carson was one, in her early twenties, just coming to everybody's attention in *Pickup*, her first big role. The caption for the movie poster read, "THEY GAVE HER A BAD NAME AND SHE LIVED UP TO IT." Beverly had full lips and dark nipples she scarcely bothered to cover with her bikini top when she was at the Carosso pool. Just like in the poster, she had a red gardenia in her wavy hair. To get her attention, Robbie and I made the biggest cannonball jumps we could off the diving board, splashing water onto the lawn by the pool where she was stretched out. Drops fell on Beverly. She looked up angrily from under her sun hat at us showing off. Then she decided to

smile. She rolled over onto her belly, undid the straps of her
top, and edged her bikini bottom down lower on her buttocks.

"Robbie, please come and rub some oil on my back,"
she purred. Robbie winked triumphantly at me and obliged
Beverly with long, easy strokes with his hands up and down
her spine and ribs and around her shoulder blades. I admired
him, envied him, and was relieved Beverly hadn't summoned
me. I probably would have made a sloppy mess of the oil and
gotten a bulge in my swimming trunks. Another day, however,
I made the biggest cannonball ever, splashing Beverly out of her
daydreams. She winked at Robbie and said, "Eli, please do the
back of my legs." Robbie whispered to me, "See how far you
can go." I sucked in my breath and stomach and ran my hand
up to her thighs. That was the last time Beverly was invited to
the pool. When we asked Anna why she was missing, Robbie's
mom said cryptically, "There is no there there."

Bette Davis was Anna's close friend, firecracker sharp.
Robbie and I still remember her stabbing her cigarette butts
into an ashtray and denouncing Senator Joe McCarthy's House
Un-American Activities Hearings. "He's nothing but a red-
faced ham trying to hog the spotlight. I know the type; I've
been in too many movies with actors like him. They fool
themselves into believing they are great. Then they fool the
audience into believing the same thing."

Bette Davis's movie *All about Eve* first introduced Robbie
and me to Marilyn Monroe's body language. The picture was
early in Marilyn's career and she had a small part playing an
ingénue at a theater party sizing up the other guests, trying
to figure out when to speak and what to say to get people to
notice her. It was a role pretty much straight out of her own
life. In the film, when a theater critic draws her attention to a
big producer, Marilyn pulls her shoulders back, raises her chest,

which is almost bare in a strapless gown, and glides toward the movie mogul, breasts forward. That bit part announced her to the world.

Three years after she appeared in *All about Eve,* we bicycled down to Hollywood Boulevard and the Walk of Stars to watch Marilyn put her foot into wet cement in front of Grauman's Chinese Theatre. Even though we knew her success had something to do with sex, and just looking at her across the boulevard or on screen made us feel warm and tingling, we didn't yet know the particulars of lovemaking. Yet we could see that Marilyn used her body so every move she made said something about sex.

After I went with the Carossos' to see her in Billy Wilder's raucous comedy *Some Like It Hot,* we came back to Robbie's house and Dr. Carosso hung out with us, which didn't happen often because he was busy with his work six days a week. He was trim with a handsomely symmetrical face, well-trimmed hair, a short, Freudian beard, a sober look, and a measured manner. If somebody ever played him in the movies, Gregory Peck would be a good choice. "You know, boys," he said, referring to Marilyn in the movie we had just seen, "she lives in her body because as a child she never had a home to live in, just foster homes and an orphanage." He told us other actresses lived in their lines and their bodies just followed along.

That was years before Marilyn came to Robbie's house. She was often in New York City then, married to Joe DiMaggio, then to Arthur Miller, and when both of those marriages collapsed, successful as she was, Marilyn overdosed on pills. Her New York therapist suggested she return to Los Angeles and referred her to Dr. Carosso. That's when she started coming to Robbie's house for treatment with his father, in our senior year at Hollywood High School.

CHAPTER
THREE

The boxes of takeout food lay pretty much empty on the coffee table. It was a warm, spring evening in San Francisco, the way it can be before the summer fog takes over, and the windows were open. The propulsive sound of Latin music drifted in from the dance hall on the corner. It would go on all night, as would Robbie's tale of his affair with his patient. He had an almost tape recorder-like memory for conversations and an uncanny ability to retrieve the content of his ill-fated sessions with the patient suing him virtually at will. When he told stories, he narrated them as if from the script of a play, with little room for interjections, and this was how he spoke that night.

"Her name was, I mean it still is, Naomi Jane Morton. Do you know how close that is to Marilyn's name before she and Columbia Pictures rechristened her Marilyn Monroe?"

"Yes." I nodded.

"Marilyn was Norma Jean Mortenson on her birth certificate. Her mother, Gladys Baker, gave Norma Jean the last name Mortenson for the birth certificate. Mr. Mortenson was Gladys's ex-husband, though nobody knows if he was actually Marilyn's father. Even if he was her father, he was never there during her life, and Gladys backtracked and later said he wasn't the father. She just put the name down to give her daughter some legitimacy.

"A few different letters and my patient's name was Marilyn's birth name. Maybe it wouldn't have happened if the names hadn't been so alike. It's as if the name triggered me into this whole terrible thing. Without that, my patient might have stayed just another depressed young woman in need of help. She calls herself NJ.

"I saw her coming up the walkway for her first visit. I'm on the second floor of a fourplex of therapist offices set back from University Avenue, walking distance from the campus. My desk faces the avenue and I like to see how my patients walk when they're out on the street. NJ was looking down at the pavement, walking slowly with very short steps, almost as if her feet had been bound up when she was a child like a Chinese woman from another age."

Robbie picked up the manila folder he'd put on the coffee table and neatened up the sheets of lined yellow paper inside. "These are notes that I make for each patient's visit. If my patient is lying on the psychoanalytic couch, I'm sitting behind it so I take notes while he or she talks; I also note my own comments. If the patient and I are sitting facing each other, I spend about ten minutes after the visit writing my notes. They are brief, a shorthand summary. They're the medical record. From them I can also remember the actual conversations we had.

"This is NJ's record." He waved it at me, placed it back in front of him like an exhibit, and opened it to the first page. "Her first visit was October 17, 2006. She was born July 1, 1973, age 33. She is an assistant professor of English literature at Stanford on the basis of her doctoral dissertation from the University of Michigan. When she came to see me, she was up for a step review on the academic ladder that would put her in line for a future promotion to associate professor, which would give her tenure. If things went well, she would move up, get a jump in salary, and keep her job; if not, the university probably wouldn't renew her contract and would cut her lose.

"Things were not going well. She was in really bad shape when she first came in. Her department chair had told her she needed help because she was erratic. She missed meetings. She missed office hours with students. She got her grades in late and returned papers late to students. Her brilliant book-length dissertation for her doctorate had gotten her a position on the academic ladder, but she hadn't published it. She just left it lying around, she said, and hadn't written anything else. Her department chair said she needed help, referred her to me, and called me with a heads-up. The patient said that what the chair had told me about her work lapsing was all true."

With that introduction, Robbie repositioned the patient's chart on the coffee table before him as if it were a script he was going to read from. With the sound of music from the club in the background, he slipped into his state of hyperfocus that had stood him so well in life up to this disaster with the patient. Hardly glancing at his notes, he began recreating the patient's visits.

Naomi: I'm in danger of not getting advanced. If I don't, they will let me go. I need help.

Note: She was sad, pale, and there was almost no expression on her face except weariness and resignation. She looked as if she might be suffering from poor nutrition. She was wearing a mouse-gray pantsuit, and her hair was cropped and colorless. Dowdy in a word.

Naomi (mechanically): I have trouble falling asleep; sometimes I can sleep, but I wake at 3 a.m.

Robbie: What do you do to sleep?

Naomi: I drink a half bottle of wine in the evening. What's left I finish when I wake up at 3 a.m.

Robbie: Why do you think you are having trouble showing up for meetings and classes?

Naomi: I think it's anxiety. I'm always tense and afraid of making mistakes.

Note: She was obviously ashamed, dealing with a lot of shame.

Robbie: What do you hope to get from therapy?

Naomi: I need a promotion, or I will lose my job.

Robbie: Is there anything more?

Naomi (snapping): I don't know. I don't know anything except trying to be at the top of my class in school and university.

Note: She was putting herself down, but at least she was getting some feeling out.

Naomi (mournfully): I want to be something other than Naomi Jane, precocious English lit grad. I keep thinking I could be a writer, make an important contribution in literary criticism, be known. To tell the truth, I want to be famous, but I don't sit down and write. I don't even send off queries to university presses to get my dissertation published.

Robbie: Why do you want to be famous?

Naomi: I shouldn't have said that; it just popped out of me. I want to show my shitty aunt and uncle I'm good for something. All they ever said was that I was useless. If my father ever thinks about me—if he's alive—I want him to know what he missed when he split. I want to do it for my mother who died before she could raise me. Enough?

"The session ended. The next time I saw her, she was huddled into herself. I figured she was timid, angry, or stubborn and needed to think through everything she said. Maybe timidity and overthinking are the same for her. She kept her face down or turned to the side our first meetings."

Naomi (in a flat voice): I'm from Chicago. My father left our family before I can remember and I've never had any contact with him; I never knew where he went or if my mother knew. I have no idea if he is still alive, and I don't care.

Robbie: Is there anyone else in your family?

Naomi: Nobody. No brothers or sisters. My mother was a school librarian, and she died of a stroke when I was eight. We were alone in our apartment, and I was in my room when I heard her talking on the phone. She was saying, "I have a terrible headache," and then I heard her fall. I ran to her and found her on the floor. I ran next door to the neighbors.

Naomi (in a child's hurt voice): I can't continue. I have to leave.

Robbie: Will you be all right?

Naomi (hurriedly): Yes. Thank you. I'll see you next week."

Robbie interrupted his story. "Eli, have you ever been in my office?"

"Not that I can recall. Describe it for me."

"Yes. You have to know what it looks like. I have a private waiting room with just enough chairs for one family at most.

I stick to my schedule and patients usually come on time or a few minutes early. When it's time, I open the door for them to come into my consulting room. It's rectangular, about twenty feet by twenty-five feet with a bookshelf, file cabinet, and door to the waiting room at one end. At the other end is my desk with the patient's file on it and the window. There is a large, abstract painting in blue and rust on one side and a large, black-and-white photograph of a trail leading into a forest on the opposite wall. I like to see what patients project onto the art. By one side wall there is a comfortable armchair for the patient, and across from a little side table is my own armchair, a swiveling one. On the side table separating me and the patient is a box of tissues and my prescription pad and appointment book."

"How do you welcome the patient?" I thought this could be important. Was Robbie old-fashioned, Freudian blank, offering no cues and letting the patient make the moves? Was he seductive? Did he shake hands? Give an embrace? Was he just Robbie: friendly, open, and a bit formal?

"I like to say good day when they come in and give them a gesture toward the chair. I give them a little welcoming smile and stay standing until they sit down. Oh yes, I forgot the couch. Or until they lie down. It's by the other wall, very nice leather with a bolster at the end so the patient's head is raised. I put a fresh, ample paper napkin on it each time a patient uses it. Some take their shoes off. My chair has a swivel on it so I can angle it toward the couch and relax behind the patient's left shoulder, out of sight but a presence. I think most patients feel me as a looming presence just behind them." Robbie gave a harsh laugh at the thought of himself being threatening.

I figured it was time to freshen our drinks with ice and water and Scotch, to take the edge off Robbie and dampen my impatience at the pace of the story. The bottle was about half empty by now. Robbie took a long sip and let out a deep sigh that spoke more of resignation than relief. He summoned his recorder-like recollection.

"A week later, I looked out the window and saw her approach. She looked up at the redbrick façade of the building and then down at the green hedge along the lower story. She began her second visit."

Naomi: I haven't spoken about my past in a long time, maybe never; nobody has ever asked me. I'm not used to talking about myself. I'd like to continue, but I'm afraid.

Robbie: Afraid of what?

Naomi: I don't know. I guess I'm afraid of feeling things.

Robbie: What things?

Naomi: I don't know.

Robbie: What comes to mind?

Naomi: Nothing.

Robbie: Do you have any friends?

Naomi: There's an older professor, emeritus, in the department, a Chaucerian. I think he is mentoring me. He and his wife have invited me to their cabin at Lake Tahoe for Thanksgiving.

"I frowned questioningly at that, wondering what kind of mentoring she meant, and she answered my expression."

Naomi: I'll be okay. They're nice people.

"She was a bit less dowdy. There was a fall snap in the air, and she was wearing a thick blue corduroy jacket."

Naomi: I bought this jacket to take to the lake.

Robbie: What happened after your mother died?

Naomi: There's nothing to say.

Robbie: Say whatever comes to mind: memories, thoughts, images. Thoughts and images float in and out of your head like clouds when you're at the beach and looking up at the sky. Don't judge, don't dismiss, and don't censor even if what comes to your mind seems silly or embarrassing.

Naomi: This is so new to me. I've never done this before. I know I need therapy, but I've never had the time or money until now that I have insurance. I've always been working or studying. I've been here three years since I got my degree and came from Michigan. This will be the first time I go to the mountains. I'm supposed to be writing an article for a literary journal, but I can't do it because I can't stop judging myself. I keep revising and revising and censoring.

Robbie: Censoring what?

Naomi (haltingly): I don't know. Probably my shitty past. My past doesn't have anything to do with what I'm supposed to be doing now at the university, but it keeps cropping in. It's like a jack-in-the box. I shove it back down, but it won't stay put.

Robbie: Okay, so let it pop out.

Naomi: Will I be able to shove it back after our session is over?

Robbie: I think you can. Maybe not today but later.

Naomi: After my mother passed away, I went to live with her much older sister and her husband. Their kids were already on their own, and they were too old to raise another child. My uncle told me he'd done his time raising kids. They were really dreary and cold. My aunt once said my father left my mother and me because he had no interest in us. Did she make that up to hurt me, or was it true? Does it make any difference? My aunt and uncle were hardly ever home, away doing whatever it is they did to make a living—accounting or something—and complaining that they didn't make enough, as if whatever I cost them was pushing them over the edge. Even when they were home, it was like death at their house, nobody ever speaking.

"NJ was less frozen in this meeting. She moved a bit, uncrossing and crossing her legs, shifting her bottom in her chair to get comfortable."

Naomi: They expected me to follow a list of rules and chores they had taped on the refrigerator. I remember so little of my mother before her death, but I know we used to laugh together before she wasn't there anymore.

"She was looking at me now with a help-me look, sensing the end of the hour moments before I told her it was time to stop. In fact, I let her go over the time, though I didn't say that to her."

Naomi (apologetically as if noting the overtime): Okay. I'm sorry.

"Going out the door, she looked away from me, absorbed in her thoughts or angry at being interrupted. I couldn't tell. Her next appointment was after her weekend in the mountains."

Naomi: The professor and his wife were very good to me. The Sierras were beautiful. We saw the first snow on the mountains. I think the professor has a crush on me; it's platonic. He's seventy-one. He says my dissertation was exceptional. It got me the job at Stanford. The hiring committee was unanimous. I can't believe it, but I've finally started to make a list of possible publishers.

Robbie: What's the title?

Naomi: *Exile and Disorientation in Shakespeare*. It's not as good as people say.

Robbie: Why would people lie to you? Is this what you mean by judging yourself? Tell me more about the book.

Naomi: It's about Shakespeare's characters who lose their moorings. You know, *The Winter's Tale,* where the king banishes his newborn daughter because he thinks his wife has been unfaithful to him. *Cymbeline,* where the king exiles his daughter because he thinks the young man she marries is too unsophisticated.

Robbie: So it's about losing love, losing home, confusion, and father figures losing their bearings. That's your life, isn't it?

Naomi: Except in those plays, there are reunions. In my life, there were just mean, controlling, substitute parents. Only losses. No mother reunion. No father reunion.

"As therapy moved from October on into November, NJ seemed to relax. It felt as if we were friends having a conversation. She continued to describe her past and give more details."

Naomi: My aunt said I had to pick up all my toys and stuff every time I played. I couldn't put my elbows on the table when we ate. I couldn't leave a book on the floor, even in my room. I couldn't touch her porcelain collectibles. Once I touched one of her so-called precious objects to see what would happen. She tried to grab me, and I ran behind a door. She slammed the door to the wall and broke my nose and a toe.

"I studied NJ's face at that point. Her nose was small and symmetrical. Her eyes were an unusual gray that seemed to change with the colors around her, blue with the color of her corduroy jacket, rust from the abstract painting on the wall, brown sometimes. They were mostly gray with brown spots in the iris, set in an attractive face."

Robbie: There's no sign now of a broken nose.

Naomi: She threatened me with a hot iron if I talked back.

Robbie: Did your uncle ever stand up for you?

Naomi: He was tuned out. He did nothing. The only thing I did right was getting good grades. The only place I had fun was in school. The teachers liked me.

"Suddenly NJ seemed to break out of her rectitude, as if she saw her good-girl self in a mirror and the glass shattered."

Naomi: That's all I fucking was—a good student, grad student, university lecturer. I'm not even sure I'm that anymore.

"We'd reached the end of November, about a month and a half into treatment."

Naomi: Do you think I can lie down on the couch instead of sitting in this chair. It might be easier for me to talk if you aren't looking at me and I'm not looking at you.

"I chewed on my ballpoint pen for a moment at her idea of the couch. I wanted to say yes, but then I wouldn't be able to see her face, which became prettier and prettier as she trusted me more and opened up. We were really very comfortable with each other, and I was always uncertain whether treatment would change for the better or worse when a patient could no longer see my face. I wanted to please her."

Robbie: Let's give the couch a try. We can start next time. Let me fill in some history today while you're still sitting up. Do you use any recreational substances, other than wine?

Naomi: I smoke an occasional cigarette. If somebody passes a joint at an off-campus faculty party, I don't turn it down. I should. Marijuana makes me anxious. Wine calms me. I drink too much; I've already told you that.

Robbie: Anything else?

Naomi: I have some Valium from my internist and take half a tablet before I lecture to calm myself down. Not every time I lecture. I also have Ambien, which I use sometimes when I try to fall asleep without wine and can't.

Robbie: How many times a week?

Naomi (evasively): Two, maybe three.

Robbie: Do you have any social life? Do you date?

Naomi: I'm alone most evenings, except for going to an occasional lecture or concert on campus. I have two women friends on campus I go with. We're not really close; we keep each other company. There's a guy in the French department I go out with about once a month. He's not a boyfriend. We were grad students together at Michigan, study partners. We had sex together, and we still do. It feels more like an obligation, a routine.

Robbie: Have you ever been in love?

Naomi: Is this important? Does it have anything to do with my work problems?

Robbie: I don't know yet.

Naomi (her voice choking slightly): Maybe I loved the first guy I ever had sex with. He was much older, a photographer. Then there was the man who taught the freshman English lit survey course my first year at the University of Michigan. I came on to him because I wanted to see what sex was like with a married man. I broke it off first because I was afraid he would. I missed him for a long time. I must give the wrong signals to single men my age because I'm afraid of being rejected.

Robbie: What was it about sex with a married man that you were curious about?

Naomi: I wanted to be more than just a student to him. I thought maybe it would be more peaceful than other, short sexual experiences because he had somebody else to fuck and wouldn't be putting so much emotion into me.

"I glanced at the clock on the bookshelf behind her, and she saw me check the time."

Naomi (sadly): We're out of time, aren't we?

Robbie: I'm afraid so. I think we might make more progress

if you come in twice a week, especially since you will be using the couch.

Naomi: Okay.

Robbie: I have time toward the end of the day on Mondays and Thursdays at 6 p.m.

Naomi: I can do that.

I broke into Robbie's treatment narrative. "What the hell was your motivation? Why did you agree to letting her lie down and then suggest she do this twice a week? Maybe to you it has something to do with treatment technique, but to the rest of the world, a young woman who is getting prettier by the hour in the mind of the man she is with and then lies down on a couch means something else. Are you tone deaf?" I snapped at him. He *was* tone deaf sometimes.

"Shit, Eli, back off. Are you interrogating me? And don't call me tone deaf."

"Why not if it didn't occur to you that you and this NJ woman were trying to get closer to each other in a way that wasn't just therapy? That's exactly what I'm doing, interrogating you. I'm trying to see how you'll answer in court. I want to see if I can put you on the stand. If I don't ask you these questions, your ex-patient's lawyer will."

"Okay, man, I get it."

"This was the beginning of the slippery slope, wasn't it? How have you dealt with being so good looking all these years and not picking up the clues women drop?"

Robbie flushed. "I've never been unfaithful to Maddie before; nothing ever happened with another patient. Women lying on a couch with a male therapist happens in psychotherapy offices every day all over the world."

"Do you hear what you are saying? Women lying on a couch with a male therapist—like the two of them together on the couch?" I chuckled at that, and for a minute, Robbie didn't even get that I was laughing. Sometimes he couldn't tell whether I was making a joke or dead serious. That's Robbie, a mite obtuse.

I wondered if most shrinks were like that, suave yet prone to blind spots. I had met a few who were that way. But Robbie was way smarter than the other psychiatrists I'd met. He was a man with good intentions. He finally caught the double sense of what I was saying and said, "I didn't mean the therapists and women lying on the couch together. That's not what I meant."

He plunged ahead. "Anyway, from the therapy point of view, it's good that NJ wanted to feel close to me. That she could actually want to be close must have been because at least for the first eight years of her life she had a mother who cared for her. That's called positive transference—the good feelings a patient has for the doctor. The good feelings are what makes the therapy go; they drive it. There is no need to interpret good feelings. It's the negative feelings a patient has about me that block progress unless I interpret them to the patient. I have to connect their hostile feelings about me with whomever in the patient's past kindled them and show how they are screwing up their life."

"Good answer. That will fly in court," I said. "Maybe a bit wonky."

"I mean I can't deny that I liked it personally that NJ wanted to be closer. I'm not going to deny that. That's what makes therapy go for the shrink. That's the reward we get, that somebody's interested in us and in what we have to say."

"What was that business about scheduling her at the end of the day?" I said sharply. "We know what happens at the end of the day, don't we? Something happens at the end of the day, and the day goes on. You call Madeleine and tell her something's come up and you'll be home late. Why didn't you find time for NJ in the morning or during lunchtime when you had other patients following this lady?"

Robbie didn't answer at first. He pursed his lips together and stood up, tense. Then he sat down before saying, "I wasn't consciously thinking of doing anything with her sexually."

"Subconsciously then. We better find out now where it was leading you rather than in a courtroom with a bunch of people listening."

"Pretty smart, Eli. I see now that without knowing it, I was already falling for her—all the resemblances to Marilyn: her life, her name, the gray eyes that could change with the light. I'd already noticed her ankles; they were pretty too. You can't find a person guilty of malpractice for their thoughts, can you?"

"Denying them, you mean. No, Robbie, not for their thoughts. For their actions. We need a break. Let's get some air."

We went to the door together. Outside a wave of music from the Pacific Mambo Club greeted us, music that we had pretty much stopped hearing as Robbie told his story. Now Mariachi trumpets quickened our pace toward the corner and across the street to the restaurant's entrance. The air was balmy and men stood around in tapered twill pants with elaborately tooled leather belts, some in suits, fancy buckaroo shirts, and cowboy boots, talking and smoking. Women in flowered, full dancing skirts were swaying in front of the club. It was a building that had been made by joining two former machine shops and putting a haphazard corrugated metal roof over it. During the rainy season, the roof sounded like a snare drum.

Inside were a stage with a ten-piece band, a dance floor, picnic tables, and a full bar and counter for ordering food.

It was 11 p.m. and the club was packed. A marimba was playing counterpoint to the horns. The bandleader and his pretty partner stepped to the microphone and sang about love. I was tempted to stay for a song or two, but Robbie was still lost in his story and wanted to get back. We bought two large cups of thick, cinnamon-flavored coffee and four caramel puddings to take with us. Back home, we spread out the puddings on the table and coffee'd up. I settled back into my couch with my legal pad and pencil at the ready to make notes. Robbie found his place across from his patient's chart. He summoned his thoughts and resumed.

"When NJ lay down on the couch the first time, she gave me a pleading look."

Naomi: This is frightening. It feels like losing you, not being able to see you. All I see is the ceiling.

Robbie: What do you see in it?

Naomi: The texture of the plaster. It's like clouds. It's very lonely.

Robbie: And?

Naomi: This is what I wanted to tell you. My uncle—my stepfather more or less—drank too much and basically tuned out when my aunt was abusive. He never did anything together with me like play a game, kick a ball, go bike riding, take me to a movie, read a book with me, but at least he respected me as a student. He said I was smart. He said I'd do well and education would make me free, in the sense of money. I think he was lonely too; we both were.

"She became silent, as if she wanted to see what I would say, but I kept my mouth shut."

Naomi: I wonder if he molested me. I never told anybody about this because I'm not sure and I don't have any memory of anything actually happening. Except when I was around eleven, I had terrible nightmares about suffocating under a heavy weight. I would wake up in a panic, gasping for breath. There was wetness between my legs and a musky smell. Was I masturbating, or was it something else?'

Robbie: What else?

Naomi: It's too embarrassing to go on. I'm glad I'm not looking at you.

"Her eyes were no longer on the ceiling but on the bookshelf at the end of the couch. At the end of the session, she swung her feet to the floor and kind of got to them unsteadily, probably because she was trying not to look at me. She was wearing very sensible walking shoes and stubbed her toe on the door as she left.

"She spent Thanksgiving dinner with her retired mentor and his wife. That Monday after the holiday, she was wearing a dress for the first time. It was a long jumper skirt that came up to her chest like bib overalls, over a flannel shirt. Her shoes were bulky lace-ups with heavy waffle soles. It was an oddly mannish outfit, not in keeping with her earlier appearance. She noticed me looking at the shoes."

Naomi: I got them for my trip to Lake Tahoe. Do you like them?

"I just nodded at the couch, and she stretched out on it."

Naomi: When I was fifteen, my aunt and uncle sent me to a girls' boarding school in Connecticut where I stayed through high school. It was wrenching yet also a relief in a way. I only came home on holidays, not even in the summer because I was away on summer programs to learn languages and get a leg up on college applications, which my aunt and uncle said was important.

Stupid because I didn't need a leg up. I was a straight-A student. They were just trying to get rid of me. I was terribly lonely at the boarding school and too tense to relate to the other kids, too much into my own head. I still am. At times I actually missed home, if you could call it that, but I was scared about going home because I was afraid the nightmare about the heavy weight on my body would return. I've never slept well since those dreams.

Robbie: Did you feel different from your schoolmates?

Naomi: I had no family; everybody else did.

"That day when she went out the office door, she paused, thanked me. She gave me a kind of appealing do-you-like-me-smile, like an orphan needing contact, which really tugged at me. We were moving into December and the sycamores on each side of the walkway to the building were shedding their leaves onto the sidewalk. When I looked out the window and saw her arriving, her step had gotten almost sprightly. She kicked at the leaves and made them jump. Her hair was brushed and longer, and she had put on a touch of lipstick."

Naomi: My work is going better. I'm now on time for office hours with students. I'm thinking of writing an article on Cordelia and Ophelia.

Robbie: Really? What about them?

Naomi: How women in Shakespeare love. I wonder what would have happened if Cordelia had not been so good to her father. Was it her love for him that drove Lear mad rather than her sisters' meanness toward their father? What would have happened if Ophelia hadn't been so close to *her* father? What would have happened if she hadn't loved Hamlet so much? Would she have thrown herself in the river in despair after Hamlet killed her father by mistake?

Robbie: What will your paper propose?

Naomi: Love and innocence are more responsible for tragedy than evil.

Robbie: Perhaps you are talking about yourself. Perhaps you are scared that you drove your real father away, and your uncle too. So now you keep men away from yourself because you feel guilty about what you think you did to your father and uncle. Perhaps you feel it's not safe to let anybody get close to you.

Naomi (irritated): How can you drive away a father you never had?

Robbie: That's the point; you can't. You didn't drive him away.

Naomi: I'm drinking less in the evening. I don't need to. Sometimes I imagine seeing your face when I go to sleep, kind of like a benign presence. It's comforting.

"As we were getting toward Christmas, she said she had a date with the guy she sees occasionally and slept with him."

Naomi: I go through the motions of having some balance in my life. Sex also is a duty to myself and to him. I think I'm in some kind of competition with other women. If they have sex, I have to also.

Robbie: What about children? Have you ever felt any desire for kids?

Naomi: If I had children, if I were their mother, they would be too lonely like I was. I think I've always been competing with people. That's where my energy has been; it takes the place of loving anybody. I don't think having sex with my study partner means anything to me except friction and response.

Robbie: Maybe that's because the men you've been with haven't meant much to you. Perhaps you're afraid to let them mean much—because your father left and your mother died.

Naomi: I'm attached to my work again. That feels safe. Safer than relationships. I read romance novels by the bushels.

"She was now wearing a trim skirt that showed her lovely figure, especially since she had just pulled it tight around her. She started to cry, and I handed her the box of tissues. She held it to herself like a child holds a doll."

Robbie: Do you realize how you are holding that tissue box?

Naomi: No.

Robbie: Like a doll or a security blanket.

Naomi, curling up more, then relaxing: I'm trying to change.

"By the next visit, she had gotten her fall term evaluations."

Naomi: My teaching evaluations are much better. The students say I'm nicer. The department chair says things are better. He hasn't gotten any more complaints about me. You know the article I told you that I'm working on about Ophelia and Cordelia? I decided the key is that innocence is the *fulcrum* upon which the tragedies pivot. That's the word I'm using.

Robbie: That sounds really good; it might be the centerpiece of a second book.

Naomi: Dr. Carosso, I wonder if Ophelia saw her reflection in the water before she threw herself into the river. Maybe she was trying to kiss her reflection or speak to herself when she fell into the water. Maybe that unfortunate woman was suffering from *not enough* self-love. That could have been what was wrong—not the Narcissus thing of too much love.

Robbie: Wrong with you or Ophelia?

Naomi: With her and me, some missing ingredient we never got. As long as I can remember, I've been playing a role—homely, intellectual, teacher-admiring student. When I got my job here, I started hating myself for playing the role, hating what my family did to me, even hating my mother for dying. So here in Palo Alto, I finally mess up to get even with them—and mess up to punish myself for being too good all along.

"That seemed a turning point. Looking back on it, I don't know if she meant she'd had enough of pleasing others, that she was done with that, or that she wanted to go for broke and be as bad as she could be to get revenge for all her past hurts. That day going out the door, she looked back at me inquiringly and thanked me. Then in the next few visits, she seemed softer and fuller, not gaunt as she was at the beginning of treatment. She came wearing earrings for the first time."

Naomi: I saw you in Kepler's bookstore yesterday. I wonder if you saw me. I think I wish you had. I wonder a lot of things. What do you think of me? Do you think I'm nuts, selfish, stupid? Are you married?

Robbie: Does it make a difference?

Naomi: I'd feel competitive with your wife. I assume you have a family.

Robbie: Why do you imagine I'd think you were nuts?

Naomi: Isn't that what therapists think of their patients?

Robbie: I think you are projecting your own self-doubts onto me and imagining that I am criticizing you the same way.

Naomi: Yeah. My aunt used to snarl at me and say, "Naomi Jane, control yourself." So now I don't know if I'm too controlled or out-of-control.

Robbie took a deep breath as if steeling himself for what

he knew was coming in the next scenes. He stood up like a conductor at his podium, the patient's chart on the coffee table before him like a score he knew so well he didn't even need to look at it.

"The next session, she arrived looking unattractive again, wearing her tough, black, lace-up, waffle-sole shoes. Her face was pinched when she stretched out on the couch." He flung his right arm and hand out, palm up, as he spoke his patient's words.

Naomi: I looked at myself in the mirror last night, naked. I'm actually pretty. You know what I did? I said to the mirror, "I'm the prettiest professor on campus." I had a taboo thought. *I can't let Dr. Carosso see me this way.* The Friday before, I fixed myself up for the faculty Christmas party for the first time since I arrived at Stanford. I bought really high heels and a low-cut blouse. It felt like the oddest, best thing in the world to have men looking at me.

"Her words made me uncomfortable. I wasn't sure what to say when she said it was taboo to think of her psychiatrist looking at her undressed. By then that's just how I wanted to look at her. So I sidestepped." Still standing, Robbie flung his left arm and hand out, palm up, to show the next words were his.

Robbie: In what way did it make you feel odd to have men look at you at the party?

But this was too much for the lawyer in me: listening to my friend and client hanging himself. I stood up and growled at Robbie across the coffee table, "Objection! Aren't you supposed to know that when you have feelings like wanting your patient to get naked in front of you it's time to get a consultation with another psychiatrist? Didn't they teach you that when you were in training?"

Robbie hung his head and sank down into his seat. "Eli, don't rub it in. Sure they taught me that; sure I teach my students that. What can I say? I wanted to keep what was occurring in my office between the two of us and keep it happening."

He sprang back up. "Eli, I'm going to finish this. Shut up. I'm going to tell you what happened even if it hangs me, even if I have to say it to a jury and *they* hang me. Enough with objections. Let the man tell his story." Still gesturing with his right hand for his patient and his left for himself, he continued.

Naomi: It made me feel strong being noticed for my looks more than my brains. Utterly new, like I had suddenly developed muscles and I wanted to show *you* how I looked at the party. But I was terrified of coming to your office looking like that, so I dressed down today.

Robbie: Terrified?

Naomi: Of looking like some blonde movie star with soft, high cheekbones, arched eyebrows, dark eyeliner, red lips, and wistful eyes. The mirror told me that's how I could look if I wanted to. Dr. Carosso, can you call me Naomi Jane instead of Ms. Morton or Professor Morton? Actually, please just call me NJ. That's the nickname I gave myself when I left Chicago for Connecticut.

Robbie: Yes, course, if you prefer.

"On December 23, the day of her last visit before the ten-day holiday break, I watched her arriving up the walk. She was back to attractive, wearing a skirt, fitted jacket, and white blouse that showed her collarbones. She was in her usual, ordinary walking shoes, not the ugly lace-up ones. But she had heels in her bag and put them on in the waiting room. They were three-inch heels, beige, with a little bow on the toe. When she lay down, she crossed and uncrossed her ankles as if modeling them for herself and me."

NJ: Dr. Carosso, I looked in the mirror again last night. I had this really creepy feeling that I saw a face in it that wasn't mine. Don't think that I'm going off the deep end. The face was mine really but also somebody else's, the face of a young woman about my age who I think I know but who is someone I don't really know.

Robbie: What are you thinking?

NJ: I'm afraid to say it.

Robbie: Why?

NJ: It's too presumptuous. She pinched her forearm hard. I think maybe I resemble Marilyn Monroe—or could. Do you see it?

"I didn't know what to say. Doctors are taught, "First, do no harm." It was quiet for a while, with her waiting for me to respond and me waiting for I didn't know what. Finally she started talking again."

NJ: (with awe): I wonder if I want to say what I'm going to say. I could make myself look like that actress. Is it horrible for me to be saying this? You have no idea how hard it was for me to come in dressed like this today. I'm scared to death.

"She covered her face with her arm and began crying quietly. I did the only thing I could do and handed her a tissue."

NJ: Can we meet over the holidays? I don't think I can go ten days without seeing you."

Robbie pushed the patient's chart away from him to the far edge of the coffee table and sat down.

"Why did you do that?" I asked.

"Because it's done. Because the chart record didn't exist

after that. I didn't make any more notes. It's blank." Robbie looked utterly defeated. "There are no more entries."

"Why?"

"She became Marilyn. That's how it happened. I made it happen. She made it happen. She wanted to, not just to please me but for herself. At some point, we both merged with the fantasy. It got to the point that when NJ would walk through the door for her appointment, Marilyn seemed to be standing there as if she'd never been gone—not the blonde bombshell from the movies and publicity stunts but the Marilyn I remembered, the one you and I knew, the demure young woman. This fantasy was helping the patient. You know that, don't you, from what I've just told you?"

"Couldn't you help her another way?" I retorted.

Robbie paused, summoning up the pensive Sigmund Freud expression that his face fell into when he was thinking about something technical from his work or some article or book he wanted to quote. "She was idealizing me into a Prince Charming who was rescuing her, and the fantasy was helping her. I had told myself that when she came to the end of treatment, I would deal with the Prince Charming fantasy, interpret to her what she was doing. But the end of treatment came so suddenly I had no chance to explain it to her."

"So part of treatment included her falling in love with you and the two of you having sex?" I said, protesting and probing.

"Bullshit. Psychiatrists can have feelings. We're just not supposed to act on them. I wanted it to end differently. I wanted to do something for her in real life, something more than the treatment."

"Such as?"

"I don't know."

"Bring her home to your house the way your dad did with Marilyn?"

"My dad wasn't sleeping with Marilyn. He tried to reparent her and show her a normal family life. He did everything he could to help her, even if it was unconventional and crossed patient-doctor boundaries. He couldn't help her, but he *tried*. I figured I could try to help NJ in some unconventional, even experimental way. I wasn't planning on it being sexual."

"You once told me how your father wrote articles about how to avoid getting overinvolved with patients."

"Yes. 'Don't enter the game.' Those were Abel's words."

"You know what, buddy? Your father brought Marilyn home for *you* to sleep with her." That just occurred to me, and I couldn't believe I said it. It was like I'd suddenly punched Robbie and his whole family in the gut. He doubled over just as if I'd knocked the breath out of him, his face in his hands.

"Man, we have to go on," I said to him. "I've taken depositions before that went eight hours. This isn't a deposition, but it's more or less the same as one. Let's push on. When did you first realize, consciously I mean, that something was happening way out of the ordinary—that your patient actually looked like Marilyn, that she was not just pretty but beautiful?"

"The day I stopped making notes in her chart. Shit, look at this." Robbie pulled the manila folder back to him and stared open-mouthed at the patient's record open to the last date he'd made a chart entry. I walked around to his side of the table and we both leaned over the chart and stared down at it. It read, "Naomi Jane Mortenson," followed by a few sentences Robbie had quickly scrawled about the patient's improved appearance and scheduling the holiday break.

"What do you want me to see?" I asked, because I didn't notice anything different.

"Just look." He tapped on the patient's name. "I spelled her name wrong. I wrote *Mortenson*—Marilyn's birth name—rather than *Morton*, NJ's last name. I can't believe I wrote that; I didn't see it until now. I knew, and didn't know, what was happening. She and I realized at the same time that something was happening that wasn't treatment. We both wanted it to go forward."

"Dr. Carosso, exactly what *consciously* stopped you from making notes in your patient's chart?" I snapped, lawyerly, at my friend, as if we were in court.

"I understood at some level I was playing with fire. I was feeling guilty already that there was something wrong, even if the patient was getting better. I didn't want anybody to know about it. I wasn't trying to seduce her. I just wanted to let whatever was going to unfold happen."

Pacing back to my side of the table, I cross-examined him. "If you had continued to make notes after that visit, it would have been as if you were still doing therapy, right?"

"Right."

"So you considered what came next as no longer treatment. Describe what happened next."

Robbie looked off into some intermediate space between the present and the past, reality and dream. He stood up. "I need to breathe. I need to talk, but give me a moment. I've never told this part before."

He went to an open window and listened to the music still coming in, less raucous now, two or three saxophones carrying a melody, a syncopated drum and bass rhythm guitars keeping time. Still standing, he said, "I gave her an appointment for the day after Christmas. She was the only patient I saw during the holiday. I knew something was wrong, and it wasn't too late. I still could have gotten some consultation. I could have called up another psychiatrist and said that I thought I was in trouble with a woman patient I had feelings for. I could have worked out a plan with whomever I called—like having me discuss each session with somebody else or my going into therapy myself. It wouldn't have been too late if I'd made the call for help."

"Why didn't you?" I asked.

He sank back down onto the couch. "NJ and I were being dragged into our pasts at the same time by a current that was just too strong. I didn't have it in me to fight it."

"You could have called me," I said softly. "Why didn't you?"

"I didn't want to hear what you'd say. What could you have said?"

"I'd have said, 'Think of the risk versus the benefit of sleeping with this woman, man.' That's what I could have said, what you doctors always talk about. I would have said, 'It's not worth it.' I would have been right."

"Yeah, I could have done a lot of things differently. When she asked to see me during the holidays, I could have answered her with a *why*, let her just project on me whatever feelings she felt about me. Explored them piece by piece after the holiday break the way I should have. Analyzed with her whether she was trying to turn me into the dream father she wanted who would never discard her."

"Were you still charging her for sessions when you stopped keeping the medical record?"

"Damn it, no, man. I may be stupid, but I'm not a thief. I stopped billing her the day I stopped making notes. It wasn't therapy anymore; we were having dates. She was happier and extroverted like she'd never been before. She'd come in with a smile or humming, almost dancing. She said her colleagues couldn't believe the change in her. It was harder for me to be lighthearted because I was having these dates with her, and I wanted to feel as free with Madeleine as I felt with NJ, but Madeleine is such a serious and busy person. My office life with NJ and home life with Maddie were totally different lives."

I made a pessimistic last stab at what might render everything up to now moot. "Robbie, how serious was all this? It may or may not be good therapy, it may be love, but did you really cross the line and have sexual intercourse with your patient? You haven't said it's happened yet."

"You'll get your answer soon enough." He poured the last of the Scotch into his glass, drained it, and returned to his story of therapy gone bad. Chart or no chart, notes or no notes, Robbie resumed his recitation.

"The day after Christmas, I was watching for her arrival. A few last leaves remained on the sidewalk and she played hopscotch with them, jumping from one to another, scrunching them beneath the toes of her high-heeled shoes. She had a shawl over her hair and shoulders against the winter coolness, looked up, saw my face in the window, and smiled. As soon as she entered the consulting room, she looked at herself in the small mirror that was on the wall over the table between the two chairs."

NJ: May I?

Robbie: Of course.

"She removed her shawl, revealing blonde hair and fluffed it."

NJ: Going to the salon scared the daylights out of me. I was afraid I wouldn't recognize myself after having my hair bleached.

"She smiled at the image of her perfectly symmetrical face that was no longer sad and downcast but gentle and relaxed. She pirouetted before the mirror, showing off in a fitted dress, and went to the couch to lie down, removing her shoes. It was winter but her toes were bare. Her delicate fingers played nervously with the hem of her dress at her knees."

NJ: Is it okay for me to be self-centered? Being with you makes me feel like fixing myself up. I want to please you; I just have to know how.

Robbie: That's not exactly being self-centered.

NJ: I'm afraid you will lose interest in me if I don't please you.

Robbie: I don't think so.

"As she left the office that day, she reached down to the table and picked up the yellow pad I use to make notes. She saw that the page was empty and nodded at me."

NJ: You've stopped writing. It's blank.

"Her next visit was three days later. She removed the shawl, revealing platinum highlights in her hair. She pirouetted gaily.

NJ: I think this will please you.

"She went to the couch, but instead of lying down, she sat on its edge of it, looked at me somewhere between shyly and coyly, before swinging her legs onto the leather. Her skirt had ridden up above her knees, and she left it there. This day she was wearing a pale-green blouse that was open deep enough for me to see the tops of her breasts."

NJ (whispering): What's going to happen next?'

"I was paralyzed. I had never been in this kind of situation, pulled between wanting to stay in my chair until some words came to me and wanting to get up and do something. She began to cry."

NJ: Are you waiting for something?

"I had to do something or say something, but I had no idea what. Finally I got up and carried the box of tissues over to her. She made room for me to sit beside her on the edge of the couch and grasped my hand tightly, as if holding on to a life preserver. Another moment passed before she brought my hand over to the inside of her thigh and moved it higher.

NJ: I feel better now.

It was after 1 a.m. and the street was silent. We had eaten our puddings and drained the coffees. "That's it, Eli. The affair continued like that until February, until President's Day approached. I think it was a lovely time for both of us. She brought me a big photo book of Marilyn Monroe in different poses and outfits and asked me which I preferred. Then she would come to the office dressed like Marilyn and pose herself, dressed and undressed like Marilyn in the album and in other ways that pleased the two of us.

"It was a huge charade. When I came home in the evening, I wanted to feel as lighthearted with Madeleine as with NJ, but Maddie is too busy to take time out to play games like that. It's not that I don't like her. I do like her; I respect her tremendously. NJ also works hard at the university, though I knew her only in this game we were playing in my office. We were like kids playing until something intrudes that makes you stop."

"What was it? You may have told me. Tell me again how it ended."

"It was the President's Day long holiday weekend. NJ asked

me if we could go away together. She caught me by surprise, completely off guard."

"You dope. How could you not have figured this in when the affair started? It had to be part of the calculation when you began." Still I also knew this was Robbie, sometimes blind to people's feelings, unaware how he could affect people, probably more adept at surgically dissecting patients' feelings with words than empathizing with them, or even knowing himself. In a way, his weakness was touching, a kind of innocence. If I could get him to show his frailty to a jury during his testimony in court, maybe they'd sympathize with him.

Robbie said again, "She took me by surprise. Life outside my office wasn't part of what we were playing. I told her that my two grown children were coming from out of town and I had to be with my family. Then she said, 'Why don't you leave your wife? Aren't you ready to move on?' I didn't say yes right away. I didn't say no. I said she and I needed to think about it.

"Me the psychiatrist, I didn't see it. She said she didn't need to think about it. She knew what she wanted. Then her anger started. She said she knew that I'd led her along all the time. I tried to say we were leading each other along with no destination in sight. She yelled at me that I'd cheated her. She left before the time was up. We'd stuck to fifty minutes all during the affair. She never came back to the office and didn't answer my telephone calls. I began to hope that it was all over and I'd never see NJ again or hear from her.

"A couple of weeks later when I came back to my office after lunch, there was a strange man in the waiting room. He asked if I was Dr. Carosso. I said yes, and he handed me a thick envelope. He was a process server. He smirked as he gave me the papers and left without a word. It was her lawsuit: malpractice, breach of contract, fraud, sexual battery with false professional purpose, theft of service. She's asking for $8 million."

For the first time, I said nothing, asked no questions. Really there was nothing I could say. The sadness of Robbie's story had wrung both of us out. The dance club's lights were off, the street had emptied of people, and the last cars had pulled away. It was time to give in to the scent of fresh fog coming in from the ocean and sleep.

CHAPTER
FOUR

What happened between Robbie and his first girlfriend in high school may have foretold his later blind spot for his patient's feelings. Actually that girl was Robbie's *and* my first girlfriend at the same time. In 1957 we were freshman at Hollywood High School. Talley Coates became our girlfriend our sophomore year, and later our first sexual partner. We couldn't resist her quick smile, dark haircut in bangs across her forehead, her restless, active body, the bounce in her walk, and her slightly slanting bright eyes. We both wanted to be close to her all the time, and she felt the same way about us. Not just because Robbie and I were good students who worked hard, not just because we were good enough looking each in our own way, and Robbie's smile felt like the sun coming up on both of us, but because our backgrounds were so different from hers.

Our parents had gone to college, and Talley's hadn't. Her mother, a prewar Japanese immigrant, was a costume seamstress on the Paramount Pictures lot; her father had been a motor pool mechanic on the same movie lot. When she was ten, he passed away from lung cancer from the asbestos in the vehicle brakes he repaired.

Hollywood High was a heady broth of students from rich and poor backgrounds—serious students like the three of us, other lackadaisical ones—and adolescent sexual desire. The common denominator was that it was a place of dreams, hope, and make-believe like the city it was in. The school team nickname was the Sheiks, after the Rudolph Valentino movie in which he played an Arab desert chieftain who seduces an innocent young Englishwoman. An image of Valentino with his sharp nose and long, flowing, black hair covered the outside of the school auditorium—glorifying young men on the prowl for *shebas,* girls. The students joked that their teams were named for the most popular condom of the day, Sheiks, and not after Valentino.

Hollywood High was also brimming with all the other currents agitating life in Los Angeles. Past graduates included Judy Garland, Lana Turner, Mickey Rooney, Joel McCrae, and Alan Ladd. The director Edward Dmytryk had gone there, the man who had given the American west its look for movie fans all over the world—deep Technicolor canyons, mountains, buttes, and deserts without end. Tuesday Weld was our classmate, and Ricky Nelson graduated our first year.

Not just stardom simmered at our school when we were there but also the brew that became the Manson murders started percolating. Sharon Tate was our schoolmate as was Rebecca Simonsen. Rebecca joined the Charlie Manson Family for tragic reasons. As a young child, she lost her parents in the Holocaust, and her second mother, the American woman who rescued her, died when Rebecca was in high school. Lonely and sad, Becky took solace in her fiddle playing. It led her to disaster for she met Charlie Manson at a music event where they both were playing. He charmed her, and she joined his harem in the Simi Hills at the abandoned Spahn movie ranch, once a set where fake cowboys had preened for B-movie cameras.

Charlie Manson himself wanted to be a star, as it is said everyone in Los Angeles wants to be at some point in life. Enraged that the songs he wrote weren't getting attention, one night in 1969, he urged his followers to make headlines another way. They crossed the San Fernando Valley, ascended the Hollywood Hills, and saw the LA Basin beckoning like a galaxy of stars. They found their way to Benedict Canyon and the home of movie director Roman Polanski, whom Sharon Tate had married. He wasn't home but Sharon was, and the Manson gang stabbed her and four friends to death. Later in court, the prosecutor said that Manson's delusional, grandiose motive was to start an apocalyptic race war by killing people that would leave him as the sole music survivor. Maybe it was simpler than that: rich and famous people drove him crazy with envy.

Jeffrey King was another one of our Hollywood High classmates. After college and law school, he become part of the team of Los Angeles district attorneys who prosecuted Charlie Manson and his cult and sent them to prison for life. In high school, I couldn't stand King for the sanctimonious way he wanted all students who broke rules to be expelled from school or disciplined to hell and gone. I couldn't stand him later because he sponsored the California law that allowed family members of murder victims to speak at convicted killers' parole hearings.

King didn't want anybody who was connected with Sharon's death in any way to get away with anything. Family members could keep seeking revenge for the death of their loved ones forever, and prisoners had no chance for rehabilitation, redemption, or release even when they spent thirty years of a life sentence in jail trying to improve the life of fellow prisoners and trying to get an education for themselves. My sympathy for Rebecca Simonsen, who was sentenced to jail even though she wasn't anywhere near the house when the killings occurred, and disgust with King's law were the main reasons I chose to be a defense attorney after law school.

I was scarcely conscious at the time of all the forces blowing in the hot, dry Santa Anna winds, except my wish to stand out and attract pretty girls. But once we got to know Talley Coates in social studies class, she was the only girl for Robbie and me. She was active in the school's theater department, and we visited her in its workshop while she cut and sewed cloth into costumes for school plays. We attended all the openings of the plays she worked on. She had a neat costuming trick that really turned us on. In a production of *Dark of the Moon,* the lead actress was playing a backwoods girl and Talley wanted her to be braless under a thin, white, muslin dress she had designed. When the drama teacher insisted on a bra, Talley dipped into her purse for some rouge and dabbed it on the actress's dress in just the right places over her breasts. On stage with a rose light on her, the girl looked as if she had nothing on under her dress. For Robbie and me, the illusion meant that Talley was thinking about sex just like we were.

Yet we were in a quandary. As best friends, neither Robbie nor I felt we could make a move on Talley. When we went to movies, she sat between us. When we got our driver's licenses and were riding in a car, all three of us sat in the front seat, Talley in the middle. We were frozen in an unspoken boys' agreement that Talley belonged to both of us or neither of us, and she too was frozen by the agreement because she didn't want to lose either one of us. If she put her hand on my knee while we were on a date, she put her hand on Robbie's at the same time or for equal time.

She watched us at soccer practices and games and admired Robbie's fluid motions, his eyes shining magnetic blue like Paul Newman's, the way his hair flew when he ran down a ball. I did too. At just the right moment after luring the defense toward him, Robbie would lift a long pass to me. I'd control it, lower my shoulders, and bull through the last defenders and pound a shot at the goal. I loved letting my elbows fly. Other times I'd plow into the fray and kick the ball out to Robbie to take the shot. Sometimes the referees blew their whistle on me and called a foul; sometimes I got away with it. Talley loved Robbie's gracefulness and my aggressiveness. Our team won the league championship our junior and senior years.

Saturdays Talley, Robbie, and I hung out together doing schoolwork, gossiping, swimming at his pool or mine— more often at Robbie's where there might be movie people sunbathing—going to lots of movies, and occasionally going to Talley's house. She lived in a small bungalow a few blocks from the Paramount lot, and we'd keep her company while she and her mother worked on costumes together.

One fall day in our senior year, we were in my bedroom with our schoolbooks spread on the floor, music playing, and I showed Talley my copy of *Playboy* magazine's first ever issue, December 1953, with Marilyn on the cover and in the centerfold. I think I was wondering how Talley would react, probing to see if she would say something about taking her own clothes off to model for pictures. She didn't say anything dismissive like "Marilyn's a tramp" the way other girls might have said or the way Talley herself might have said about other nude centerfolds if we had shown them to her.

Instead she studied Marilyn's face and said, "She's beautiful. There's something about her expression."

"What is it?" Robbie asked, trying to understand what Talley was seeing, maybe also hoping to draw Talley out and get her to segue into modeling for us.

Talley didn't bite. "I think she's hiding something that hurts." She closed her eyes for a moment, mulling some kind of protective feeling toward Marilyn. Then she got up from the floor, took the magazine over to my dresser drawer, and put it back in its hiding place beneath my underwear.

For years Robbie kept a copy of the famous Marilyn Monroe 1949 nude calendar under his mattress, which she'd posed for before she could support herself with acting. Her image didn't intimidate Robbie and me the way some pinups did because there seemed to be a hint of ironic laughter on her face and that sadness in her eyes. Her moist, half-parted lips made her look tentative, the way a lot of the girls in school seemed to be before they became sure of themselves. Marilyn looked clueless and clever in her movies, virginal and carnal all at the same time, depending on the angle from which we looked at her picture. Her dewy, innocent face disarmed her in our eyes, disarmed us, and made her seem approachable, unlike actresses like Beverly Carson with her full, red lips. Marilyn didn't seem haughty the way we felt many of the girls at Hollywood High were, which I later I realized was just a pose some teenage girls used to keep boys at length until they were ready to get closer.

Some months later in the spring of 1961, just as the weather started going from winter chilly to spring warm, we were spending a Saturday afternoon in Robbie's backyard and feeling bored. We'd done some lap swimming in the heated pool, clowned a bit off the diving board for Talley, our homework was up to date, there were no interesting guests that day, and spring fever restlessness was in the air.

Talley sat up from dozing. "We need to find something exciting to do."

Robbie's father happened by that moment, retrieving a book he had left earlier and heard her. Experienced shrink that he was, he probably figured that we kids needed some kind of outlet for our sexual feelings. He saw that Robbie and I were not touching Talley nor she us—we were keeping our hands to ourselves-—and probably knew that we had not done anything seriously sexual yet. He smiled paternally at us and walked on.

I said to Talley, "Go for it; exciting like what?"

"An adventure. I'm thinking of something." Sitting cross-legged on her towel, she closed her eyes and put her index fingers to her temples, holding our attention. "I've got it. Let's see how many famous actors' pools we can swim in tonight. Let's call it 'pool hopping.'"

Instantly the idea ignited. I announced that I'd sneak out of the house with the keys to one of my parents' cars way after dark when they were asleep and pick Talley up, then Robbie after midnight. Talley said she would invite one of her girlfriends, who would probably bring her boyfriend along. We would be five.

The night was warm, perfect for our adventure. When we were all in the car, we circled back to my Beverly Hills neighborhood and drove a few blocks to a large, white, colonial mansion that belonged to movie people, which I knew had a swimming pool in back. The house had a large lawn with grass as perfect as a golf putting green. There were tall, dark hedgerows on the sides, perfect for creeping swiftly along to the fence that fronted the backyard.

I parked the car next door and we walked back to the

hedge, moving quickly to a gate in the fence at the back of the front yard. We paused to listen for noises, such as a barking dog or window opening, or signs of life like a light coming on. There was nothing but silence and dark.

We opened the gate to the back and saw a round swimming pool lying black in an unlit yard. Swiftly and silently, we stripped down to our swimming suits and slipped into the water. The point of this game was making ourselves at home in a famous person's pool as if it were ours and we were part of the family. That and the risk, the possibility of getting caught, the caressing night breeze, the sense of danger, and the thrill of success seemed worth the chance. We dog-paddled for a minute and blew streams of water at each other through gapped teeth and pursed lips, then at a nod from me or Talley or Robbie, we retraced our steps. "Ersatz sex" Robbie's dad no doubt would have called it.

The next house our group went to was Edward G. Robinson's Italian villa. We parked two houses down, walked back, and worked our way among large, planted urns and shrubbery to the fence. To mount it we dragged over a concrete bench to get a leg up. Robinson's swimming pool was a huge, elliptical affair. There were Roman columns topped with a lintel at each end of the pool. It was as if Robinson had created his own Roman Empire so he could continue to play his *Little Caesar* gangster role long after the film had wrapped. For a few seconds, we played hide-and-seek among the columns and Talley's girlfriend's guy threatened to climb a column and dive into the pool from the lintel. The girls shushed him down. Talley's girlfriend slipped off her bikini top and we all slipped into the water. Just then, a light in a second-story window came on.

A light in a window might mean nothing; nonetheless,

we started climbing out of the pool. Almost immediately as we were getting back into our jeans and shorts, the whole downstairs and the grounds lit up. Simultaneously sirens started wailing the approach of the police. E. G. Robinson had evidently learned how to set a trap from playing in so many mobster movies. He'd probably spied us minutes earlier, called the police, laid low letting us think all was well, and triggered the lights when he heard the first siren.

The window in the corner of the second floor swung open and the star appeared, silhouetted by the room light, jowly cheeked, beady eyes looking down on us. There was a cigar in his mouth, and the scent of good tobacco wafted down. It was a perfectly executed trap for getting us arrested for trespassing. On the other hand, the sirens gave us a little head start chance to escape, a dumb warning if they really wanted to catch us. Maybe that was the cops' point—put on a show for the neighbors to let them know that the crime fighters were on duty and at the same time scare us but let us get away to save themselves the trouble of arrests and paperwork in the middle of the night. This was still a mostly peaceful time in upscale Los Angeles, a decade before the Manson murders made everybody keep their doors locked forever.

All five of us started moving as fast as we could in the first direction that came to mind. Robbie and Talley reached a locked back gate first and started clambering over it. Rather than waiting for a turn to climb, Talley's girlfriend and her boyfriend and I dashed back the way we had come and reached my mother's car. I hit the ignition but stupidly turned on the headlights—stupidly because the police were just rounding the corner and might not have seen us if I'd left the lights off. The cops were on us instantly and took us to the precinct station.

The two arresting officers were laughing with the desk

clerk about throwing the book at us, reciting a list of offenses they were going to charge us with, such as destruction of property, theft of statuary, intent to commit assault, trespassing, and breaking and entering. I told my friends to stay silent and told the police to call my father. He arrived within minutes. In a stern, lawyerly voice, he announced, "I'll take responsibility for these youngsters." To me he chuckled, "Kids will be kids." The Beverly Hills police almost pushed the group of us out the door. I doubt the police ever intended to do anything, let alone paperwork at two in the morning.

Meanwhile, Robbie and Talley were walking back to Hollywood, four and a half miles along Sunset and Hollywood Boulevard to Beachwood and up to Robbie's house. It was four in the morning when they got there and went into the backyard. Almost simultaneously they said, "Let's go skinny-dipping." They were so pumped up over escaping that they wanted to keep the excitement going and amp it up further.

Robbie told me how he unscrewed the backyard light and they stepped out of their clothes and swimming suits. They paddled around and drifted into each other, then into each other's arms as if they jointly knew it was time to kiss, really kiss unlike the polite ones they'd shared already. Talley put her tongue into Robbie's mouth and wrapped her legs around him. They floated to the shallow end of the pool and staggered to the steps where Robbie lay back and Talley straddled him and pressed onto him.

"Are you all right with this?" Robbie whispered.

"There has to be a first time."

After that evening, before Robbie told me what happened, I knew something was different when he and I and Talley met after school to sit in the bleachers or walk for a while before heading off in our own directions. Our easy rhythm together was gone. It was not as if Robbie and Talley had suddenly become intimate with each other in the sense of holding hands, touching, or kissing, but their speech wasn't spontaneous. The way they talked with each other became slower and calculated. Instead of leading with ideas, Talley seemed to be waiting for a signal from Robbie or me what to do, when to get together. We all felt the strangeness and didn't talk about it for almost three weeks until one day when Robbie and I were in the locker room after soccer practice.

Speaking low so nobody else could hear, Robbie said, "Talley and I had sex."

"Shit, you didn't," I said, so surprised that heads turned and looked up. I knew almost instantly that was why things had been so different among the three of us. And I felt betrayed even though I didn't know if I felt cheated by Robbie for taking Talley away from me, or by Talley for not choosing me for her first time. "That's not fair," I whispered.

Robbie bristled, "What's not fair?"

"I don't know," I admitted. "How did it happen?"

"The night of pool-hopping. We went skinny-dipping when we got back to my house. It just happened." Robbie wouldn't look at me. "She looks really good with her clothes off. She really liked it. She'd never done it before." He told me the whole story of what happened in his swimming pool, including that it had also been his first time.

Filled with envy, all I could think of saying was "Okay, man."

We left the locker room and I took the Santa Monica Boulevard bus west to Beverly Hills. After that, I turned numb. Robbie and I were both unsure of our feelings when we were together so we became tight-lipped, stiff upper-lipped with each other. There were no words about what was going to happen next, about whether Robbie would want Talley to

himself, whether they were a couple or even dating. I didn't
even know whether I was okay with Robbie having Talley if
that was what was going to happen. But soon enough, I began
to wonder if Talley might sleep with me now that she had had
sex with Robbie.

That's what I really wanted to know, and I had no idea
where Talley's head was. I asked her out to see *Cat on a Hot Tin
Roof* starring Elizabeth Taylor and Paul Newman, which had
just opened. The movie was about a southern family that was
a hothouse of sexual frustration, which is how I felt and hoped
Talley felt when we came out of the movie. We lowered all four
windows of my dad's car and let the wind blow through as we
drove way up on the Palisades and found a wooded viewpoint
facing the ocean. We turned off the headlights and watched
the waves slowly and steadily roll in, cresting that night with a
froth that caught the moonlight. Everything felt slowed down,
as if the waves would never change their mild pace and we had
all the time in the world.

Talley snuggled in close and I put my arm around her
shoulder. "Eli, what does the ocean make you think of?"

"It's endless. So empty. I'd like to know what's out there.
I'd like to go around the world."

"Me too," said Talley.

I thought of Robbie gazing at the distant ocean from high
on the hill above Beachwood when we were in middle school
and his saying he'd like to sail across it sometime. I thought
of Robbie going all the way with the girl seated right next to
me before I had. I told myself to stop being a competitive shit
about everything, including sex.

"You could get lost out there," Talley said dreamily about
the sea. "Maybe that would be good, getting lost and finding

someplace completely new. Then we'd find our way back again. That would be the best part."

"We could do that together," I said. She snuggled in closer and I asked, "What else do you want to do, Talley?"

"See my father again. Maybe he's out there." She was staring at the water. "At least I was old enough to have memories of him before he died—doing homework together, shopping, kite flying, swimming, jigsaw puzzles. He was a lot of fun." She turned her face up at me and kissed me on my neck.

"Why did you do that?"

"I like who you are."

"What are you going to do after high school?" I asked.

"I just want to get my scholarship to art school and move to New York. I want to live in a different place than LA, someplace where the whole world isn't focused on who's important and who isn't. I need to put some distance between my mother and me. I think we're too close; we can read each other's minds." She looked at the starshine and moonshine on the water, then turned back to me. "Where will you be, Eli?"

"I'm going to Cal Berkeley. Then probably law school after that." More waves rolled in before I kissed her, and before the kiss was over, I felt her tongue slide into my mouth. I slid my hand under her dress and moved it up her thigh. She let it stay there for a second, her breathing getting faster. When I began to slide it under her underpants, she sighed. "Eli, don't."

"Why not?"

"Because I don't feel good. Robbie's a shit. He hasn't spent more than a minute with me on the phone or in school since the night of pool-hopping. He's always too busy; he has to get home or something. You know what happened that night between Robbie and me, don't you?"

I nodded yes.

"I am so angry I feel degraded. Not about the sex but the way Robbie is treating me now. I don't want it to be like that with you."

"I'm not Robbie."

"I know you aren't. You wouldn't do something like that." She pressed down on her dress and stopped my hand; she slowly took my wrist and removed my hand from under her dress and put my arm back around her shoulders. "Not tonight. I can't."

That was the moment when I fell in love with Talley. There was nobody else like her in the school. Maybe a few girls who were more beautiful or got better grades or told jokes better, but none of those girls had feelings and cared about things the way Talley did.

A few days later after school, Talley and I were headed toward Larry Edmund's bookshop a hop, skip, and jump away, which was crammed with everything Hollywood, to look for a volume she wanted on 1930s movie dresses. Halfway across the athletic field, Robbie intersected with us heading for Highland. The three of us walked together a few paces until I couldn't hold myself in check any longer and blurted out at him, "How could you do that?"

"Do what? What the hell are you talking about?"

I stiffened, getting taller, and felt myself wetting and pursing my lips with determination. I saw Robbie balling his hands into fists at his sides. I wanted Robbie to apologize, but he still had no idea what was going on. Talley stepped aside trying to figure out what the hell was happening also. Then I couldn't stand how I was feeling any longer and lunged low at Robbie like a football tackle and took him down to the ground.

"What the fuck?" yelled Robbie, trying to roll me over and hold me down. "Why are you doing this?" We rolled over and

over as I kept trying to pin Robbie, he tried pinning me, and neither of us could hold the other down.

Finally Talley yelled, "Cut it out, you jerks!" She scooped a handful of dirt and threw it into my face and then one into Robbie's. The fight was over because we couldn't see. Wiping dirt from my face, I confronted Robbie. "How could you sleep with Talley and then just drop her? How could you do that? It's not right. How did you think it would make her feel?"

Robbie was stunned. "I didn't think. I didn't realize. I thought the three of us would just go on being friends." We stood brushing ourselves off like two movie cowboys after a dustup.

That was Robbie's obtuseness, having no idea how having sex with Talley and then almost ignoring her would hurt her and not realizing how furious it would make me for his treating her that way. In high school, I came to Talley's defense. Years later I was coming to Robbie's defense when his stupidity about how his affair with a patient would make her feel blew up into a disaster for him.

Talley was more generous than the patient. That day on the school field, she said,

"We are friends. It's going to stay that way." She brought out a handkerchief, went up to Robbie, and wiped dirt off his face, then did the same to me, whispering as she wiped my face, "You didn't have to do that. I can take care of myself."

Robbie was ashamed and confused. Yet there was still more to it. Suddenly as he brushed his hair back from his face, he broke into a huge half-proud, half-apologetic smile. "There's something I haven't told you. I kept it a secret because my dad asked me to, but I have to tell you. Marilyn Monroe has moved into our house. My mother isn't inviting her friends over now. They don't know."

"Whew." I let out a whistle. "You're making this up." But I knew it was true because Robbie would have laughed by now if he was joking and he was teasing us.

"No. It's true. My dad wants her to have a family because she's never had one. He thinks it may give her some stability if she can lean on us. She has appointments with my father in his office at the house four or five days a week and often stays for dinner with us. She can stay overnight in the studio by the pool whenever she wants. She had been living at the Roosevelt Hotel." Robbie flung his hand up, pointing at the tall, redbrick hotel rising up a couple of blocks away. "My dad's helping her shop for a house in Brentwood. Not a fancy house but one that's small and private."

Talley and I both got it. Robbie had dropped her because of Marilyn. That was why he hadn't called her. That was why he always wanted to get home as soon as possible after school; he had eyes only for the star.

Our curiosity took over. "What's she like?" Talley asked.

"Nice, really nice. She's funny; she's smart. She's nothing like she is in most of her movies. The hard part is she's really moody. Sometimes she barely says a word over dinner; sometimes she's chatty as can be. It's like having a big sister."

"Some big sister, lucky bastard," I said.

"Like an older sister I never had."

"Beautiful, big sister," I added.

Talley decided that was enough and brought us together with a hug. "Friends," she said. Then she gave Robbie a push uphill, me a push west, and turned and walked lightly toward the flats.

In the spring of our senior year, we all stayed really busy, with Robbie and me playing soccer and keeping up our grades and Talley doing the costumes for the final play of the year. I also volunteered to help build the sets for her play and position the lights so I could stay close to her. She and I pumped Robbie a couple of times about how things were going with Marilyn and asked him if he would invite us over to meet her, but he prevaricated. All he said were things like "She has bronchitis" or "She's away for a few days." He told us that Marilyn was feeling down because a lot of reviewers had panned her new movie, *The Misfits*. Their criticisms were making her feel like hiding.

She'd made the film a couple of years earlier on the Black Rock Desert north of Reno and it was there that her marriage to Arthur Miller had fallen apart. He'd written the script to give her an opportunity to do some real acting in a serious role, an experience Arthur and Marilyn could bond over. Instead he took up with the still photographer on the set. Marilyn probably wasn't faithful herself. And now she was also grieving the death of her costar Clark Gable, who'd died from a heart attack a few weeks after the film was finished, and hurting for her other costar, Montgomery Clift, who had started using drugs again. Both things haunted her.

Talley wouldn't let go of it. "Robbie, your dad wants her to feel like your house is her house, her home. So it's normal for you to have a friend or two over. That means kids like us."

"My father wants her to have her privacy. Even my mother doesn't invite her friends over anymore unless she knows Marilyn won't be there."

Talley played the guilt card. "Robbie, you owe me."

I piled it on. "Prove she's there," I said.

Finally he agreed. "Okay. I'll ask her about Saturday afternoon. She usually finishes her session with my father around 2 p.m., swims a bit, suns a bit, reads, takes a nap in the studio, and has dinner with us. I'll tell her my two best

friends would like to come over and meet her. See what she
says. I think she may say yes because she actually likes being
with people. She feels lonely and shut in when there is nobody
around. My father is trying to get her to pace her social life
and learn to be alone. But no autographs and no talking to her
unless she starts a conversation. And you can't stay for dinner."

I think when you come right down to it, Robbie wanted
to get us off his back by agreeing to set up our visit to his
house. And deep down, he wanted to show off for us, at least
a little, like most everybody in Los Angeles likes to do. Talley,
generous as she was, felt there was a part of him that just wanted
to please us and make amends for dropping her. She was pretty
sure Robbie himself didn't know what his feelings were.

"Can I bring my camera?" she teased, and Robbie growled
at her like a wary dog.

In preparation for the visit, Talley and I went to see *The
Misfits* that night. It was a strong movie, filmed in black and
bright white to show the heat radiating off the desert stretching
to eternity with black lava mountains rimming it right and
left. The story was about a woman in her thirties: a blonde
downtrodden in marriage and life who comes alone to Reno
to get a simple, quick divorce. There she meets two aging
cowboys—Clift and Gable—and they become friends. Maybe
her character and Gable's become more than friends; it is
unclear. However, when she sees the cowboys driving wild
horses down from the mountains into a corral on the desert
floor in order to sell them to be slaughtered for dog food, she
rebels. At the climax, Marilyn rips timbers off the corral and
sets the horses free.

Afterward, Talley said to me, "I bet Marilyn *is* that woman!
Marilyn became that desperate woman in the story who is
trying to free herself from everything that has held her down.

When she lets those horses go, she finally stops doing what everybody expects her to do and becomes real for the first time."

There was scarcely any romance in the film because a story of lives going nowhere or almost nowhere can hardly be romantic. Marilyn's triumph—or her character's triumph— seemed too little too late to presage anything particularly great to come later in life. I read Arthur Miller's memoir, which described the Marilyn he married as "a whirling source of light," paradox, and mystery who was street tough one moment then "lifted by a lyrical and poetic sensitivity that few retain past adolescence." In the end, Marilyn couldn't help Miller stop being a bookworm, nor could he help her change from being an insecure youngster into a settled, educated person.

It was the unspoken bargain they thought they were making when they married, just like so many years later Robbie and his patient thought they had a bargain—each a different one it turned out—when they began their affair.

CHAPTER
FIVE

As that Saturday approached in our senior year, Talley was in a snit over what to wear to Robbie's pool. She hesitated. "Is it really fair to Marilyn to have us staring at her?"

I too had picked up the tension about seeing her and tried to defuse it. "This isn't a party we're going to, just hanging out at Robbie's. She's not supposed to be in a cloister."

"I've got to think of something special to wear," she insisted. It was the LA breeze blowing the desire to look good and be seen through the air like perfume. After all, part of glimpsing Marilyn was being noticed by her, as if that might open a door. A door to what? Something special?

On Friday Robbie caught up with us after school and led us to the bleachers. "It's a go," he said. "Sometimes a chauffeur brings her even twice a day for sessions with my father. It's all very private."

"No reporters lined up with cameras?"

"No, nothing. Nobody sees her coming or going. She has a scarf over her hair and dark glasses. She wears slacks. She has her own house now only twenty minutes away, but she's with us almost as much as she's there. My dad is helping her cut down on all the pills she takes to sleep at night."

"How does she get them?"

"From other doctors and friends. My dad is trying to get her off them. Sometimes she starts the day with champagne to keep from feeling nervous. This is only between us, right?"

We nodded yes.

"Her treatment is confidential," Robbie maintained.

If it was confidential, I wondered why Dr. Carosso had told Robbie so much. It didn't seem like Robbie should know all this about Marilyn.

As if reading my thoughts, Robbie added, "My father says since we're trying to help her, there shouldn't be secrets in a family; a healthy family doesn't keep secrets from each other so family members can support each other." Nonetheless, Robbie seemed troubled by being so close to Marilyn's treatment, maybe even being a part of it himself. He was frowning.

I offered, "My dad talks about some of his law cases, even mentions names sometimes. I wonder if that's right. My mother weighs in with ideas about his cases and so do I. He listens to our questions even if they are out in left field."

Talley added, "My mother tells me about actresses who are witches and men who are bastards when she is trying to fit their costumes. They blame her when a dress or suit doesn't fit the day of filming because they binged the night before."

"My father says the only sure way he can stop Marilyn from drinking and using barbiturates is to send her away to live in a rehab program, but he thinks that would be even worse for her. She would probably feel that our family was abandoning her, like everybody else did when she was growing up. He says he has to keep her working, keep her on the set, because her identity as an actress is all she has."

"Is it true that she's having an affair with President Kennedy?" I asked. My parents had put me up to questioning Robbie about what they'd read in the gossip column. My question caught him off guard; he didn't say anything, and I didn't push.

The next morning when I went to Talley's house to pick her up, she made her entrance in a sarong she had put together from batik-dyed fabric remnants her mother had brought home from the studio. Talley had sewn the exotic materials together in a way unlike anything I'd seen in a Hollywood shop window to really bring out her curvy shape.

"That's great," I said. "I've never seen anything like it."

"Come on, Eli. Don't you know the sarong Omar Kiam did for Dorothy Lamour in *Hurricane* in 1937?" Talley was poking fun at me, and maybe putting herself down at the same time for not being completely original with her creation. Underneath the sarong, Talley had on a modest one-piece swimming suit.

She saw me looking her over and bristled, "I'm not going to compete with Marilyn's body!" She stamped her foot. Her figure was soft, a bit round; she didn't work out every day or count her calories. She was very cute.

Marilyn wasn't in the backyard when we arrived. Robbie drew us over to something on a table by a lounge chair—a worn, black, leather notebook with gold letters embossed on it that said, "Record." "It's her diary," he said.

Talley frowned at him.

"She leaves it all over the place; she leaves everything all over the place. She likes to write. Sometimes when an idea pops into her mind she just takes a piece of paper—from by the phone, from the kitchen, from anybody's desk—writes it down, and just leaves it, forgets it. We give them back to her and she puts them in her diary. So she doesn't care who sees them." He picked up the diary.

Still uncertain, Talley said, "Should you?"

"It's her way of using what she writes to talk to us and to herself."

We laid towels out on the grass and sat leaning over the diary, looking at the pages together, a few lines here, a few lines there. Talley picked out a section and started reading Marilyn's words quietly but loudly enough for us to hear, and they were scary. She was writing about wishing she were dead and nonexistent and gone away. Talley repeated a line from the diary, "But how would I do it? There are always bridges, but I love bridges."

"That's awful," Talley said. Do you suppose she's thinking of jumping from a bridge?"

I thought of the actress hanging herself from the Hollywood sign. "Remember Peg Entwistle?"

"Peg who?" asked Talley.

"An actress who hanged herself from the Hollywood sign in 1932, when the critics panned the play she was in."

Robbie interjected. "Entwistle left a suicide note, but that doesn't prove she killed herself. It still may have been an accident. She may have changed her mind and broken her neck from falling. Nobody knows."

"Do you think Marilyn is that depressed, Robbie?" Talley asked.

Robbie became very serious. "She's very depressed sometimes. That's why my father has her almost living here. He even found her a housekeeper who is almost a nurse and reports to him. Peg Entwistle died because she lost her family and the critics dumped on her. Marilyn never had a family to lose. My father says she wanted to have a family but hasn't been able to have a baby. And the critics dump on her too. Some of them say she can't act."

"Blow after blow," Talley responded.

"But look at what Marilyn writes at the end. There's hope and beauty. She says she loves bridges; she says that everything looks good from a bridge," Robbie said, pointing to lines in the diary.

"If you go high enough and look far and wide enough, you can always find beauty," Talley mused.

I wasn't satisfied. "She also says she doesn't want to exist."

Robbie grinned like the top English lit student he was. "Maybe she wants to be an existentialist—present but not present."

"Maybe she wants to stop being famous," Talley suggested. She read another diary entry that was in the form of a poem. It began with the words "An actress must have no mouth, no feet, no shoulder" and ended with urging herself to think only of her partner and the feeling in the tips of her fingers.

"Thought without a body," Talley reflected.

"Just the tips of her fingers" came to me.

"You can't focus on feeling, on thinking, on your partner all at once. She's trying to do too much," Robbie said.

"Maybe it's an acting exercise," Talley said. "Let's touch our fingertips together." She raised her hands and Robbie and I followed, fingertips to fingertips. "Feel the feeling."

We closed our eyes to feel the feeling. We heard birds chirping, the hum of the pool pump, a neighbor's music.

Talley started reading the next entry in which Marilyn wrote about listening to her body for feeling and having no brakes and letting go of everything.

"That's very fine writing," Robbie observed.

"Having no brakes, letting go. That's the way I think of her," Talley said.

Robbie added, "My dad says that's what they're working on in therapy—not being all wound up inside, knowing when to apply the brakes."

"Look at this one." I pointed.

"Read it, Eli," Talley prompted me.

It was about how Marilyn felt she was hanging upside down but "strong as a cobweb in the wind." Marilyn said she was like "old glistening frost" yet also had "beaded rays" like "colors I've seen in a painting."

"Her words are really good. 'Strong as a cobweb in the wind' sounds like Walt Whitman for the drama, Thoreau for the nature, even Robert Frost for the images," Robbie said with his usual acumen.

"And so sad," Talley concluded.

A piece of paper fell out of the binder onto the grass, and a puff of wind lifted it into the air. I jumped up, ran under it, caught it, and brought it back. "Robbie, it's a letter to your dad."

Robbie took it and bent over it. It was dated March 1, 1961, just a few days earlier. We looked at each other, knowing we shouldn't continue, but Robbie read on anyway.

In it, Marilyn asked Robbie's father if he had seen *The Misfits* yet. She implied that she was like the bare, strange tree that appeared in the movie and said tears were falling on the page as she was writing to Dr. Carosso but she didn't understand why.

Later in the letter, she wrote that a person could change but wouldn't. That was the original theme of *The Misfits,* Marilyn said, but she lamented that nobody had picked it up because it had gotten lost in too many script changes and the way John Huston had directed the movie.

Near the end, Marilyn said she knew she would never be happy but could be gay. It sounded like an epitaph.

Talley took the letter out of Robbie's hands, put it back in the binder, and closed it. Her eyes were glistening, brimming. She dabbed them with her towel. Robbie looked sheepish and apologetic. I felt that way too, as if we had walked in on Marilyn and seen her blemished without camouflage or makeup.

"She left her binder out," Robbie said, justifying himself. "She wants us to know about her."

"Maybe she likes to show people what she's thinking, the way she likes to show her whole body for the camera," I put in, defending Robbie's impulse to exonerate himself for reading Marilyn's writings.

"She must be very lonely," Talley said.

Just as she said that, Marilyn appeared, materializing like a wisp of blue in a faded work shirt and jeans with short, curly, blonde hair. She smiled at the three of us as if she were pleased to see us and crossed to the studio just beyond the pool at the back of the garden. Minutes later, she came back in a one-piece knit swimming suit with many bold horizontal stripes—black, yellow, blue, white, green, purple, red—cut high on her hips. She laid her towel and book down, pulled on her swimming cap, and made a little dive into the pool, like a lithe kid whose legs stay neatly together almost all the way into the water. Then she swam laps in the forty-foot-long pool.

While she was swimming, Robbie took Marilyn's diary back to the lounge chair where we had found it and put it under her towel, which was held down by a big book she had brought out to read: James Joyce's *Ulysses*.

Marilyn steadily ate up the pool lengths without pausing or breathing hard: fifteen laps of crawl, fifteen of breaststroke, and fifteen of sidestroke. She was smooth, not Esther Williams smooth but totally lost in her rhythm and completely isolated within herself. On her last lap, she raised her head and emerged from her isolation. She smiled at Robbie, making a quick little kissing gesture toward him from the few feet away, maybe to all three of us. Between exhaling and inhaling, she took her last strokes. It felt as if she were one of us, just a girl with the most charming and modest smile we'd ever seen.

She climbed the steps out of the water, pulled off her cap, and toweled off. Her figure was in great shape, nothing fat or over-the-hill about her as the tabloids and gossip columnists rumored she had been while making *The Misfits*. She almost looked the age of the three of us at the pool. Eighteen years older than us and her stomach was flatter than Talley's, as if her looks had been frozen in time when she was about twenty.

Talley saw us looking at Marilyn. "She's an actress. She exercises every day. All those laps—it's her *job* to look good. What am I supposed to do, go to a gym or pool every day just to look good?" She was irritated as if she were asking herself as much as us.

Marilyn had settled at the other end of the pool. She waved at us and said, "Hi, kids," barely loud enough for us to hear. Then she patted the edge of her lounge chair and said, "Robbie, keep me company." Her voice was in its high, breathy register. She spoke differently than other actors and actresses who almost always spoke with a self-conscious intonation and modulation in public, a bit like Robbie's way of speaking. Marilyn's voice was breathy in real life the way it was in the movies, not deep from her vocal cords, not from her body. Her drama was in her body, which had a life of its own apart from her words.

Standing up, Robbie sneaked a self-important *ciao* grin at me and Talley as if to say, "I told you she's my friend," and walked to Marilyn's side.

She turned face down on the lounge chair and pulled her arms out of her swimsuit straps, baring her back for Robbie to rub suntan lotion on it. He worked it into her shoulders, down her back, calmly, patiently, all the way along her spine down to where she had rolled her suit down. Talley and I took it as our cue to leave. We bid our goodbyes and walked out on the path by the side of the house, stilled by Marilyn's words in her diary and our time with her.

PART 2
PROM NIGHT

CHAPTER
SIX

When I asked Talley to go with me to the prom a few days later, it almost seemed like an afterthought. We both knew we were going together. She gave me one of her bright smiles and quick chaste kisses and said she was going to make something special to wear. Before Marilyn came into Robbie's life, it would have been very complicated figuring out who was going with whom to the dance. Probably the three of us would have gone together. The bombshell dropped when Robbie told us that he was bringing Marilyn to the dance. Talley's eyes widened; I squinted disbelievingly. Robbie added self-effacingly, "It's my dad's idea. She's never been to a prom." Of course that didn't dim our understanding that Robbie had an opportunistic streak, though our anger at him had dissipated. After all, I had Talley; his bombshell made life simpler.

The night of the dance, I drove to Talley's home in my mother's new Chevy Bel Air, a car with a lot of shiny chrome trim, one of the first with power windows, and no center post between front and back windows. Her house in a neighborhood of one-story bungalows off Highland, just up from Melrose, was pale-blue stucco built over the garage. Like so many of the little homes on the block, it had a touch theatrical whimsy. Its façade was a miniature of an Andalusian villa with a small dome and two tall, arched windows with wrought iron grills.

While her mother and I waited for Talley to make her entrance into the front room, Mrs. Coates tried to make small talk. She asked me what my plans were after high school.

"I'm heading up to the Bay Area for college. I'm going to Cal Berkeley." We'd seen each other many times when I was in and out of Talley's house, but we'd never really talked. She was trying to get a sense of whom she was handing her daughter over to for the night of the grand ball.

"Good for you. They say that's a really good school."

"Thank you."

"Do you have any plans for afterward? I suppose you'll be a lawyer like your father."

"How did you guess?"

"Kids who grow up happy in good families often want to do what their parents do. Boys follow their fathers; girls follow their mothers. I'm a studio seamstress; that's all that was open to me. Talley's taking it a step further. She wants to be a costume designer. She's determined to go to school in New York City"

"That's what I hear," I said somberly, not liking the idea of Talley being so far away. "There's no good program for her in the Bay Area."

"Maybe if her father was still with us, she would stay closer to home." Mrs. Coates was rolling her eyes down the hallway toward her daughter's room. "Talley never does things halfway. Wait until you see the dress she's concocted."

Talley finally emerged. "Mom, get the camera."

I'd brought a corsage for Talley. Her mom said, "Eli, I'll snap a photo while you pin it on."

I tried, but the bodice of her dress was so tight that I started fumbling with the pin, afraid of running it right through the material into Talley's breast, and pricked myself. Mrs. Coates rescued me and pinned the flower on.

She positioned us side by side, arms around each other's waists, and snapped a picture of us in our prom outfits. Talley was in layers of diaphanous chiffon and organdy over a silky blue slip with white polka dots, ending in a poof at her knees. Her shoulders were bare except for the two spaghetti straps that hardly seemed sufficient to hold up her dress creation, with enough of her breasts showing to keep me looking all night long.

I wore a rented tuxedo with a white jacket and my father's black wingtip shoes because I couldn't stand the shiny rented ones that seemed more like plastic than leather and didn't have any dress shoes of my own. Stepping lightly, Talley didn't seem to notice how stiffly I was walking, feeling like I was encased in cardboard. Practical Mrs. Coates said, "Call if you're not going to be home by two."

As we drove the few minutes to Hollywood High, we both felt that we were on the brink of something more than a fairy tale. Storytelling was in the air and in the neighborhood that was busy with movie palaces, Ripley's Believe It or Not, the Wax Museum, big and little movie studios, little theaters here and there, film processing labs, acting schools, talent agencies, the Writer's Guild, movie equipment and costume rental shops, prop emporiums, and more. In an ill-defined way, we felt that the night's story was incomplete because Talley should have been in the middle of the car's front bench seat between me and Robbie. A new script was unfolding.

During the drive, Talley mused, "Do you think Robbie's really coming with Marilyn tonight?"

"Who knows? They say she's really fickle. She gets nervous about going on stage; sometimes she doesn't show up."

"She is not going to be before a lot of cameras tonight. It's just a bunch of high school kids. Maybe Robbie will end up coming alone and join us."

"I hope not; I like it just this way," I said. Talley scooted in closer to me, her hips and legs against mine, both of us feeling our bodies' warmth.

We pulled into the school parking lot that was already mostly filled, with hardly space for the eight hundred seniors in the class, even with many coming two or four to a car and many in rented limos. A line of Cadillac and Lincoln stretch limos disgorged kids, piling and laughing their way out of the doors in finery that made them trip and stumble as they walked.

The walkway went past the football field with a big billboard over the bleachers that read, "Achieve the Honorable." The walk continued to the tall gym and theater building with the huge profile of Rudolph Valentino on the side. Talley was on my arm, and my heart skipped a beat and my stomach fluttered because seeing "Achieve the Honorable" made me think about a Sheik condom, any condom. Was that an acceptable thought? What the hell does Sheik Territory mean? What are the rules? I had never bought a condom in my life because I'd never had the opportunity to have sex, but maybe it would happen tonight with Talley. The way she had scooted so close to me in the car seemed like a sign, and I should have been prepared.

The prom crew had turned Sheik territory into a sumptuous, elaborate Egyptian fantasy. All they had to do was ask some of the school's famous graduates for help. This year, they'd hit up Judy Garland and Alan Ladd; the money flowed and doors to the big movie studio prop warehouse opened. They had borrowed pieces of sets from *The Egyptian* and *The Ten Commandments*. Two big plaster of Paris elephants straddled the gym entrance along with a gauntlet of admonishing notices nearby put up for the evening: "No alcohol, no fireworks, no smoking." There were no signs about drugs; it was before students began bringing marijuana, LSD, and ecstasy to the dances. A cop, two parent chaperones, and a dean stood by, as if to give emphasis to the rules.

Twenty feet or so from the door, students clustered, taking last drinks out of flasks and bottles, last drags on cigarettes before ditching them in the bushes or slipping them into jackets and purses. Everybody, including Talley and me, was straightening jackets, hitching up trousers, and adjusting necklines and hiplines to make grand entrances into a netherworld that was between high school and a new stage in life.

"When it's eight, nine, ten, eleven too, I'll be going strong and so will you. We're gonna rock around the clock tonight" blasted through the fake palace doorway cadged from the set of *The Egyptian*. We followed the red carpet inside. On the left stretched a long bar serving root beer floats, Cokes, and popcorn. To the right of the red carpet sat café tables, chairs, and potted palms. Faux steles and columns with pretend hieroglyphics turned the cavernous gym into little private places perfect for clustering, gossiping, playing hide-and-seek, and making out.

The scent of perfume, cologne, and aftershave hung heavy like incense, heightening our senses. The prettiness of the girls in their gowns and boys in suits was such that Talley and I needed to do double takes to recognize our classmates. Every once in a while, a sparkle of colored light from the rotating mirrored ball flashed on faces that were still unformed, unwhiskered, pimply, or shaved in a hit-and-miss way.

Talley pointed up to the gym rafters where little electrified fixtures like ancient oil lamps and fireflies swayed. "It's a night sky," she said. "Make a wish." She squeezed my hand.

I fumbled my words. "It's ... uh ... secret."

"I want to go up into those stars. See what's there."

"Can I go with you?"

"If you tell me your secret."

My secret? I wanted to have sex with her that night but wasn't sure how to say it, so instead I looked around and came up with "Robbie's not here yet."

"Not unless we didn't see him come in," Talley answered, leading us past a huge sphinx borrowed from a movie set. Then we passed a ten-foot statue that was a cross between the Oscar and a Nietzsche superman, and it was standing on a can of movie film while brandishing a crusader sword—the work of the senior art class.

Talley was swinging her hips to "Jailhouse Rock." The crooner was good, curling his upper lip like Elvis. A beast—a gryphon with the head and wings of an eagle and body of a lion, borrowed from yet another movie set—was draped over a basketball standard and formed the band's backdrop. Little plastic angels hung from the rafters: beauty and the beast.

"Dance with me, Eli," Talley trilled.

At home in outdoor sports, I was clod-footed on the dance floor, not very good, but the darkness and little points of light dancing on our clothes helped. I just mirrored Talley twisting her hips, doing the windmill with her arms, doing the mashed potato with her fists and wrists hammering like little mallets. She'd skip in close and signal me to put my hand on her waist and spin her away. Then I'd do a turn and she'd spin her way back to me. Somebody passed a flask of vodka. My dancing got better.

A new band took the stage, older guys to do the slow music. The gryphon's eyes winked little red lights at them. Another flask went around, and it all got wonderful: the kitsch, the fantastical movie world grafted onto our familiar school, the perfume and teenage sweat, the music, and pretty girls in party dresses. The band sounded as if the Platters were actually in the gym singing, "My prayer is to linger with you in a dream that's divine." Talley let me hold her as close as I could, as if she was feeling exactly the way I felt. Her breasts, in a pointed bra, pushed into me, and I moved my right hand behind all the layers of chiffon and organdy she'd used in her dress. I could feel her spine and, just like the song said, "our hearts were aglow."

All at once, there was a murmur, a rushing sigh. The wind of hundreds of breaths sucked in, let out, inhaled, and exhaled again, blew across the gym, gathering force until it became the sigh of a thousand people flowing toward the two sphinxes guarding the dance. Up in the rafters, a student quickly crawled along the catwalk and trained a klieg lamp on the entryway.

Robbie had arrived.

On his arm was Marilyn Monroe.

As they walked along the red carpet, the crowd parted for them like the Red Sea for Charlton Heston in *The Ten Commandments*. The band found its footing and struck up "Love Is a Many Splendored Thing," and students tugged on the guy-wires holding the papier-mache Oscar so it moved to the music. Robbie was standing tall, formal, and confident. He had an air of practiced graciousness and noblesse oblige. His black tuxedo added a few years to his looks.

He and Marilyn paused under the spotlight, kids fell back, and he took the actress in his arms. They began to dance as if it was a normal thing to do—come to the prom and dance with his date just the same as with any girl. Except this one happened to be the most famous movie star in the world. How did he do it? How did he keep his head about him? I marveled while adjusting my movements with Talley to try to look calm and sure like Robbie.

Marilyn wasn't trying to outshine Robbie; she wasn't acting special or anything, just following his sure lead, looking comfortable and almost small in his arms, modest and undemonstrative. But we could see that the spotlight and throng of staring teenagers were making her glow with pleasure. Plus she looked golden from her afternoons by Robbie's pool, her lipstick bright red, and her hair more naturally honey than platinum this evening, falling in gentle curls around her face.

"Look at her dress," Talley was saying as she pulled me toward Robbie and Marilyn. "It's the white one from *All about Eve*." Strapless, it pushed her bosom way up and half bare, tight as an hourglass at her waist and flowing down to her calves. She looked older than the other girls, sure, but hardly thirty-five, more college sorority age. Talley showed off some more cinema knowledge. "Charles Le Maire designed that dress for her for the movie. My mother told me. Edith Head did all the other dresses in the film."

Then Talley noticed Marilyn's shoes. They were red satin with thin high heels and two narrow straps with silver buckles near her toes, red satin foot pads, and a red strap crossed behind Marilyn's ankles tied in a bow in back. Her socks, like bobby socks but something else, were thin, fitted white nylon just over her ankles with tops embroidered in red lace. Talley seemed puzzled and troubled by them. "I wonder where they came from."

Then the next song broke out, a fast Jerry Lee Lewis rockabilly number. Robbie and his date stepped apart, facing each other for this dance, mirroring one other in perfect synch with the beat. Marilyn could dance though she wasn't nearly as loose and fluid as Talley. Most of Marilyn's rhythm was in her shoulders; they seemed to lead for her, constantly moving to and fro. Even when she was standing still, her shoulders absorbed the beat from the song and kept it. Her hips and butt followed along, while her face stayed quiet in a sweet little smile. Talley led with her hips.

Suddenly my date stamped one of her pointed heels down on my foot, and I yelped and jumped in pain. My dad's thick leather wingtips had blocked part of the blow, but it still hurt like hell. Talley was angrily facing me. "You can look at me a little bit too. Marilyn's shoes aren't everything."

"I'm sorry." I hadn't realized how long I had been staring at them.

Between dances, a lot of girls were looking pissed because they'd planned their dresses for months and now their guys were gawking at the movie star. Yet other girls wanted to get close enough to touch her, as if some of her stardust would rub off on them.

Finally Talley and I were in close enough to claim our friendship with Robbie. The klieg light had sensibly turned away and there was a space. Robbie gave me a guy's shoulder pat and leaned forward to kiss Talley on the cheek, which made her beam as if Marilyn herself had embraced her.

Then he did what we hoped he would. "Marilyn, you remember my best friends, Eli and Talley."

Marilyn smiled at us, kind of giggling with her bare shoulders, and said in a tremulous, sincere voice that could have been a teenage girl's, "Of course I do; we had such a nice afternoon together. It's so nice to know people Robbie is close to." She extended her small hand to each of us and seemed to start to make a little curtsy and then held it back as if she was as unsure as we were about who was paying respects to whom. "I've never been to a graduation dance before, you know. I moved so much when I was your age that I never had a high school class I belonged to."

Robbie said to our little group, "My dad's idea was pretty good, don't you think?"

Marilyn said, "I think it's such a nice idea being Robbie's date." She touched Talley's chiffon and let it run through her fingers. "I love your dress. Who did it for you?"

Talley flushed from her face all the way down her throat and bare shoulders. "I designed it myself."

"I wish I could do that. Everybody dresses me, tells me what to wear. This works pretty well, don't you think? I picked the shoes out by myself; I hope they're right for a prom. I really have no idea." Marilyn moved her torso for Talley, made half turns right and left, modeling her outfit.

Talley stared, bit her lip, stood up straight as if summoning courage, all five foot, two, of her to Marilyn's five foot, six, both boosted even higher in their heels, and said to her, "Where are you going after the dance? There's a party at the Roosevelt Hotel two blocks away. Would you like to come with us?"

Robbie cut in purposefully. "We're going back to Beachwood Drive after the dance."

I wanted to ask if Talley and I could go back to Robbie's house with them but remembered I had other things on my mind.

Robbie asked, "Who's giving the party at the Roosevelt?"

"The theater gang," Talley answered, still hoping to follow Marilyn to Robbie's.

"Oh the Roosevelt," Marilyn cooed. "I lived there for a while, after Joe and I broke up and before Arthur and I got together. I had a little apartment by the pool, that great pool that a famous artist filled with his designs. When I dove in, I felt I was diving into a painting."

There was a pause. We were running out of small talk and nothing else was possible with so many people about. Marilyn, holding Robbie's hand, said, "The theater gang. Oh, that sounds like too many people. I think we'll pass. I'd rather go home to your house, Robbie. Is that okay?" She seemed to be really flirting with him now and also getting tense, searching for words. "Our house, Robbie, your mom and dad's house," playing with the different meanings with a sly smile.

Robbie grinned agreeably. "Yes, of course."

Marilyn continued. "It was so nice to meet you two again. I have never done anything like this before except maybe in a movie. Maybe in *All about Eve,* the movie in which I wore this dress. In one scene, I came into a big, beautiful party, and the script says I'm not sure how I'm supposed to behave. So I was just myself, unsure about everything, pretending. You two are so lucky to have parents who showed you the right way to act at a dance like this. I bet you two come from happy families. I know Robbie does."

Marilyn paused, readying a thought. "I just want to go back to my family on Beachwood. Just me and you, Robbie." She gave Talley *and* me little pecks on the cheek. "Good night, you two."

I shivered up and down my spine from the kiss and the whole bewildering few moments together. The gym was really black now, quiet time at the prom, just the dancing flecks of light on people's outfits. We couldn't see Marilyn and Robbie anymore or much beyond our own feet as if we were dancing in a dark fog. Talley whispered in my ear, "What was that about? Is there something going on between the two of them? Are they dating or is it just a big-sister little-brother thing?"

Johnny Mathis's song "It's Not for Me to Say" warbled. I flashed to the image of Robbie massaging suntan oil into the small of Marilyn's back at the pool and started getting an erection. I forced myself to find something to say to Talley, which came out, "Your dress is just as pretty as hers."

"Thank you, Eli. I'm sorry I stomped on your foot earlier."

"It doesn't matter." We were dancing as close as two people can get, just swaying and hugging to Tab Hunter climbing the chords as he sang, "Young love, first love, filled with true devotion." We hugged even closer and I slipped my hand down Talley's back and over her behind as the lyrics of the last song of the prom echoed, "Whenever I want you all I have to do is dream, dream, dream, dream."

The Roosevelt Hotel was Hollywood's biggest—twelve stories high with an underground garage, Spanish-style décor inside, and the Blossom Ballroom where they held the first Academy Awards event in 1929. Talley's theater gang had a top-floor suite rented with money from another one of the alums, Lon Chaney.

There were no chaperones there, no teachers or cops, just kids getting drunk everywhere, in clumps seated on the carpet, piled on he couches, all over the king-size bed, getting sick in the bathroom, girls craning to get a peek at the mirrors to put on lipstick. Lots of cigarette smoking. Harsh lights in some rooms, no lights in others.

Fats Domino records seemed to be the favorite, Fats growling, "Ain't That a Shame" and "Blueberry Hill" over and over again. The big, thumping, insistent bass beat made everybody feel they'd crossed over onto the other side of the tracks where rules were different. We'd left Marty Robbins's "White Sport Coat" and "Pink Carnation" behind when we left school property. Some of the kids were making out—long kisses and furtive groping hands. A lot of girls didn't seem to care how high their dresses had hiked up on their legs, but there was not enough privacy to let it go further. A lot were talking about Marilyn and Robbie. Talley and I heard stuff like "Robbie better watch out. That guy is getting too big for his own good." A guy made a cock-grabbing gesture at that comment. One girl snapped at her date, "This prom is turning into a story about you and Marilyn Monroe. I get it; all you'll talk about in the future is that you went to the prom with Marilyn."

All the alcohol consumed was revving people up, making them head to the bathroom to throw up as if it were a rite of passage to be able to brag about puking on prom night. Voices rose. Through the din, we heard one blonde with freshly reapplied lipstick as red as Marilyn's sneer, "She's a whore."

"She's a nympho!" another shouted back.

The party had turned nasty.

Talley and I had been drinking too, and we were sitting on the floor back against the wall, heads light, leaning on each other's shoulder, my right leg over her left leg. It was past 1 a.m. and we wanted to go back to where we had been months ago in the car—touching and kissing with the radio on low.

"Let's split," I said.

"Yes, I want to be alone. But not some place where we sit in your car in a parking lot on a cliff overlooking the ocean with a lot of other cars parked all around us with prom kids doing the same thing. Everybody will be waiting for dawn so we can go home and say we stayed out all night after the dance. We'll be feeling like we have to neck because that's what we're here for and that's what everybody else is doing."

"Maybe go to your house or my house," I ventured.

It took her a good long moment to weigh the question, the pros and cons and chances of being alone, and if we couldn't have a place to ourselves, where would we rather be. "My mom's a light sleeper; we'd wake her, and the house is a mess because of all the sewing. There are cloth samples all over the place. Let's go to your house." Neither of us was sure how that would lead to finding a way to be alone except that we would have to play it by ear and see what happened.

I drove slowly, really slowly, fifteen miles an hour. I didn't know how my reflexes were after I'd drunk so much.

My house was silent and dark except for the sitting room light. Once inside, Talley said, "I've got to call my mother and let her know where I am. I'll say we're here and that we're really tired and I might not be back until morning so she can go back to sleep. If we were at my house, she'd never be able to sleep."

Talley had just started talking with her mother on the phone, explaining why she needed to stay over at my house, when my mother came into the room rubbing her eyes and got the gist of the conversation. Sometimes my mother was very motherly and did the right thing. Sometimes she was tense, absorbed in the demands of volunteer work at a school and running the house. She liked to make life as easy as possible for my father and needed things to be really orderly and without surprises. When she was like that, she got irritated easily, made me the family scapegoat for whatever went wrong, and couldn't do anything spontaneously. I never knew ahead of time which way she would be.

This evening she began with "Eli, you left the garage door

open when you left, and it's open now. Do you want rats to come in?"

Rats in Beverly Hills? What kind of rats? I was preparing to defend myself. Then she looked at Talley, standing by with the phone in her hands, and remembered hearing Talley asking her mother if she could stay over. My mother did a double take, took the phone from Talley, and said to Mrs. Coates, "Of course Talley can stay with us tonight." She looked at Talley again, took in her prom dress, and said to Mrs. Coates, Talley, and me, "I'll give Talley a nightgown and she'll be fine. We don't want her to mess up that beautiful creation of a dress she made."

Maybe my mother smelled the alcohol on our breath and figured there was no choice but Talley staying. Hearing my mother speak about Talley's extraordinary dress straight-faced without a touch of irony, I realized that Talley had made her prom gown with a leap of daring, convention be damned, and this was one of my mother's good moments when she could go with the flow.

She added to Mrs. Coates, "She will have the guest room to herself." She turned to us. "Anything else, Talley? Eli, please check if the guest room is made up for your girlfriend."

My girlfriend. I liked the ring of that; maybe it was true. Talley caught the words and smiled at me.

I showed her the room; it was all ready with a bathroom between it and the library. The rest of the bedrooms were upstairs. My mother padded away in her slippers and came back with a pale-blue, worn, cotton nightgown. She was yawning and rubbing her eyes again as she climbed the stairs, already falling back into sleep.

We locked ourselves in the room and curled up beside each other, the urge to make out and sleepiness fighting each other.

Talley's dress had so many layers of chiffon that I couldn't find the zipper on the back, and she couldn't make the little studs that served as buttons on my formal shirt come out. Suddenly she stopped pulling at the studs, alert. "Eli, what do you suppose *they're* doing right now?"

"Who?" For a second I couldn't follow her, deep into the moment as I was.

"I'll bet they're in the studio by Robbie's pool."

"Think so?"

"She's prettier than I am, isn't she?" Talley was frowning.

I knew this was some kind of a trap even in my half-passed-out, half-sex-focused mind. I couldn't say the truth that Marilyn was more beautiful than Talley, and if I made up that Talley was prettier, she would know that I was flattering her. I found the words that I really felt. "It's perfect being here with you."

"Me too with you. This feels so much better than last time, in your car after the movie."

"Yes." I didn't want to think about anybody else but Talley or anything else except how much I liked her. We started kissing, tongues exploring deeper and broader. Talley's breaths were getting faster.

"Can your parents hear us?"

"They're upstairs; they're pretty deep sleepers, and the door is locked." Sometimes they weren't deep sleepers, but tonight they had to be.

"Eli, help me with this." She turned her back to me and pointed to the zipper. When I had the zipper down, she picked up the nightgown my mother had left and went into the bathroom.

I wasn't sure what to do. I sat on the bed working out the last of the studs on my shirt, watching the bathroom door and listening to the water running and the toilet flushing. Then

Talley came out of the bathroom in my mother's washed-out nightgown that was too long and too big for her, so much so that the bodice was well down and hanging off one of Talley's shoulders so her breast was just about all out of it.

She saw me looking at her. "This thing's too big," she said, pretending to look askance at herself, her cheeks getting pink and her eyes crinkling into a smile. I sat still, fighting the feeling of being turned off and rebuffed by my mother's nightgown. My girlfriend came to the bed and pulled the nightgown up over her hips and over her breasts so I could see all of her, her skin faintly luminous in the moonlight coming through the window, all of her including the dark triangle between her legs. That was what mattered, the place between her legs. I quickly stepped out of the rest of my pants as she pulled my shirt from my shoulders.

Then she said, "Eli, do you have anything?"

The condom. I'd forgotten about it, the one Robbie had given me ages ago, in my wallet behind my driver's license. Talley saw me startled; she reached down by the side of the bed to fish the little foil package of Sheiks out of her purse and give it to me. A minute later, her arms were around me again and she was pulling me into her, with a lot of help from me.

It was over really quickly, just a few seconds it seemed—or maybe a minute—even though I wanted it to go on and on. I wasn't sure what had happened; I didn't even know if I'd been inside Talley when I came. My body quivered, her body had quivered for a long moment, and she sighed and held me tight.

In a few minutes, we were both asleep.

The first light of dawn woke me, and I tiptoed upstairs to my own room. Then I slept some more and had a terrible dream. I heard the Platters' song from earlier in the evening and the words "My prayer and the answer you give, may they still be the same for as long as we live, that you'll always be there at the end of my prayer" while in my nightmare, disembodied hands and arms were pulling Talley from me. Or she was floating into the distance, going away on some strange trip. I kept making the song repeat in my dream, hoping for a different ending, but each time it came to an end, she was farther away, staring at me with a long, lingering, wide-eyed look like a movie scene shot through the wrong end of a telescopic lens. I tried desperately to change the lens to bring her in close, but I couldn't find the right one or make it work.

Robbie would understand the dream better than me. He liked to read about dream analysis. When he was sick at home his freshman year for three weeks with a mild pneumonia, he'd walked into his dad's office and stood looking at the book titles on the shelves. He'd scrolled his fingers along the bindings and they'd stopped on Freud's *Interpretation of Dreams*. By the time he went back to school, he'd finished the book and discovered the secret world of the unconscious, as he said. He was the first in our English lit class to write about the unconscious motivations of the characters we read about in books and plays, before the teacher had even gotten to the subject. It gave him a big leg up. I knew my nightmare had something to do with not wanting Talley to leave for the East Coast. But it also felt like the dream was a premonition of more than not seeing each other for a while.

In the morning when I stepped into the breakfast nook, everything seemed okay. Talley stopped buttering a piece of toast and blew me a quick, silent kiss while my mother, her back to us, scrambled eggs. Tally was back in her prom dress. By now the stiff organdy and chiffon looked like a creased and bent multicolored window screen that had been twisted and walked upon. Barefoot, she had on one of my mother's shawls over her shoulders and hair that didn't look as if a brush had touched it. She wasn't making excuses for how she looked and didn't need to as far as I was concerned, pretty as she was. I felt there was some excuse I should make for myself, though for what and what I should say I wasn't sure.

My father put down the sports section of the *Los Angeles Times* and asked knowingly, "How'd it go last night at school?" But nobody in the kitchen was sure exactly what he was talking about. He added, "Talley just told us about Robbie's date."

My mother asked with a touch of superiority, "How much makeup did she have on? Did she try to show all the girls up?"

"She was a honey, sweet as can be," Talley answered. "She could be one of the Hollywood High cheerleaders. Nobody would know the difference unless they recognized her. But wow, that dress she wore last night, straight from a movie."

My mother looked at Talley's dress, "Oh, it couldn't have been nicer than the way yours looked last night, before it got all battered and crushed."

Talley said, "Maybe I used too much starch."

"Robbie and Marilyn must have been a handsome couple," my mother went on.

My father said, "Pretty fortunate guy, that Robbie. Eli, you should dress more like him."

That was a low blow—my parents' habit of comparing me to Robbie, implying that I should be more ambitious, more intellectual, more clothes-conscious, and more gentlemanly like Robbie. Basically they were envious of the Carossos for the way Robbie brought home honors culminating in class valedictorian. They wanted me to garner some honors, but inwardly, I recoiled when Robbie seemed to be apple-polishing the teachers. Besides Talley didn't seem to mind the careless way I dressed. I didn't answer my father.

My father continued. "I don't think *I* could have handled dancing with a woman like that when I was seventeen. I'd have had goose bumps. Couldn't have uttered a word. Now I meet with famous actresses and actors all the time to discuss studio contracts, and I know about their warts. They have flaws as bad and worse than me, than you, than anybody in this kitchen. It takes a while to see below the surface. What do you think an experience like that will do to Robbie? I wonder how he feels this morning."

That was the question of course—how did Robbie feel, not necessarily just that morning after the prom but deep inside his polished patina every day. I'd wondered about that ever since we had become friends. Was he as excited as I was when we flew down Beachwood on our bikes? As wound up and elated as I was when we played together to win two soccer championships? Did Robbie's outward self-assurance mirror his inner feelings? Did things just come to him effortlessly, as a matter of course? I had to work hard for my successes. I felt sure that Robbie and Talley must have felt more satisfied after they had sex last year at his house than I felt this morning. She probably felt let down because it had been so brief between us. I'd hardly even touched or kissed her breasts.

"I think Robbie's a pretty levelheaded guy; he gets what he wants," Talley said to the table.

"Seems to have won the lottery," my father mused.

Between the spring prom and graduation, Talley and I were no more ready to go steady than she and Robbie had been after their one-time making love. We had our final exams to study for; Talley needed to polish her portfolio for art school and fill out financial aid applications. Soon Talley learned that she had gotten a full scholarship to Cooper-Union art school on the Lower East Side of Manhattan plus all expenses paid. She told me at school, and when we hugged, she pressed into me really strongly. Standing in the school hallway, I pressed back. We determined to finish what we'd started on prom night in the right way.

My house wasn't right. The specter of my mother's faded-blue cotton nightgown on Talley still haunted us. A motel seemed shabby and evasive. Where to have sex again came to us one hot weather evening—on a little balcony just outside the dormer on the half attic of Talley's house over her backyard. We had to cross the low-roofed attic stooped over to get to the balcony, but once there, we spread out a mat and had all the time in the world to watch the sun go from orange to purple to blue. Nobody knew we were there; nobody had ever gone to that balcony. It was completely ours. Yet at the same time, we also knew our time was up. High school was over. Talley and her mother would go east to look for a place for Talley near Cooper-Union. We couldn't make any promises to each other because we were on our separate paths, secure enough that we didn't have to cling to each other or our families. Yet our bodies fit together so well that night on the balcony that we had to come together again.

CHAPTER
SEVEN

Talley and I weren't sure what Robbie was up to during the last days of school, or if it was with Marilyn, and we still didn't know what Robbie and Marilyn had done together after the prom. I figured Robbie would tell me in the summer when the two of us went rafting. It had become a tradition for us ever since we got our driver's licenses after our sophomore year. We both talked our best and deepest when we were floating down a river on a stretch of slow water between rapids and at night over a campfire on a sandbar.

Our dream of running rapids had begun when we were boys watching a flash flood cascade down Beachwood Drive after a winter storm dropped ten inches of rain in one day, two-thirds of a whole year's rainfall. We'd stared at the cascade tearing away chunks of macadam, mailboxes, and front gardens. It set our blood flowing, and as soon as we could drive, we'd gone to the Sierras and started running rivers. The Beachwood flood had fixed in us a sense of excitement about water—its rush, its power, its ebb and flow. Robbie said he'd also felt it when Sterling Hayden, the actor, had talked with him when we were kids about the romance of sailing the seven seas. Robbie still wanted to go out to sea in a boat of his own someday.

In late July, two months after graduation, we packed our camping gear and drove north for seven hours to the high country on the northwestern rim of Yosemite National Park. An outfitter in the hamlet of Big Oak Flat drove us down a steep, rutted dirt road that descended into the Grand Canyon of the Tuolumne River. As we went deeper and deeper into the canyon, parched tall grass gave way to stubble, cactus, cliffs, and boulders until after an hour of hairpin switchbacks we reached a gravel bar at the bottom. A grove of tamarisk trees stood near a small spring that came out of the rocks at the base of the cliff. We unloaded our gear, the truck left, and we set to pumping up our raft.

The canyon floor was about 150 feet across. Boulders, gravel, and sand edged the stream that flowed fast and clear, fed by melting winter snow in the high Sierras. The sides of the canyon were so tall and steep that we had to crane our necks to see the sky. Just downstream of our gravel spit, an eddy formed a deep pool of water that was perfect for cooling off. The air was good and hot but neither sweaty nor exhausting. After we'd cooked and eaten dinner over a driftwood fire and laid out our sleeping bags, we broke out a bottle of Scotch. We poured shots into our tin cups, mixed it with spring water, and felt like we had arrived in paradise.

"I like it here," I said to Robbie.

"To Clavey Falls tomorrow," we toasted each other. It was legendary white-water every rafter dreams of running.

"We've got the whole world here, right now. Who needs anything else?" Robbie assessed. He turned serious, even stentorian. Raising his cup to the canyon wall, he repeated his lines from Herman Melville that he'd put in his valedictorian speech in June. "We are the pioneers of the world; the advance guard sent on through the wilderness of untried things to break a new path."

Up high, shadows were descending the sandstone and granite; soon our beach would be dark except for the campfire and pinpoints of light from stars in the strip of black overhead. Maybe the moon would come over at some point that night, but who knew?

"How do you get your bearings when there is no horizon, nothing, nothing, nothing, just water flowing?" Robbie soliloquized.

"Who needs bearings?" I countered.

"Bearings, bearings, bearings!" Robbie yelled at the rock walls.

They echoed back, "Bearings, bearings, bearings."

"*Does it matter?*" I yelled.

"*Does it matter, matter, matter?*" came back at us.

"Seriously, seriously, seriously," I mocked. "If we rip the raft on the rocks tomorrow, no matter. We just make our way downstream on foot, swim a little if we have to. Sooner or later, we reach Moccasin Reservoir and civilization."

"What does it matter if we reach civilization?" It was Robbie's turn to mock fear. I sensed he was building himself up to something he wanted to talk about by beating around the bush with philosophizing. He was getting ready to talk about what we wanted to talk about and hadn't yet.

I gave him a push. "Robbie, you haven't told me what you and Marilyn did after the prom." I said this with bravado, expecting him to follow suit in a show-off kind of way.

Instead he prevaricated. "Shit man, haven't I told you? I haven't?"

"Not unless you did and I didn't hear you."

He stared at the fire; he made sparks fly by poking it with a stick. He wet his lips with a sip from his tin cup. "She took me around town," he said.

"Like clubbing?"

Robbie looked sad and uncertain in a way I had never seen. "Not clubbing, nothing like that. She took me to all the places she'd grown up." He became soft-voiced and distant, as if receding into himself, and began to tell me what happened that night.

"You know what she said when we were in my car? 'Robbie, honey, I want you to get to know me. I've never shown anybody all the places I've lived before.'" He was summoning up his amazing memory for words and conversations. It was just the way he was able to describe for me word for word years later his encounters with the patient who was suing him. I listened to him raptly.

"Maybe Marilyn felt comfortable with me because I was so much younger; she didn't have to make an impression on me. Maybe she wanted to show my father the places from her past but felt she shouldn't or couldn't because he was her doctor. Something like that."

We stared at the flames and I put another stick of driftwood on, not that we needed the heat because the rock walls and boulders at the bottom of the canyon would give off warmth all night long, but to keep some light so we could see each other's face.

"The first place Marilyn told me to drive was just a few blocks away on El Centro, you know, the Hollygrove Homes. It's that redbrick, two-story building that takes up most of the block. You can see a playground behind the tall bushes and chain-link fence that surrounds it. It isn't ugly, just plain. Nobody's thought of giving it any decoration or is willing to spend money on how it looks. Across the street are those plain, four-story, stucco apartment buildings, really basic buildings, and a few little houses that haven't been torn down for more apartments."

"She said to me, 'This is where I lived when I was about nine, after my mother went into the mental hospital for good. It was called the Los Angeles Orphanage then. My mother was prettier than I am. Her hair stayed brown with a lot of red in it, kind of coppery all her life. My hair started blonde, turned kind of dark honey colored, and now it's bleached all platinum. I think my mother was smart; she was a film editor. Maybe I'd be happier if I worked behind the cameras instead of in front to them. Do you think so, Robbie? But I know it makes me happy when people are looking at me and when there's a camera on me.

"'It's saying my lines that makes me nervous. Your dad says it's important for me to keep working. I don't think he knows how hard it is when I have to speak. I start trembling. That's why I drink too much and take pills.'"

"I didn't know whether to say anything to her or just let Marilyn talk. I could see she wanted to, that sharing this was important to her. I had no idea how hard it was for Marilyn to speak her lines in front of a camera before she started telling me this. Mostly I let her talk because I didn't know what to say anyway—me, who can usually recite an assignment in class without breaking a sweat."

Speaking came to me easily also but in bursts and thrusts in contrast to Robbie's mellifluous style. And I had no idea how hard it was for Marilyn to speak her lines until Robbie told me. "She told me that she was happy in her orphanage with the other kids, that the people were nice, except, she said, 'I didn't have a mother to smile at me like you did when you were growing up, like you still do, Robbie.' She said my mother was really sweet.

"And then she said, 'Do you know what it's like waiting for the phone to ring, wondering if it's your mother calling? That's an actress's life too, waiting for the phone to ring, wondering if it's your agent with a part for you or a boyfriend.'"

Listening to Robbie, I thought Marilyn was describing a really nasty life, yet so many people wanted stardom. Even me from time to time, imagining having the fame of a big-name lawyer.

"She told me to drive around the corner to the Vine Street School," Robbie continued. "It's red brick too, with big, white-trimmed windows, and a block long and three stories high. It has those broad steps in the center that lead up to a row of white doors.

"Marilyn said she and the other kids walked there from the orphanage with a counselor and back to the orphanage after school. She remembered being happy there and skipping along the sidewalk. 'But that's before my body started to mature and sex set in,' she said. 'Do you know about sex yet, Robbie? It changes everything, especially for a girl. You begin to think about whom you can get together with; whom you can make a baby with; who'd be a good father. When do you want to do it? If you're a girl, that's when you stop skipping along the street.

"'I never had a child, even though Joe and I and Arthur and I tried. I kept losing the baby. Do you think it would have made a difference in my life if I did have a kid? Your father thinks so. The doctors think it was because I had an infection when I was young, but I think I was afraid I'd get sick like my mother and have to leave my baby with somebody else. God knows I wanted to be a mother. I think I could have done it.'"

Robbie said to the firelight, "I told her that maybe it was not too late.

"'But I don't have a man in my life now, Robbie,' she responded. 'Not the kind of man you want to be the father of your child, someone who's good, steady, and around. Your father is that kind of man, but he's my doctor. I never knew my father.'"

Robbie shifted his attention to me and said, "I asked her if she knew anything about her father." He turned back to the flickering light as if looking in it for the faces of the people he was talking about. In the background, the river was pattering.

I interrupted his reverie. "What did she say?"

"Nothing about her father then. She told me to drive south two or three miles toward Compton, then turn right and left toward the ocean. When we came to Hawthorne, she said, 'This is where I lived before the orphanage. I can't remember exactly, but it was with the Bolenders who took me in when my mother couldn't take care of me anymore. She was in a mental hospital almost all the time after I was born, but she visited me once in a while. It was a small, one-story house, and in those days, the little hills around us hadn't been all built up with houses. They were like beautiful, round, yellow and tan pillows, green in the spring. I could smell the ocean. I called the Bolenders Mom and Dad except when my mother visited. Then I had to call them Aunt Ida and Uncle Albert. They were really just neighbors who took me in. I never met my father, yet even with all that I didn't have, I think I was okay with my life there.

"'When I was seven, my mother got better for a while and she and I moved into a boarding house in Hollywood near her work. She told me we'd have our own house soon. Once she showed me a picture of a really handsome man who looked like Clark Gable, and I wished he was my father. Of course it wasn't Gable because I was born in 1926 and Gable was just a kid then. I don't know the name of the man in the picture.

"'The name on my birth certificate was somebody named Edward Mortenson, though he and my mother weren't living together when I was born. She and Mortenson had been married but got divorced, and I think my mother just put his name down so I would be legitimate.'

"When Marilyn said the word *legitimate*, she scoffed at it really scornfully."

Robbie poured more Scotch into his tin cup. He drained the pungent liquid, seeming to want to feel and wash away Marilyn's bitterness in the same swallow. "'*That* word,' Marilyn said. 'Who decides? Who decides? And if you are not legitimate, how are you supposed to be different from other people? So I was born Norma Jeane Mortenson to Gladys Baker. Now all that people care about, including me, is whether I'm a legitimate actor.

"'I called myself Norma Jeane Baker growing up. If a teacher asked our names in school, I said *Baker* because that was at least the name of one of my parents; sometimes I spelled it Norma Jean, sometimes Norma Jeane. That's how uncertain I felt about who I was. Any guy who might have been my father never took an interest in me when I was growing up. I was twenty when I signed with 20th Century Fox, and twenty-two with Columbia. Together we came up with Marilyn Monroe—a studio exec liked the name Marilyn and I chose Monroe because it was my mother's maiden name. They sound good together. That's who I've been ever since.'"

Robbie stopped talking and ran the heel of his shoe back

and forth, deeply into the sand. He engraved parallel lines in the sand and then scraped a diagonal across them as if mimicking how deeply his experience with Marilyn had imprinted itself in his mind. He started speaking again. "Marilyn said that she didn't know who she was and that was her problem. 'Your pop says that when I start to feel panicky and that everything is falling apart, I should take a deep breath and ask myself, 'Who are you?' and let myself be that person. The name that always comes up first,' she said, 'is Marilyn.

"'My mother's friend Grace took care of me when we lived in the boarding house and my mother was working or out in the evening. I still remember watching my mother put on her really red lipstick before she went out to dance. I loved to see her smile into the mirror. Grace loved the movies; she told me that someday I'd be important, someday a movie star. She let me wear makeup and curled my hair like Jean Harlow's, and we went to a lot of movies together. That was it, Robbie. Maybe that's what did it to me. Grace had this fantasy about me. Maybe she just said those things to make me happy, but I held on to them. I never let go of the idea that I'd be famous someday and people would love me and I'd feel secure.

"'Then my mother got sick again and couldn't afford to pay Grace to care for me. That's when I went into the orphanage. Later Grace got married and she took me back to live with her. You know what happened next, Robbie? I was getting breasts and a man in the house started coming into my room at night and touching me under my nightgown. So I had to go live with one of Grace's aunts not far from where I live now in the house your dad helped me find in Brentwood. I was in junior high school there with a nice foster mother named Ana for three years, but her husband got sick and so I was back with Grace who had moved to the Valley.'"

Robbie broke off his narration and turned to me. "I think it occurred to me that Marilyn was turning *me* into my father, or at least talking to me the way she talked to my father during her therapy. Except she was telling me all this in my car instead of his office."

I was thinking that there by the campfire Robbie was turning me into his confessor, so to speak. "Do you think she's told your father these things?"

"I didn't feel right about it when she was telling me what they talked about in therapy or should talk about, but what could I do? It wouldn't have been right for me not to listen. And I wanted to hear it; it made me feel close to her and that she was close to me. Not just physically because we were in my little two-seater but in a real emotional way. She said we should drive to the Valley next—take 101 through Cahuenga Canyon and get off at Sepulveda Boulevard. She said to follow that to Van Nuys past the high school and turn off onto a little street called Archwood. It had small, one-story, ranch-style homes that were separated by narrow driveways. She told me to pull over at number 1473. It was dark, but I could see a large front yard with a house that had a door in the center, a modest picture window on each side, and a roof that sloped down from a low peak. There was no porch, no trees, just scrub grass and a waist-high, metal-grill fence around the property. There was a lot next door with a tall palm tree that towered over some ancient fruit trees that looked as if they hadn't been pruned for decades. The whole area was probably once orchards.

"Marilyn told me, 'It hasn't changed a bit, Robbie, since I lived here in the 1940s.' She kept saying my name as if I meant something special to her. It almost felt as if she was saying she loved me, and it made me love her in return.

"'Lord knows I've changed, Robbie sweetie,' she said.

'Sometimes I wish I could be a teenager here all over—go to Sepulveda High again, join the chorus, and get good grades like you and your friends. When do you think we are what we are? How far back do we really have to go in life if we want to start over?'

"She told me to shine the car lights into the driveway. At the end of it was a little house with a flat roof, a place that was once a garage or had been built in the backyard as an afterthought. It must have been two in the morning. A dog started barking, and Marilyn asked me turn off the engine and lights. It was silent and pitch-black when she started talking again. I think she was trying to make sense of her life.

"'That's where I lived next,' she said. 'In the cottage at the end of the driveway, with Grace and her husband. I was fifteen. My life was pretty normal for a while, and I was kind of happy. I'd walk to school and hang out with the neighborhood kids. Jimmie Dougherty who lived in the front house was one of them, but when his parents and my foster parents found out that we were having sex, they decided we should get married. It was that or I had to go live somewhere else. I still saw my mother once or twice a year, but I knew there was no chance she'd ever be able to take care of me again. I was just sixteen and Jimmie was twenty-one.'"

At this point in the story, I was wondering if Marilyn and Robbie were touching each other while they talked, the way Talley and I had been cuddling briefly in my car after the dance before going to my house. Robbie's parents had given him a forerunner of the Ford Mustang for his birthday, a blue two-seater, kind of boxy, with a short rear deck and long hood. The gearshift was between the bucket seats, and the narrow bench in back scarcely fit one person, so how could they touch?

"Marilyn told me she copied the styles she saw in movie

magazines, how she practiced smiling in the mirror while she put on eye shadow and lipstick. 'People said I was pretty the way I was, but I wanted to be prettier. Grace had gotten weird about me using makeup, but she kept buying Hollywood magazines and telling me that I looked as good as this or that actress. I liked to dance, and she believed dancing was sinful. Somehow I don't have hang-ups about sex. I like it. It makes me feel close to another person. My hang-ups are with needing love and doubting it when somebody gives it to me or picking guys who say they love me and don't mean it. Dr. Carosso knows that.'"

Robbie was talking so softly now, and his face had faded into the dark so that I felt I was almost hearing Marilyn herself. He paused and we stared at the campfire flames, their sinuous waves and curves bending to and fro like Marilyn and Talley dancing at the prom.

"'People are so hypocritical about sex,' Marilyn said. 'They probably thought it was my fault that Jimmie came on to me. He was nice to me, but we were just kids with nothing to talk about. He was more interested in hanging out with his friends and playing pool.'"

I broke in on Robbie. "Could be *me* acting like Jimmie Dougherty. Hanging out on a river with you, buddy, rather than spending time with Talley. Anyway, she has plans of her own."

Robbie looked up, maybe registered or maybe didn't notice what I said, and turned back to his story as Marilyn wound hers down. "'You know the rest, Robbie. Everybody seems to know. The war was on and Jimmie joined the merchant marine. I moved into the front house with his parents and started working in a parachute factory. I'd lost interest in high school. If people hadn't been so scared of my sleeping with guys and hadn't married me off, I might have stayed in school and gone to college like you're going to do. I wish I could put ideas together the way people who have an education can.

"'One day an army photographer came to the factory to do a photo shoot for an army magazine and picked me to be his model. I was a brunette when he picked me, my natural hair color, and from then on, I realized men would pay to photograph me. Jimmie's parents thought I was trash for that and kicked me out of the house. After that, I had to make my own way. I actually wanted to. I started modeling and taking acting classes at a little school in Hollywood. I'd do anything to become known, even sleep with guys if I thought they could help me get somewhere. I learned that photographers paid me more if I took my clothes off for the camera and paid more if I was blonde, so that's how that happened.

"'I got my first studio contract that lasted with 20th Century Fox when I was twenty-four, thanks to my first agent from an important agency. That was Johnny Hyde. He was much older than me. Before him, I only had bit parts with no lines or just a line or two to speak. Johnny was my real father, the most like a father of anybody I'd known. He took care of me more than anybody else did until your dad came into my life. If Johnny hadn't died just when I was starting to get good film roles, I wouldn't feel so nervous all the time now. He'd have made sure that I became more than a sex symbol.

"'My life is so complicated. I'm not even certain whether I've remembered everything I've told you tonight correctly. So much of my life has been in my imagination. I just let the idea of being a star pull me along. That's not exactly honest. I grabbed every chance I had, and I made chances. I'd do whatever I thought was best at the moment. I don't think very much. Your dad says I pay the price for that. That I'm impulsive and pay the price later. He's right. He keeps asking me why I don't slow down and start respecting myself more now that millions of people love me. He says I don't have anything more to prove, but if I slowed down, I'd have to kill time alone and that terrifies me.'"

Robbie stopped talking, got up, and walked to the edge of the water. He picked up a disc-shaped stone and skipped it across the river. It made three hops. He scowled and threw another—four skips—and another. The stones smacked the water, bounced, and bounded farther and farther across the river. He was flinging them as if I weren't there. He wasn't having fun; his body was stiff and robotic. It was nothing like when we'd stand side by side and skip stones for fun, egging each other on to see whose stone made the most skips. I had no desire to get up and join him. He was angry; the memory of prom night had upset him. Seven skips was the most he could get, not close to our shared record of eleven skips. Then the disc-shaped rocks he threw started falling shorter and shorter— four hops, three hops, then nothing but a plunk and the stone was gone beneath the surface. He turned from the stream and came back to the fire.

We poured more Scotch and sipped from our cups. Then we toasted marshmallows over the embers. Robbie's flamed up. He blew it out, took it off the stick with his mouth, and scorched his palate. Then he cooled his mouth with whiskey and water.

I couldn't control my impatience any longer. "Come on, Robbie, did you make out? Did you have sex with her or not?" From the moment Marilyn and Robbie had left the prom, Talley and I had wondered whether he and Marilyn would do it. And how? Would she hug and kiss him like in a movie scene, stagey and polished? Would she and Robbie really get into it and lose themselves like Talley and me that first time on prom night—at least until we paused to take off our clothes and something got lost? I both wanted and didn't want to know because I didn't like feeling that I was competing with Robbie over who would have the best first sex. The competition was not about him having Marilyn, however, because I couldn't imagine me with her. Marilyn's host of past lovers and male fans would be looking over my shoulder and rating me and her on some kind of performance scale: prowess for me and artistry for her.

Robbie stirred the flames once more with a stick, weighed his words, and said stiffly, "We went to bed. I mean she went to sleep. She went to the studio by the pool and I went upstairs. I can't say more, Eli. You know why." As if rehearsed, he added, "My father says what happens with Marilyn at our house is part of her treatment and has to stay private." A Cheshire cat smile slowly appeared on his face, the kind of smile he has from time to time that makes him appear all-knowing and utterly at peace. But his next words came out forced. "She was great, man. That's all. Let's pack it in." He sounded as if he was copping out. There was something else unspoken.

The next morning as we packed our gear on the strip of beach by the river before we shoved off, Robbie told me he'd had a bad dream during the night. "You know the movie *Niagara?*" he asked.

"Sure, the one in which Marilyn and Joseph Cotton are visiting the falls on their honeymoon. Cotton plays a disturbed war veteran and he sees Marilyn's character having an affair with another man who has followed them. Cotton chases

Marilyn to the top of the lighthouse by the falls and strangles her to death. She dies screaming."

"Yes, terrible scene. In my dream, the four of us—you, me, Talley, *and* Marilyn—are sitting in a movie studio screening room watching Marilyn die in the film. Horrible, the sound of her screams and the sound of the water drowning them out so nobody can hear her crying for help. What was even more horrible in my dream was Marilyn sitting next to us watching herself die. In my dream, she can't tell if she is seeing herself die in real life or just in the role she is playing, and we can't do anything to help her. We were all terrified. I think she really *is* afraid of dying and that there is nobody who can save her."

He brooded as we sealed our stuff in the waterproof sacks. I sensed that there was more to Robbie's nightmare than sympathy for Marilyn, for her life and the grief in it. Like my dream about Talley floating away from me, I thought Robbie's dream also meant something about his future. The part of his story about his night with Marilyn that he had not come clean about had more in store for him.

Just before shoving off, we sat on the side of the rubber raft and studied a map showing the whitewater for the day. There were three rapids to run: Clavey Falls, Devil's Garden, and Blind Ambition. The name of the last one triggered Robbie just the way we primed each other in the old days—our kid days—jumping up shouting, "No fear!" and racing down Beachwood Drive on our bicycles. Robbie yelled, "Blonde Ambition!"

We jumped up and pushed the raft into the current.

PART 3
AFTERMATH

CHAPTER
EIGHT

Our first year of college, Robbie and I got together infrequently. We continued our quest for good grades with our eyes on what it takes to get into graduate school. Robbie's gift for drawing people to him and the entertaining know-how garnered from his parents got him drafted by his peers into being an officer in his fraternity at Stanford—and two years later president. He didn't go out for the university soccer team but played for the fraternity.

Talley didn't come home for the holidays. I called her house. Her mother said she was spending Christmas with Talley in New York City. When June 1962 came around, I drove by Talley's house, but the shades were drawn and there was no answer at the door.

By August I was back in Berkeley early to find an off-campus place to live my sophomore college year because I didn't want to be in the dorms a second year. I moved into a beat-up, old, brown-shingle, former family home in the Elmwood neighborhood just south of campus. The landlord had crudely split it up into six bedrooms, and the students living there had slapdashedly painted them different colors from pink to black to Day-Glo green. Mine was purple. It was not my doing. I wished I could just call Talley over and let her redecorate the place. But I had no phone number for her. The realization finally sunk in that Talley wanted to be free. It was not that we had broken up; we had just taken separate paths, and I wondered if they would ever come together.

I switched my sport from soccer to rugby because it was a rougher game, and practice had begun. By playing rugby, I could release my frustration and drown my sadness at missing Talley better than in soccer. It seemed to be working; I shoved bodies with all of my strength in the scrum and slammed and tackled opponents as hard as I could without referees blowing their whistles the way they did in soccer. I didn't have any school assignments yet so I followed what the news and gossip columns were saying about Marilyn in the summer of 1962. She looked beautiful and performed well on the set of *Something's Got to Give,* as long as her acting coach was by her side. She came down with laryngitis and couldn't work; she had gone to the Cal Neva Lodge at Lake Tahoe with Frank Sinatra; she disappeared from the movie set to fly to New York City to sing "Happy Birthday, Mr. President" to John F. Kennedy in Madison Square Garden. Then she was back at work, and then she was missing again.

Some columnists said the Cal Neva Lodge was Mafia owned and Sinatra had taken her there to meet Bobby Kennedy, who was arranging an assignation for her with his brother. Most seemed to agree that she had become intoxicated on something at the lodge and had to be flown back to Los Angeles. Then 20th Century Fox fired her from *Something's Got to Give.*

Marilyn seemed to take being fired with equanimity. In July she told *Life* magazine, "Fame is fickle. I now live in my work and in a few relationships with the few people I can really count on. Fame will go by, and so long, I've had you, fame. If it goes by, I've always known it was fickle. So at least it's something I experienced, but that's not where I live." Maybe Dr. Carosso was wrong. Maybe he should have just let her have her moments of fame and drift out of the spotlight instead of pushing her to show up on movie sets and keep working. Maybe Norma Jean was trying to liberate herself from Marilyn, as Talley had thought she had been doing in *The Misfits*.

On August 5, 1962, I woke up late in my purple cubicle of a bedroom while hearing the television blaring in the distance. Usually no one turned it on until the Oakland A's or San Francisco Giants baseball game started later in the day. I left the girl in bed beside me, who was still deep asleep, and followed the noise through the litter from a party the night before to the living room. Marilyn's image filled the TV screen.

She was dead.

The announcer was narrating her life as the screen showed her in many poses—stills taken from movies, studio publicity photos, scenes with her ex-husbands DiMaggio and Miller, the film clip of her singing "Happy Birthday, Mr. President" a few weeks earlier. The dress she was wearing was so tight she had to be sewn into it, they said. The news also ran pictures of her with other people from the entertainment world who were important to her: friends, colleagues, and costars, such as Peter Lawford whose wife, Patricia, was Kennedy's sister, her acting teachers the Strasbergs, Yves Montand, Laurence Olivier, Jack Lemmon, Tony Curtis, Clark Gable—it went on and on. On the screen were glimpses of Marilyn happy, laughing, outrageous, and doing cheesecake poses. There were also glimpses of the Marilyn I'd seen myself—the studious, pensive, wistful girl.

The newscasters repeated the police report over and over.

Robbie's dad had found her in the early hours of the morning in her bedroom in her home in the Brentwood section of LA. Her housekeeper, the one Abel had picked for her, had called him when she couldn't get Marilyn to come to the locked bedroom door or answer her calls through the door. Dr. Carosso rushed over and, when he couldn't rouse Marilyn to come to the door, climbed through her bedroom window. He couldn't find a pulse and called the police at 4:25 a.m. The TV kept replaying footage of the front of her modest, one-story, Spanish ranch-style house with thick, tidy landscaping blocking the view from the street. A police spokesman recited for the camera that there were pill bottles by her bed. Foul play was not suspected. Suicide wasn't suspected. There was no note. Further details would have to await an autopsy.

Of course no sooner did a TV station show the police spokesman announcing that foul play and suicide were not suspected than so-called Hollywood experts and sources popped up on the screen saying she might have been killed because her liaison with the Kennedys was a threat to the White House. Or perhaps the Mafia had done her in because she had seen too many Mafia bigwigs on her trip to Lake Tahoe with Frank Sinatra earlier in the year.

Psychiatrists came on to suggest that 20th Century Fox drove Marilyn to suicide by firing her in June. Friends said she had everything to live for and was upbeat because she and Fox had resolved their dispute. They said she had just signed a two-picture deal with Fox, and they were going to resume shooting *Something's Got to Give*. Peter and Patricia Lawford said they had seen her recently and insisted that far from depressed, she never looked better and was looking forward to their next party. A woman whose name meant nothing to me, identified as a Hollywood spokesperson, with lacquered hair and a gravelly voice, said it was "morally outrageous" the way Lawford had "pimped Marilyn off to the Kennedys" and that he was to blame for her death.

I sat on the sofa glued to the TV for two hours, wanting to call Robbie and Talley but not wanting to miss a single word or picture. I was completely unmindful of the dregs of pizza, beer bottles, chips and dip, overflowing ashtrays, and my housemates drifting in and out. Even the dark-haired girl I'd slept with the night before, who looked like Talley, drifted in and out, unable to get my attention off the Marilyn news on TV.

Finally when the news was into its third recycle, I was ready to get up and call Robbie but wasn't sure if he'd arrived at Stanford yet and had no phone number for him there. I tried his home in Los Angeles, but the phone had an endless busy signal. I reached Talley's mother, who commiserated with me over Marilyn's death but said that Talley had moved out of her dorm in New York and didn't have a phone yet. Mrs. Coates didn't sound worried and said she would tell her I'd called when Talley got in touch.

A few days later, I watched Marilyn's funeral at Westwood Village Memorial Park Cemetery on television. At the grave, her acting teacher Lee Strasberg said that he *did not know* the Marilyn who was a legend. The Marilyn he knew was a poor girl without a family who by dint of will attained stardom and became the symbol to all the world of the "eternal feminine." Those were his words. He said the Marilyn he knew was a shy and expressive acting student who had nurtured all her life a dream of talent that was real and not a mirage. He said her radiance and freshness never dimmed and made everyone who came into contact with her want to be a part of it. On TV I saw Robbie and his mom and dad standing by her casket with their heads bowed. Incredibly handsome, they had become the closest thing to family Marilyn had ever had.

As the eulogies droned on, I thought about what ambition had done to Marilyn and what it could do to me if I wanted to make a name for myself doing something, probably law. My father wasn't famous, just a successful corporation lawyer working for a famous movie studio. It seemed to suit him; I didn't know yet what would suit me. Robbie's dad, Abel, had been a famous doctor with an international reputation in psychoanalysis, and now he was infamous; his mother was glamorous, and now she was publicly grieving. I remembered my childhood fantasy of seeing my name in headlines floating over Los Angeles saying, "Famed Lawyer Wins Big Case," but how many doors would I have to knock on? And how many parties would I have to go to and make small talk with people I didn't know or care about in order to beat out somebody else for a big-name client or case in order to make the headlines? That's what I thought it entailed, and I had a built-in brake against tooting my own horn.

I started feeling angry that Marilyn couldn't have saved herself from crashing and burning and turned the TV off. I'd shaken her hand hello at the prom, and she'd brushed her lips against my cheek to say goodbye. Why couldn't she have been smarter than letting her life end this way? Dr. Carosso was probably right when he told Robbie that there are some traumas people have when they are very young that they can't get over. I kept reassuring myself that my role in this world was going to be doing something with my head and education rather than seeking headlines.

Robbie and I finally had time to sort out our feelings about Marilyn's death the next summer, 1963, on the Stanislaus River. It comes out of the Sierras farther north than the Tuolumne and flows into the San Joaquin Valley near Stockton. It has big drops and whirlpools and deep limpid pools at the end of long stretches of whitewater. Along its course is the detritus of mines and dredging from the California gold rush of 1849—large dirt mounds and twisted, rusted steel. Every once in a while, there is a campsite where a man or two still labor to make a strike. Standing half submerged near the riverbank, they scour it away with a high-pressure hydraulic water hose. The *pockety-pock* of the little gas engine that powers their hoses echoes off the canyon walls. Then they swish the sand and pebbles in a pan with water or through a screen while looking for the yellow glint of gold to make their strike. It is a different route to fortune than the trade in glamour I'd seen around me growing up. Both kinds of work are as gritty as it gets. Gold miners are covered in mud—seekers for fame in Hollywood trash their spirits. Today in San Francisco, a different breed of laborers mines the internet by clicking on computer keys all day long to make their fortunes.

Our first night by the campfire on the banks of the Stanislaus in the summer of 1963, Robbie cut to the bone. "Marilyn called me the day she died."

"Oh man, what did she say?"

"I didn't get the call. Maybe if I'd gotten it and called her back, I could have done something to keep her from dying."

"What happened?"

With measured words, he said, "I was out playing tennis and our maid forgot to give me the message. Marilyn also called Dad the day she died and he called her back in the evening after he finished with his last patient. Her housekeeper answered and said she had gone to sleep early."

"The big sleep."

"My father said not to wake her; he'd talk with her the next morning."

Robbie got up and kicked a chunk of burning driftwood out of the fire, skittering it sparking into the water where it hissed itself out. He sat down again and said, "I haven't told you this. I'd gone into my dad's office the week before she died, when she was having all the trouble staying on the set of *Something's Got to Give*. I could see how scared she was about going to work at the studio, and I read her chart. I wanted to see what he was writing about her."

"You did that? Isn't it supposed to be private?" I was surprised by what Robbie had done yet too curious to resist hearing what he had found out.

"I shouldn't have; I couldn't stop myself. She was almost living with us, and I told myself that you are supposed to know the people you live with. I was too interested to stop myself. I wanted to know what she was like that I didn't know, like maybe who she was sleeping with and other stuff that nobody but my father knew."

"Doesn't he lock his files up? What if some tabloid guy broke into your house looking for Marilyn's file or some other patient's?"

"He keeps the key across the room in a coffee cup on a bookshelf. Nobody would guess. They'd just find a locked cabinet."

"So what was in her file?"

"This is private, Eli. My father kept it out of the public record."

"I know." Though I wondered how confidential doctor-patient conversations are after the patient has passed away or if it mattered.

"He wrote that she could barely manage without him, even

when she was having almost constant therapy sessions with him. He said he needed to intervene with the movie studio at least once a week to reassure them that she'd pull herself together and ask them to give her one more chance. One day she was too discouraged or anxious to leave the house to work. Another day she was too restless to sit still. He said in his notes that he was worried he'd taken on more responsibility than he should and that it wasn't going to work out. He was thinking of calling in another doctor to do a consultation.

"He wrote, 'Like a moth is to flame, Marilyn is to fame.' He said that she needed recognition—attention from boyfriends and husbands; that she was a starved-for-recognition orphan and being noticed gave her confidence, but pursuing attention drained her. He wrote that when she is exhausted, she longs for anonymity and peace. Sometimes she finds it briefly and can retreat from sight. Sometimes she turns to drugs and alcohol to find a *warm soft place.*' Those were her words to him."

Robbie had a clear memory for what he'd read in his dad's office. He was describing "our" Marilyn, the young woman whom Talley and I had briefly chatted with at the prom, the unprepossessing, calm girl reading by Robbie's pool who wanted fame yet just wanted to be a regular person and couldn't be both.

Robbie went on. "My father wrote, 'She's too ambitious to just stay out of sight. She goes from ecstatic one day to despondent the next day because she's trying to have a long-distance relationship with important men in Washington and never knows when they'll get in touch.'"

"Did he say who?"

"No. We can guess. He said this was making her stage fright worse because she was scared she was having more success than she deserved. Each time she went on stage, she was sure she wouldn't be able to hold her audience's interest. He wrote down that he said to her, 'You feel guilty because you're glittering like a diamond and your mother is in a mental hospital. You're afraid that you don't deserve to be a star and will be punished for trying, but you earned everything you've achieved.' He underlined that. Then he wrote, 'She started crying.'

"His goal was to get her to wait until 5 p.m. to drink and to only use the pills he prescribed for her. But he was afraid this wouldn't work because she had too many other sources for pills and there were too many temptations to drink at all the events she attends. She'd met a new guy just before she died, a handsome Mexican businessman with nothing to do with the movie industry. Dad wrote that for Marilyn a new relationship was always a *leap of faith* that it would make her happy, and a *leap of fear* that nothing would come of it. He warned her not to jump into it, to just see how it developed. He wrote, 'My presence comforts her, but can I replace what she didn't have as a child? Can I give her the power to calm herself? Even when she's doing great in the world, she feels it's not enough.'"

Robbie dug at the beach by the shore with a paddle and flipped a bunch of pebbles into the stream. He said, "I was worried about my dad; maybe that's why I went into Marilyn's chart."

"How is Abel doing now?"

"Not well. He's absentminded about things; he's irritable. He's had some chest pains and is going to get it checked out. My mom isn't inviting her friends over the way she used to. He still loves his work, but he's tired."

"Does your father think Marilyn killed herself?"

Robbie looked at the river. The circle from the pebbles he had flipped into the water had grown, merged, and disappeared. "No. He thinks she accidentally took too many pills because she had drunk too much Champagne and couldn't remember how many pills she had already taken. She had barbiturates and chloral hydrate in her blood. He'd prescribed the chloral hydrate to help her sleep because it's pretty hard to overdose on chloral hydrate. She got the barbiturates from somewhere else. He blames himself for not doing more, like telling the housekeeper to wake Marilyn up when the lady called him at 9 p.m. For not sending Marilyn away to rehab. And for not doing less like *not* intervening with the studio to keep her on the film and allowing her stop working."

Robbie got up, pulled a piece of paper from his jeans, and stood by the fire facing me.

"What's that paper?"

"Remember Marilyn's diary?"

"Sure."

"I copied this from it back then. It's a poem about a river, really beautiful in a scary way. I thought it would be perfect to read this evening."

Over the patter of the Stanislaus's flow, Robbie started reciting like a thespian, getting into the rhythm and drama of the words. Soon he wasn't reading, just remembering Marilyn's words. "'I love the river,' she said, but there's a 'thunderous rumbling of things unknown, distant drums. The sobs of life itself.' Those are the poem's last words."

"Amazing, man. She wrote that?"

"It's so good I wrote it down to keep it." The light had changed, and as Robbie spoke, his face was half in a shadow. One side was lit by the glow of the fire, and the other side was hard to see. It was a split face, earnest, sad, composed on the firelight side, and inscrutable on the dark side, something missing or invisible. He moved his lips and feet for a moment as if he wanted to say more, or turn to the light, but decided he couldn't or wouldn't. Like on our last river trip, I thought what was on the tip of his tongue was about the part of the story he hadn't finished, about his night with Marilyn after the prom.

Maybe I was way off base, simply projecting my own fantasies onto him. The more I wanted to know, the more Robbie seemed to hold back. He'd said all he was going to. Just as he had done before, he changed the subject. "Let's look at the map, see what we're doing tomorrow."

Our first two rapids the next day were sporting—bouncing up and down straight shots of rushing water and making tight turns to avoid midstream boulders. Robbie was in the stern, ruddering, and I was in the bow, providing power as he pivoted our raft around obstacles. Sometimes I thrust my paddle into a rock and pushed off to keep us from riding up on it and tipping or ripping the craft. This was the warm-up for Charybdis, class 4 to 5 whitewater, which means, depending on the season, almost unrunnable or unrunnable. Most people portaged around it but not us. Before we actually saw or heard Charybdis, there was a long, calm stretch, then came the sound of the rapid—a gathering roar and rumble like drums or a train coming upstream. It got louder and louder, closer and closer.

"Distant drums!" I yelled over the roar, echoing Marilyn's poem.

"The whisper of things!" Robbie yelled back lines from the poem.

"Moans beyond sadness."

"Terror beyond fear."

We buckled our life vests tight around us. Robbie yelled forward to me,

"Risk-benefit, man! Doctors' Mantra. *River of No Return.*

Remember that movie, Marilyn and Robert Mitchum, 1954, fleeing the bad guys on a log raft?"

"Cheesy movie. All fake. This is real!" I shouted back. It was our last chance to bail out and pull over to shore.

"Things unknown. Let's do it!" Robbie shouted.

We knew from the map that we were entering a narrow chute between stone walls and that at its end the chute dropped eight feet into a deep pool that sometimes whirled so strongly that rafts couldn't break free from the spin. We knew we had to have enough speed going down the chute to fly over the waterfall and land beyond the whirlpool. If we got caught in it, we'd have to abandon the raft and go deep below the surface below the current and swim free underwater.

We raced ahead, bouncing like a pinball from rock to rock and wall to wall, levering and digging at the waves to keep on course. Two-thirds of the way through Charybdis, a boulder spun us around. When we straightened out, we'd lost so much speed that there was no chance of our raft going over the fall fast enough to get past the whirlpool. We were going over the waterfall right into it the cauldron. But on the shore there was an ancient live oak tree, which we'd heard about from river runners who'd gone before us. The tree stretched its rough limbs across the spinning water, and I reached up and grabbed a limb. A second later, Robbie was hanging on to the oak too, gripping the furrowed bark and swinging from the limb like from a trapeze. Water spray rose around us, draping us in a rainbow, and we started laughing with glee.

With last swings from the trapeze, we cleared the whirlpool and dropped into the warm, quiet eddy just beyond the whirlpool.

Five minutes later, our little craft joined us.

We beached, bailed out the boat, and climbed aboard again.

The rough water was behind us, and basking in the sun, we dreamily floated down the river.

As the takeout point came into sight, Robbie said, "How are *you*, man?" in that voice of his that projected warmth and closeness that invited me to open up. "You haven't said anything about yourself. How are you doing?"

"I miss Talley. I miss her so much." My voice broke, and my eyes were tearing up.

"Do you date?" Robbie asked, his easy smile calming me, his hands open and arms extended toward me from the stern of the raft.

It was a bit theatrical, I knew, because he used it with other people to show care and support. Still it always worked with me. At that moment, I loved him and spun around in my seat in the bow to face him. "Yeah, I date. I pick girls who look like her, but they aren't, so nothing comes of it. They get that I'm not really there with them. I don't know what to do."

"Go find Talley, man. Get on a plane. Hound her mother. Get off your ass."

"She doesn't want me to find her or she would have gotten in touch. That's the worst part. Do I go looking for her to make myself feel good or leave her alone so she can find out what she feels like doing?"

"Maybe she doesn't know how she feels; maybe she needs you to let her know." We drifted some more before Robbie said, "I think I've found somebody. Her name is Madeleine. She's premed like me; she's got it all together. She's really beautiful, a head-turner. Tall, slim—if you can imagine Lauren Bacall and Katharine Hepburn all rolled into one. She's perfect for me."

CHAPTER
NINE

When Talley graduated from high school, she disappeared in New York, at least for me, and pretty much for her mother who was uncomfortable the two or three times I asked her for news about Talley. So I stopped asking. Mrs. Coates told me that her parting words to Talley at the airport were "I know you will be a great success. Your father told me so." To my questions about Talley, she gave stock responses like "Talley will be all right. I have confidence in her," her stiff upper lip masking any uncertainty she had about her daughter's fate. She and her daughter had been like sprightly twins after Mr. Coates passed away, and she felt Talley needed to separate from their virtual twinship to come into her own. Mostly Mrs. Coates did have faith in Talley who was going to New York to fulfill the costume design ambition that Mrs. Coates once had had for herself.

Mrs. Coates said proudly, "Talley's going to design the clothes that will give actors their personalities. If I trust her, she will trust herself to find her way. That will make her strong." In a way, her words echoed the way my parents had raised me; they'd given me lots of freedom, and so far, I'd stayed

out of trouble. In retrospect, Robbie's parents had too much
confidence in him, the way from an early age they threw him
in with movie stars and other famous people, not the least of
whom was Marilyn, and were sure he could handle anything
socially. As a result, he became too self-assured, like a rock
climber going too far beyond his last piton.

The truth is Talley did not last long at Cooper-Union art
school. The railroad yards across town on the Lower West
Side of Manhattan near Hudson Street drew her away from
her studies. This was where the freight trains came across the
Hudson River from all points to the west and down from
upstate New York to unload the goods that kept Manhattan
humming. The boxcars often sat in the yards for days. Their
big, broad sides faded and rusted into many hues appeared to
Talley like canvases waiting to be painted. She liked to walk
among them, listening to the rattle and bang of the snail-slow
boxcars and the trucks unloading them, listening to the lap of
water at the nearby freighter docks. She had discovered Jack
Kerouac's writing and felt as if he were a soul mate in his search
for liberation through free association. Walking down the rail
yard tracks, Talley hummed his "Railroad Earth" in a jazzy
rhythm, the way she'd heard it sung in a club.

> the boomcrash
> of truck traffic
> wild-neon twinkle fate there in all
> that eternity
> too much to swallow
> and with that pleased semi-loin-located shudder
> energy for sex
> not knowing who I am at all

In her paint-spattered, torn bibs and black night-watch cap, she could be taken for one of Kerouac's "lost bums so hopeless and long left of meanings of responsibility and try." Little did she know then that her hero Kerouac had no bearings of his own and was being led by the nose by his manic friend Cassidy, who was high on speed.

Before long, Talley joined a gang of taggers who painted the sides of the railcars with graffiti. It was not the typical graffiti of cartoon figures and designs tagged with the artists' names in bold, idiosyncratic lettering but art in the fashion of Mark Rothko's bands of sunset colors, Franz Kline's jagged black slashes, and Jackson Pollock's drips. She and the other members of her gang hurled balloons filled with paint at the freight car rolling stock and watched the paint run down the sides; they sprayed colors from cans. They painted in the railroad yards under moonlight. The thrill was seeing the sun come up to illuminate their art then running from the cops. It was a thrill like Robbie and I had crashing over Charybdis, the waterfall on the Stanislaus River, and swinging from the tree limb that saved us in a rainbow spray of water.

Talley also missed me and was tempted to come to San Francisco to see me. The idea of a reunion with Robbie also had appeal now that she thought he was freed from his enthrallment to Marilyn because the actress had passed away. Talley couldn't help but be drawn to Robbie's courtliness and looks, yet his courtesy and tightly ordered life didn't leave her much space to fuck up. I was different for her; she and I had traded verbal punches back and forth as well as blathered nonsense. And while Robbie's manners and smile radiated warmth that at times made him seem more caring than me, Robbie was that way with almost everybody. When she and Robbie were together, Talley was never sure how much of his thoughtfulness was for her alone. She'd noticed that Dr. Carosso acted that way too. She figured it probably endeared him to his patients.

Talley didn't get on a plane to return west because she wanted to be far away from all of us—from anybody she knew or cared about so she could figure out who or what she wanted to be by herself. The glowing neon night colors of the huge city seduced her away from learning to design costumes in art school. Her favorite costumes were not what her instructors were teaching about how people dressed in a bygone time but the costumes people her age were wearing in the 1960s. She moved out of the school dormitory and into the second-story loft of an old, brick warehouse off Hudson Street. When tagging boxcars stopped being sufficiently liberating, she surrounded herself with vats of colored dye and pots of paint. It wasn't simply art that drew her but color. She needed to become color—to be color, to feel color—which she couldn't do thinking of her mother or me or Robbie. Because her mother had faith in her, she had it in herself, and she used that faith to cut loose from past ties.

Most nights she was at the Fillmore East Ballroom, where the great bands performed: Jefferson Airplane, Big Brother and Janis Joplin, and the Grateful Dead. She liked to dance in extended free-form improvisations to music that ambled along until it picked up tempo, swelling and swelling with sound loops echoing in ways never made and heard before by anybody. In those days, with dance partners who appeared and disappeared, Talley became a swirling stream of light and color under the strobe lights that were bouncing off the spinning kaleidoscopic ball hanging from the ceiling.

In a few months, she was pouring colored liquid and clear oil into large, colored glass slides in the loft. She took them to the rock concerts and from high up she projected the slides with the swirling color onto the stage screens. Within a year, she had the largest worktable in the loft with an industrial sewing machine and bolts of white cotton. She and her crew dipped fabric into cauldrons of Rit Dye to make backdrops for rock concerts around the country.

Talley also began inventing new ways to dye cotton by bathing it in her vats of color tied with unique knots and wire ligatures. Soon she was making bolts of cloth for friends from art school who were designing clothes. Then she turned to adding color patterns to silk, batik, and cloth made from bark.

She and her friends in the loft commune had a ritual. Once a month when the moon was at its highest and flooded through their skylight, they unrolled a large Navajo rug on the floor and scattered Indian blankets and pillows about. A kettle of peyote tea and battered mugs sat on a low table in the center space of the warehouse. Talley, three other women, and four men sat on the pillows as one of the men started softly beating an Indian drum. A woman began shaking a rattlesnake rattle. Talley filled their mugs with tea, and as they sipped, the sound of a Navajo flute filled the room. Pastel lights began to play on white scrims that circled the space, creating a rippling forest of color to get lost in.

As the music segued into acid rock, the seven men and women would rise to wander and disappear in the forest of colored lights and waving cloth. Soon they danced free of clothes, drifting in and out of alcoves to make love, scarcely caring or seeing who their partner was each time.

About two years later, Talley started getting in touch with me and her mother again. She sent us occasional postcards with miniature self-portraits of herself floating in a pastel bubble with the words "Love you, missing you, doing well!" written in spiral, candy-stick colored script. The return address was a New York City post office box. Her mother and I wrote to her from time to time, but I didn't know if Talley would answer me and when she did it was perfunctory—excited words about the fabrics she was making and splashes of paint from inside her pastel bubble—that there seemed little point.

I shared one of her cards with Robbie, who studied it carefully and said, "You've got to see if you can find where she lives, trace it back from the post office box. She's the one for you." By that time, Robbie and Madeleine were planning their wedding, and Maddie had in mind that one or two of her bridesmaids would click with me.

CHAPTER
TEN

All of this was far behind us in July 2007, when I was at the wheel, driving with Robbie from San Francisco to his hearing with the California Medical Licensing Agency in Sacramento. We were a little more than halfway there on the two-hour drive, speeding along the Yolo Causeway through some of America's richest farmland now in full bloom. At the hearing, Robbie would have an opportunity to appeal to representatives of the agency to be lenient with him when they handed down his final penalty. I would be present and could assist Robbie.

The agency's disciplinary choices included permanently prohibiting Robbie from practicing psychiatry or permanently revoking his medical license and banishing him from medicine completely. Lesser penalties were also possible. They could just suspend him for a year or two or put him on probation for one to five years and allow him to continue to practice if he presented his work to a supervisor and took refresher courses in psychiatry. They could allow him a limited license to practice some form of medicine not involving contact with patients, such as radiology where he would only look at the shadows patients cast on x-rays or scans. If that happened, Robbie would have to go back to school to learn a field other than psychiatry. At the very least, he would have to take remedial courses in medical ethics.

After NJ reported Robbie to the Medical Licensing Agency, a female agency investigator interviewed NJ at length. Then two investigators, a man and woman, jointly interviewed Robbie. He'd admitted outright that he had an affair with NJ in his office. NJ gave consent for the investigators to have access to her medical records and they photographed her patient's chart on the spot. Within two weeks, the agency sent Robbie a certified letter stipulating that his license to practice medicine was suspended.

As we drove toward Sacramento, I asked Robbie, "Why didn't you call me as soon as the Medical Licensing Agency notified you that you were under investigation rather than waiting until NJ filed her lawsuit against you? I could have been present when the investigators interviewed you, told you when to shut up."

He said, "There was no point in lying to the board. I crossed the line, pure and simple. I've got to face the consequences, Eli. That lady's anger at me, Maddie's anger, having to leave my house were all so humiliating that I caved instantly. I would have said yes to anything. I don't think I'd ever been called on the carpet before." Nothing like this had ever remotely happened in Robbie's charmed life, and he was totally unprepared to fight it.

"I think this is how my father felt, defeated, when Marilyn died. After her death, the Medical Licensing Agency had investigated him also to see if he had improperly prescribed medicines to her. In fact, my father was very careful, and there was no evidence of wrongful death. Marilyn was in fair spirits the last time he saw her. She called him that day like she did often and didn't say it was urgent. He called her back, but it was too late. A tragedy."

"The world can't live with tragedies, Robbie. People think that if they blame someone, anyone, the next one won't happen. Bullshit. There will always be tragedies."

"That's where you come in, isn't it? Taking the side of the person being blamed. Thanks for being with me today," he said. "Way back in high school, you were siding with the students against the administration when you thought they were sticking kids with unfair discipline. Jeffrey King always got your goat, didn't he, when he went along with the principal against the kids." Robbie smiled wanly at me.

I grinned at the memory of our classmate who always agreed with the school administration when they suspended a student for doing something stupid like throwing water balloons on campus or starting a wrestling match in the hall. "Yeah, he got my goat." I gave Robbie my stock answer for defending some of the guilty people other lawyers wouldn't touch. "Even if a person is guilty, somebody has to try to get them a fair shake."

I also had my mother to thank for helping me decide to be a defense lawyer, because during all my growing-up years, she'd flung accusations at me for silly things gone wrong at home without getting all the facts. Things like the dishes not being clean enough and rodents living in the garage because I hadn't closed the door, even when it was my father who'd left it open. My future profession was fated.

I said to Robbie, "You know you have choices in the meeting that's coming up."

He looked at me strangely. "What are you talking about? I'm guilty as hell."

I measured my words. "You can still deny the whole thing. Tell them the patient is making it all up because she fell in

love with you. Tell them you were sick and confused the day
the investigators interviewed you and felt so betrayed by your
patient making up a false story about you that you confessed
to something you didn't do. Tell the agency that you had so
misjudged your patient—the truth, by the way—that you just
wanted to be rid of the whole thing. You can tell the agency
that you said yes to her false allegations just to make it go away.
You can add that you weren't thinking clearly that day with the
investigators because your wife had just told you to leave the
house because of your patient's story."

I was testing Robbie, to see if he would lie to save his
career by denying his transgression. It was my habit as a defense
attorney. I didn't think Robbie would lie. But I gave this
possibility to all of my clients who had to know their options.
It was a test. If I knew they were lying to me, I would not tell
a prosecutor or jury they were innocent, but I would still try
to get the best deal possible for them. Some would-be clients
got angry at me because I wouldn't defend their lies and went
elsewhere. I didn't need or want their money if they wanted
me to knowingly lie for them.

"I can't lie," Robbie said. "I'm not an actor."

"I didn't think so." I took my hand off the steering wheel
and gave him a thumbs-up of support to show him I was on
his side. Sacramento was just appearing on the horizon, tall
buildings and the capitol dome rising out of the farmland.
"One strategy is to ask the agency for time in order to get
statements of support and gratitude from your patients to show
to the agency. Testimonials that you're a good doctor, that you
are a valuable asset to the community. You can also suggest that
the agency interview your patients to see how they felt about
your treatment and to find out if you crossed any boundaries
with other patients. You'd have to get releases first from your

patients to give the agency information about how to contact them. All of that is legally complicated."

"I can't do that to my patients," he said. "It would compromise all the work I've done with them. It would set some of them up for their symptoms to come back. I have no idea how tactful the agency would be if they actually contacted my patients. They could get nasty interrogating them. As it is now, I just told my current patients that my license had been suspended because of a sexual transgression. I asked nothing from them so they could deal with the news without any pressure from me."

"A twist on the old risk-benefit equation, isn't it? If you ask your patients to help you with the licensing agency, you may get the benefit and they may be hurt."

Robbie nodded. We had crossed over the Sacramento River, passed the freight yards, and reached the green, neatly landscaped state government center. The building in which the Medical Licensing Agency had its offices had drab brown plastic siding, windows that never opened, and dreary sheetrock corridors inside. We paused for coffee and rolls in the lobby and took the elevator to the fourth-floor room, where the committee was already seated around an oval boardroom table, chatting together amiably in leather swivel chairs. The American flag and the state flag stood in a corner, and flashy color photographs California scenes adorned the walls. The ugly office building architecture rebuked the beautiful images of mountains, beaches, and streams. Or perhaps it was the other way around; the scenes softened the room. The tone of the hearing would ultimately set the mood. On the table were transcripts of NJ's interview with the agency and Robbie's agency interview, which we had all read.

At the table sat a surgeon, a woman who was chair of the

committee; a lawyer; an OB-GYN specialist; a psychiatrist; the layperson representative to the committee, who owned the state's largest medical supply business; and the Medical Licensing Agency's executive secretary. It was all stone-cold, audio-recorded formality. There was no sharing of names of mutual acquaintances that we and they might have to break the ice, no offers of coffee or water, no apologies for leveling charges at Robbie.

The chairperson began by looking at me. "Dr. Carosso, I see you have brought an attorney, Mr. Eli Meyer. Both of you understand that this is an administrative process today, not a courtroom. It is not a time for arguing right or wrong or procedure. We are here solely for the opportunity to meet you personally, having received a full report from our investigators. There is always an appeal process if you don't agree with our decision. Mr. Meyer may make a few suggestions to you from time to time, may offer an idea or two, or give you advice, but that is it. We only have an hour."

Then she got to the point. "The psychiatrist-patient relationship is a legal and moral contract that begins when the patient agrees to pay for treatment in keeping with accepted standards of care. That contract defines the physical, psychological, and social boundaries between the two individuals, and you broke that contract. Thankfully, only 4 to 9 percent of doctors commit sexual boundary violations, most of them psychiatrists like yourself." She stared hard at Robbie and paused to take a sip of her coffee, never taking her eyes off him. Next she summarized the facts of the allegations to him and entered new territory. "Did you routinely offer to prepare a cup of hot tea for other patients the way you did with Naomi Jane Morton?"

Confused, Robbie said, "I do that to be kind, to put a patient at ease who is sitting and talking with me. I often like to drink tea when I'm having a session in my office, and it wouldn't be polite to not offer the same to whoever is sitting opposite me. Even when a patient is in psychoanalysis and lying on the couch, sometimes we chat over a cup of tea before he or she lies down. Is there anything wrong with this?"

The psychiatrist on the committee signaled the chair that he wanted to speak. He was younger than Robbie and me, about fifty, with thinning hair grown long and tied back in a ponytail. Unlike the other men in the room, he didn't wear a tie. He gave the appearance of being laid-back, and his voice was soft, but his words weren't. "Dr. Carosso, isn't this overly casual, this sharing refreshments with patients? Couldn't it be misconstrued?"

Robbie asked, "Misconstrued? How?"

"How do you think? I'm trying to get an idea of your thinking."

Robbie answered, "Isn't it common courtesy?" Then testily, he asked, "Is there something wrong with courtesy?"

The ponytailed psychiatrist responded, "Couldn't offering a patient something to drink or eat be taken as inviting the personal? You also kept granola bars on the side table. Couldn't that be construed as asking them for something in return? The very gesture of offering the cup of tea or snacks to them could lead to a brushing of hands."

Robbie's jaw was tightening. He was chewing on his cheek. I put my hand on my friend's shoulder, a calming, restraining touch. Perhaps I shouldn't have; perhaps I should just have let Robbie have free reign to talk his persuasive best. To the committee, I said, "Can I say something as Dr. Carosso's friend, professional though I am?"

"Feel free," the chair said. "Remember this is not a legal procedure and you are here solely to provide support. We will consider everything. We have until noon. Then we break for lunch and resume with another case in the afternoon."

I asked, "Does the committee think that there is something that Dr. Carosso did wrong from the very beginning, even before the sexual relationship started, by occasionally touching Ms. Morton on the shoulder as she left a session when she was very upset? Does the committee feel that it was wrong for him to take her hand in his hands for a moment as she left when she was distraught after talking about her mother's death and the way her aunt and uncle mistreated her?" It seemed as if NJ had demonized Robbie's kindness in her interview with the investigators. I was trying to humanize Robbie in the committee's eyes, trying to normalize his professional demeanor before the affair started.

Piggybacking onto my question, Robbie came to his own defense. "Touching patients to offer reassurance is an acceptable part of medical practice. Standing in the face of someone who is crying and not offering them a hand is not human."

The psychiatrist said curtly, "Touching is never a part of psychiatric practice."

Robbie was chewing on his cheek again, preparing to respond, but I couldn't see any point using our time debating this.

I tried a new tack. "Dr. Carosso is a highly respected member of his profession, a clinical professor at the medical school, in charge of conferring degrees at the psychoanalytic society, a sought-after teacher by trainees. His transgression with Ms. Morton was a one-time offense. He has never done anything like this with another patient, and Ms. Morton consented to the affair. The Medical Licensing Agency can best serve the community by suspending Dr. Carosso's license for a period of time while he takes appropriate remedial courses on ethics and courses on how to treat patients who eroticize their treatment. After that, I suggest letting him return to work on supervised probation. As you know, 85 percent of physicians who commit boundary violations and receive retraining and psychotherapy have no reported future violations after four years."

The chairperson retorted, "We don't know if this is a one-time offense. There may have been other patients. Your point about the patient consenting to the affair is a matter of legal definition. We won't go there, but it is debatable whether a psychiatric patient is even able to freely give consent because of the strong influence a therapist may have over a patient."

The gynecologist added, "The Medical Licensing Agency *never* considers consent when a psychiatrist or gynecologist engages sexually with their patient. It is a blatant failure of impulse control to satisfy the doctor's personal needs even if the patient is willing. It is sexual battery."

The committee members were all nodding. The psychiatrist added, "Your behavior with your patient was a gross mismanagement of the transference that was likely secondary to delusional fantasies about your patient."

Robbie visibly flinched in his chair yet gathered himself. He raised his hand to speak again. "May I stand to talk?"

"If you must," said the chair.

Robbie stood and fixed his eyes for a second at each person in the room and gestured to them with open hands to show he was defenseless. "If you please," said Robbie, "I have the greatest respect for medical ethics and for you, members of the committee." He extended his right arm broadly over them and even gave them a half smile as if he were pleased to see them. The layperson on the committee squirmed in his chair uncomfortably, uncertain whether to lower his guard; the executive secretary's face softened. The others sat stolidly.

"There is an explainable reason, not a sinister reason, why I crossed a boundary with this patient. There are extenuating circumstances. It had to do with Marilyn Monroe spending time in my house when I was a teenager. I didn't understand how that affected me. I didn't address it in my own psychoanalysis, which was part of my training."

Robbie had said he wasn't an actor who could tell a lie, but he performed better as a speaker than anybody else I knew. This time it wasn't good enough. The lawyer on the committee cut him off. "We know about that. You told our investigators. Your patient told us about your fixation on the actress."

Robbie surrendered to them. "I will go back into treatment to address it, if you will give me a chance." He was pained, desperate, feeling betrayed by life in a way I had never seen before.

The chairperson looked at the clock and said, "Duly noted. Expect to hear from us within a month."

Our hour had passed and the hearing was over.

On the drive back to my office, I told Robbie that I expected we would have a date for the trial in about ten months, approximately May 2008. People charged with a crime are entitled to a speedy trial, but Robbie's case was not criminal; it was a civil lawsuit. The district attorney wouldn't be interested in prosecuting him since in his view the case was just about an aggrieved person trying to win money and a charge of rape was not provable. The lawsuit NJ's attorney had filed was a shotgun blast of charges against Robbie that included physical and sexual assault, but assault wouldn't make it past day one of a trial because Robbie's patient returned time and time again to the office after the first sexual encounter and continued the sexual relationship.

As misguided as Robbie had been to enter the Marilyn charade with his patient, it remained to be seen in the civil trial whether NJ's decision to have an affair with her doctor was misguided on her part or not. Robbie would have to endure the uncertainty of his economic future and reputation until the trial came around as best he could. In the meantime, I would be busy with various kinds of discovery and look for expert witnesses to testify on Robbie's behalf. Maybe also there was evidence out there to be found of Robbie's innocence, as preposterous as that seemed. Evidence of some kind, not just arguments to present to a jury.

Back in San Francisco, as I let Robbie off at the Civic Center garage where he'd parked, I said, "We have to meet. We've got a lot of planning to do, and there's more I have to know."

"Any time. You know where I am."

"Your boat?"

"Come visit me. We'll take the *Impulse* out. Call me. I'll come to San Francisco, whatever you want."

"Do you think Maddie will come around and let you back in?"

He crossed his fingers signaling hope. We bear-hugged each other, and he folded his lanky body into the molded driver's seat of his car, a sky-blue Ford Mustang. His car was always a Mustang, from the time he had driven Marilyn to the prom in the prototype his parents had given him for graduation. It was the car they were in when she had told him about her childhood. He had hung onto it as long as he could, and when that car got very old, he bought a new Mustang, and every ten years or so another—always sky-blue. The models changed shape over time and became sleeker and more powerful. However, it wasn't the car's power or cachet that drew Robbie but his memories of that night in his first car with Marilyn when she whispered to him, "Robbie, honey," that never faded. Each new Mustang rekindled them.

CHAPTER
ELEVEN

Sometimes the California Medical Licensing Agency moves swiftly, the way they suspended Robbie's license within weeks of NJ reporting him and Robbie acknowledging it, and sometimes slowly. Robbie didn't hear anything during the summer, then a week after Labor Day they sent him another certified letter. The agency had permanently revoked his medical license.

When he called me, he knew he could appeal the decision but he felt so chastised he didn't want anything to do with the agency. Maybe in the future. Philosophical, he said, "I've had my day in the sun, I guess. Not fame like Marilyn told *Life* magazine shortly before her death, but lots of professional limelight. Now students are shunning me. So I'm getting by just coaching, advising, fortune-telling, whatever you want to call it, because I can't say the word *patients* anymore, can I?"

"Legally no, they're clients; it's a business arrangement. You can't have patients. That suggests you are offering care you aren't licensed to give. Some people would say that would make you guilty of being an imposter."

"A few new faces appear in my office now and then to tell me their stories and hear what I have to say. Shit, maybe I should call them customers, pretend that they are clients, when in my mind they're always going to be patients. The good thing is I don't have to be on call twenty-four hours a day anymore. On call is only for people who treat patients." Robbie smiled self-disparagingly.

"Are you making it?"

"Financially I can make it if the lawsuit doesn't take everything away and sink me in debt. Sooner or later Maddie and I have to talk about money."

"Okay. How about if I come down to Half Moon Bay and go out on the boat with you? It's been a while."

"Let's do it."

I wanted to know what Robbie meant by being philosophical about losing his license or whether he was just pretending to accept the agency's judgment. I was worried about him. I cleared my schedule for a day and headed south from San Francisco. In Daly City, I veered off 280 toward the coast on Highway 1, and in twenty minutes, I was in the oceanside town of Pacifica. It sat on bluffs and in coves where streams from the hills had eroded the cliffs. Typically it was fog shrouded, and every winter, bluffs eroded and a few more houses fell into the surf. From there the road traversed Devil's Slide, as treacherous a route as existed in California, clinging to a ledge on the side of a cliff that fell to ocean. Finally the road descended into Moss Beach with its truck garden farms, and then it was smooth sailing for twenty minutes to Half Moon Bay and the Pillar Point Harbor where Robbie kept his boat.

The land was unstable, so much so that the state was digging a tunnel through the mountain to bypass Devil's Slide; people were unstable; and life was unpredictable. By the time I had arrived late in the morning, the fog had lifted and the day had turned windless and hot. As I walked along the pier past the

side jetties and floating docks with their tangle of deep-sea
fishing boats, sailboats, yachts, and rigging, I wondered what
mental state I'd find Robbie in. His boat appeared, its name,
the *Impulse,* boldly painted on the stern. He'd told me that the
"Old Man," meaning Sigmund Freud, had led him to the name
because Freud had written that impulses had been given a bad
rap. Impulses weren't necessarily bad, but often good—to be
enjoyed, indulged, and managed. "You have to know when to
say yes to them, when to suppress them," Robbie said.

He had been wanting to have his own boat for a long time
so he could go out on the ocean whenever he felt like it. It
was the dream Sterling Hayden had planted in him so many
years ago when he'd said, "Hey, kid, come and crew with
me." When Robbie saw the ship for sale one Sunday when he
and Maddie had driven the gentle route from Palo Alto to the
ocean, it was love at first sight. He'd written the check for the
down payment on the spot and named it instantly.

Crafted from wood and classic white with green trim,
at thirty-five feet long, the *Impulse* was medium size for the
fishing vessels that put out to sea from Pilar Point. She had
been built by Portuguese fishermen at the Half Moon Bay
Boat Works in 1923 and just restored to mint condition before
Robbie bought her. She had a cocky-proud bow, a broad beam,
and a squared-off stern that rode low in the water for pulling
nets on board or reeling in lines. Net fishing was a commercial
enterprise; Robbie and his guests went fishing for sport with
hand lines. The wheelhouse, just aft of the bow, was a finely
crafted antique cabin, kind of boxy like his first car, with two
ample windows close together facing forward and two on each
side. The roof sprouted aerials and electronic gear. The narrow
door to the wheelhouse was in back, a step up from the deck;

alongside, another door opened to the cabin three steps down inside the ship's hull.

Robbie was dozing in one of the stern swivel chairs bolted to the plank deck, his face hidden by steel-rimmed aviator sunglasses and a long-billed cap, Ernest Hemingway style from the writer's Cuban days. Uncoiled ropes littered the deck, and a rod and reel rested in his lap, fishing line dipping into the murky harbor water. I made the floating slip bounce as I reached the boat, and the rocking woke him up. He reached into an ice bucket and beckoned me on board with the offer of a bottle of Bucanjero Fuerte, Havana beer, Hemingway's beer. He popped the cap off another bottle for himself.

"Let's head out," Robbie said. "I'm going to power it up." He entered the wheelhouse and I went down into the cabin to use the john. The cabin was the size of a big camper van with cushioned benches for sitting and sleeping on the sides, built-in cabinets, a center table, a tiny galley with a one-burner propane stove, the head, and water-level portholes on each side. In a moment, the rumble and vibration of the diesel engine came to life. The deck litter extended into the cabin—dirty dishes, a black trash bag filled with garbage and bottles, and clothes piled in the corner. Robbie had small mementos framed behind glass and screwed to the plank hull. There was a picture of me, Talley, and Robbie with our arms around each other taken on our Hollywood High graduation day. She was in the middle, beaming. There was a photograph of Robbie, Madeleine, and their two children when they were small, in their backyard. The Half Moon Bait and Tackle 2007 calendar hung on one side of the cabin. It had high and low tide charts and small pictures of salmon, tuna, and haddock and their fishing seasons.

On the opposite bulkhead was the cover of the famous Marilyn 1949 calendar—the one with her arrayed on red velvet—framed and screwed into the planking. It was the same picture he and I had lovingly pored over in our middle school and high school freshmen years, and he'd anointed the cabin of the *Impulse* as his man-cave by mounting this souvenir in it. I had seen it other times when I was out with Robbie on his boat and may not have noticed it this day if the glass over it hadn't been shattered into vicious fragments. Robbie had thrown something at Marilyn's picture or hit it with a mallet, and pieces of glass now speared her body.

The *Impulse* had never been damaged or let go like this; it had always been shipshape and ready for guests to admire it. Nonetheless, I was glad that he had some anger in him, some fight instead of total gloom or what he euphemized as philosophizing. Marilyn must have become his scapegoat. I went topside to the wheelhouse as the boat gained power and its bow rose to meet the first swells outside of the harbor. Robbie was standing by the high captain's chair, lightly spinning the wheel with his right hand and throttling up the engine with his left hand. I settled onto the chair beside his. He was scanning the sky, the ocean, the scattering of other craft, the dashboard instrumentation: compass, engine gauges, sonar for locating schools of fish, radio, barometer, GPS, and shortwave radio.

He caught me admiring the dashboard and said with pride, "Not bad, all these controls. We can go anywhere on the *Impulse*. I can load it up with food and fuel and we can go to Mazatlan, Acapulco—you name it. Come on, buddy, crew for me."

"Why did you smash Marilyn's picture?" I asked.

Robbie turned bitter. "She's a fucking vamp. She sucks the life out of you. Look what happened to everybody she got close to: Clark Gable, Montgomery Clift, the Kennedys, Sinatra, me, my dad."

"Sinatra died of old age, Clift had drug problems before he met Marilyn, Gable had heart disease before he went out on the Black Rock Desert to film that movie with Marilyn. He never should have signed on to make the film in the beastly heat. And by the way, buddy, just how close did *you* get to Marilyn?"

Robbie pushed the throttle forward, gunning the engine to drown out anything more I would say. The *Impulse* came down from a big swell and sliced into the next one, spray flying over the bow and onto the windshield. He eased off the throttle and for a while we just cruised, heading out to the horizon where a handful of fishing boats lingered. Robbie activated the sonar that swept a needle over a gray-green optical screen with depth and compass readings. "When the sonar hits a school of fish, it bounces back to this gizmo and shows us where to drop our lines. Not today, man. I know you don't like to fish. We're just out here for our health." Robbie had pulled his long-billed cap down over his forehead against the sun, which was now past its peak and in the west. He was squinting into the distance like Humphrey Bogart playing Hemingway playing a Caribbean rumrunner in *To Have and Have Not*, poised between relaxation and worry. Being Captain Robbie was good for him because it shook him out of his usual gentlemanliness.

Several years ago, he'd invited me to join him for a day of tuna fishing, bullshitting, drinking Cuban beer, and smoking Havana cigars with his psychiatrist colleagues. Captain Robbie had somehow scored the beer and cigars in spite of the American embargo against Cuba, and doctors cherished invitations to join Robbie on his boat as much as guests had cherished invitations to Anna Carosso's poolside afternoons in Hollywood. Robbie's guests thanked him with patient referrals.

When the *Impulse* had reached the fishing grounds, there were no other boats in sight, and Robbie set the autopilot on a slow, broad circle. He had a young deckhand who handed out rods and reels and baited hooks and told the doctors how to let the fishing lines trail the boat. When a fish took the bait, he told us that we'd feel it, know it by the tug, and then we were supposed to gradually reel the fish in, coax it in, not yank the line or we might lose the fish. Robbie and his deckhand coached us all the way. "Give it line, reel in, let 'er run, reel in, not too tight, wait till it tires, and reel in."

Finally the tuna they'd hooked and reeled in, forty or so pounds each one, appeared in the water at the side of the boat. They had a greenish-silver, waxen sheen, blue-gray eyes that stared at us, and pink, hook-ensnared mouths. When the first ones appeared alongside, Robbie yelled, "I see color!" Soon the doctors themselves were yelling, "I see color!" as their fish fought the lines by the side of the boat. The deckhand took a long-handled pole with a steel hook-shaped tip, speared the fish, and flipped them onto the deck where they flopped about until Robbie swung a wooden mallet and crushed their skulls. Then the fish went into an ice bin under the hatch cover. The doctors learned fast and soon did their own gaffing and killing.

By the end of the day, everybody had caught their limit of three and the deck was awash with blood. That was the last time I went out with Robbie on one of his party cruises.

This particular day, Robbie set the autopilot so we could leave the wheelhouse and talk without the distractions of instrument readouts staring at us. We settled into deck chairs, and I asked what was on his mind to give him the lead.

He went right to the point. "How can you prevent that woman who's suing me from forcing me to sell the *Impulse*? I love it. It's me, you know; it's part of me. I'm at home here. I can be myself."

"What do you mean?"

"I don't have to act like a doctor, caregiver, medical school professor, psychoanalyst, intellectual. I can just hang out here." A beer in hand, he waved his arm in a big arc, taking in the ship's cabin and the expanse of ocean. "I bought the *Impulse* after the kids were on their own so it doesn't mean much to them, and Maddie never took to it. She doesn't like to be out of sight of land. She says it is too much of a guy thing."

I figured maybe Robbie had taken her out on a fishing day and she didn't like the killing any more than I did. A boat deck slippery with gore was probably no more for her than it was it was for me. Plus lawyering to defend people charged with mayhem was close enough to violence for me without adding killing for sport.

In fact, early in my career, I had been involved in defending a San Francisco politician who had murdered the mayor and a city supervisor in City Hall. The assassin was addicted to Hostess Twinkies pastries. I was a very junior member of the defense team at the time. I'm not sure who on the defense team came up with the notion that all the sugar the defendant was consuming had driven him to murder. It could have been me, but I wasn't the attorney who argued the strategy in court. The lead defense attorney did the arguing so eloquently that it worked. The jury and judge bought it hook, line, and sinker, and the killer got off with a puny manslaughter conviction and eight-year sentence.

Somehow word leaked out that I was the legal boy genius behind the scenes, and it made my career; I never lacked for clients after that. But it screwed with my conscience, and I never took on another murder case. The light sentence also screwed with the murderer's mind. Out of prison in five years, he couldn't live with how he had virtually gotten away with a double murder and people shunning him wherever he went. He committed suicide two years later.

I said to Robbie, "I'm working on an angle. I subpoenaed your patient's university personnel file and department file. The university said they were confidential; NJ and her lawyer also resisted my subpoena. I told them that I would move for dismissal when the trial came up on the grounds that they were hiding material evidence. NJ's attorney finally convinced her to sign a release. The school is dragging its heels, but when we get the files showing how the professor remarkably improved her performance beginning with the first month of therapy with you, we can turn the jury's attention from sex to the outcome of the treatment and win the case."

"You can do that?"

"I'm going to try."

"What witnesses are you going to use? Who the hell is a witness to this?"

"I'm hoping our best witness turns out to be your patient herself. Is she going to come off as a frail, pathetic victim or as competent and forceful as you said she has become on campus? We won't know until the trial begins. I want her to be strong when she testifies. I don't want her to be timid and unattractive the way she was when she first came to you for treatment. I want her to be the beautiful Marilyn look-alike she was when she left your office the last time."

"Why?" Robbie was confused.

"Because I think most of the jurors will admire her that way—the person you and she created together. Part of success will require selecting jurors who will respond to NJ as strong rather than responding to you as a sexual predator. In other words, we don't want moralistic people on the jury."

"Can you do that?"

"We can try. Her attorney will no doubt go after law-and-order types. During the voir dire, means the show and tell, we get a chance to screen the potential jurors by asking them questions about themselves. I can also listen to their answers to NJ's lawyer's questions. I can exclude a limited number of potential jurors if I have a bad feeling about them without giving any reason. I can exclude some jurors for cause if they have experienced sexual trauma themselves, which may make it hard for them to be impartial."

The ocean swells had grown and the ship was rocking a bit. We stood up and stretched. Robbie went to the railing and stared at the water splashing against the side of the boat. I watched a seagull gliding overhead while looking down at us. A thin layer of clouds had moved in and dark heavy clouds were building on the north. Soon we would have to head for the harbor, but first we broke out sandwiches.

"What's with smashing the photo of Marilyn in the cabin?" I asked Robbie. "What's with calling her a vamp, let alone a vampire? She's the last person I would think of as exploiting men. Wasn't it the other way around with her?"

That startled Robbie, but he didn't answer. I persisted. "You and I and Talley didn't see Marilyn as dangerous, did we? Didn't we think she was vulnerable as hell and wouldn't hurt anyone intentionally? Remember her diary and her poem about terror?"

Robbie shook his head, clearing it like a terrier shaking off water. "Sometimes I want to blame her for all this shit I'm in."

"Be careful. Juries don't take to people trying to scapegoat somebody the jurors might feel kinship with or sympathy for—like Marilyn. Those are the jurors we are going for, the ones who admire her and feel kindly toward her."

"I've got another idea. Maybe you can use this one, Eli. It's really a story from the past." He put on his professorial face, his father's face. "Freud wrote about a case that was similar to what happened between NJ and me. It was in 1909, and his colleague Carl Jung was treating a beautiful, young woman named Sabina Spielrein. Jung wanted to sleep with his patient and had the good sense to ask Freud if he should. Freud told him, 'No, don't become intimate with her.' Freud said to Jung that one must dominate the *countertransference*.

"That's the first time that the term *countertransference* appears in psychology. It means the feelings a particular patient creates in a therapist that come from issues in the therapist's own past. Jung didn't follow Freud's advice. And I probably wouldn't have followed your advice if I had called you before it happened. NJ stirred up things in me that were simply too strong to resist." I watched him pause over his sandwich and swallow a draft of beer, wondering where his story was going.

"Jung couldn't control his countertransference any more than I could control mine with NJ. He had an affair with Sabina. Then they both had nervous breakdowns, and they both went to sanitariums for treatment and rest, different ones. She recovered and went on to have a fine career as a physician and psychoanalyst. Three years after the affair in 1912, Sabina published a paper titled "Destruction as the Cause of Coming into Being," which became famous. Jung also recovered from his breakdown, more slowly than Sabina, and went on with his important career.

"Out of destruction, who knows what I'll become? Maybe a new, better Robbie." He'd had enough beer by now that he was feeling less pain. "Sabina had a good life until the Nazis killed her much later."

I was thinking maybe a new, better Robbie if the furies didn't get him too.

"Maybe you can use something from this story in court."
He was right. I would keep it in mind.

The wind had really picked up, and the sea was rising more. Dark clouds were lowering about us, and visibility was way down. Getting back to the harbor would be by compass and radio signal. As drops started falling, we retreated to the wheelhouse. Robbie picked up the harbor signal on his radio, and he set the compass on a northeast setting. Soon we could see nothing but whitecaps, large swells, spray breaking over the boat, and fog through the flapping windshield wipers. We could almost have surfed our way to the harbor just by riding the crests of the waves as they flowed toward land, but that wasn't good enough for Robbie. He gunned the engine to its maximum as if to prove the *Impulse* could beat the elements and then some. From the crest of a wave, he powered down into the trough at the bottom and then charged through the next wave, heedless of the tide that could have carried us to the harbor.

After two hours, we heard the Pillar Point foghorn sounding through the storm, and fifteen minutes later, we saw land.

CHAPTER
TWELVE

Thanksgiving followed close on the heels of Robbie's and my day on the *Impulse*. The Wednesday afternoon before the holiday. I was alone in my office. My secretary had gotten off early, and my last task of the day was catching up with my assistant Julia's progress with the professor caught in the imbroglio with his graduate student, the university, his tenure promotion, and his Signs of Love research.

Julia appeared looking even more like a Cal graduate student in her getup than when she started her investigation. She now had a bulging daypack strapped to her back. "What do you think I have in this sack?" she asked.

"The professor's computer? The student's computer? The dean's file cabinet?"

She raised her backpack over our conference table and poured law textbooks out on it. "After this investigation, I'm going to start studying for the Bar exam."

"Hanging out at the university got you down?"

"Yeah, I need to get school behind me once and for all, grow up, and become an attorney instead of a law school graduate who can't practice," Julia announced.

"What did you find out about our professor Aldenbrand?"

"He has an anger management problem. Otherwise, he's brilliant, fine, clean as a whistle. Charming, some people say. Apparently Aldenbrand was over the top suggesting to his grad student—named Louis Hansen and handsome to boot—that he was plagiarizing Aldenbrand's work. That felt like the kiss of death to the student. The professor could have politely asked the student to add one or two references to his dissertation about his mentor's work and their work together. That could have stopped everything in its tracks. The student could have saved face and said that he hadn't completed the references yet. He could have said he was saving the most important for last. Instead the student became defensive. According to Lou, Aldenbrand started heaping scorn on him, calling him disloyal, a thief, a liar, a shit, a whole string of epithets. The professor was completely in his face, and the student was ready to choke him. He went to the dean instead. It all wasn't necessary."

"Aldenbrand has done this before?" I asked.

"Once, when he was taking his oral exams for his PhD, fifteen years ago. One of his examiners, known as Old Fart behind his back, liked to put PhD candidates on the spot by hazing them with silly questions nobody could answer. His questions triggered our professor. Aldenbrand shut down, refused to say anything. Then he started verbally tearing into the Old Fart. The oral exam fell apart in shambles. Lucky for Aldenbrand, the other members of the committee saw what was happening and really wanted Aldenbrand to get his degree and join the faculty because he was so gifted. The professors reconstituted the oral exam committee without Old Fart, and things went well from then on—until now."

"How did you find this out?"

"Two of our guy's colleagues remember. They shared it with me."

"What else?" I asked.

"Hansen is going around bad-mouthing the professor. He's hell-bent on getting even with the professor for suggesting he was plagiarizing, so he's spreading rumors to other faculty and to other students—whoever will listen—that Aldenbrand stole the idea for Signs of Love from *him*. That's not true because the professor's first paper on the idea appeared before Hansen even graduated from high school.

"He's smearing Aldenbrand, and the professor can't fight back. Because it's a university personnel issue, he has to keep his mouth shut about Hansen even with his friends on the faculty. Personnel issues are confidential, and a student complaint against a faculty member is a personnel issue. So Aldenbrand can't defend himself. The investigator is going to get an earful when he interviews people, so will the tenure committee, and it's all one-sided because it's all coming from the student."

"Good work, Julia. When is the investigator's report due?"

"In about a month. She's supposed to be a really thorough person; she takes her time. She usually gets called on to chair committees handling sexual harassment cases and tends to give reports that protect the university's ass."

"Whatever protecting the university means in this case— siding with the student or the prof? Let's sit tight until the report comes out. I have an ace in the hole, if we need it."

"What is it?" Julia asked.

I winked at Julia. "You'll find out, if we need it."

Julia left and it was going-home time. I locked the file cabinets and swept papers off my desk. On it, I kept a small picture of

Talley facing me because I didn't want some of the miscreants who came into the office to see it. I picked up the picture and gave it a little kiss, my ritual at the end of the day to drive out the meanness that goes with defending people caught in nasty fights. The photo gave me warmth to carry into the evening.

Talley. She had come back to California thirty-five years ago, in the fall of 1972. Her mother had given her my address and me a heads-up that she was coming. I was living in an apartment in the Richmond District, a foggy neighborhood of faceless, post-earthquake streets with modest houses and small apartment buildings. Talley arrived in a peasant blouse with a huge smile on her face, hoop earrings bigger than the smile, and a tie-dyed headband around her forehead and straight black hair. With her was a little girl slightly fairer than Talley, squeezing up against her leg, casting her eyes up at her mother and peeking a look at me. Mrs. Coates hadn't said anything about a child.

"Here's the wonderful man I told you about," Talley said to her daughter. And to me, she said with the same twinkle in her eyes I knew so well from before, "I'm ready to move in with you if you have room for Lucy."

I scooped Lucy up in my arms.

Her mother laughed. Talley was filled with delight. "I knew Lucy and I were home when I rang the bell, before you even opened the door."

That evening, after the little girl was asleep on the couch, we retreated to the bedroom where Talley explained a lot. "Lucy is four. I knew now was the time. She is old enough to travel and to understand leaving our commune and making a new family with you. And you're the best man I can think of to be her father. Did I say that wrong? You're better than the best man."

I could have stopped her talking there and kissed her all over, but she wanted to continue. "There's more. The psychedelic art and music world I've been part of has turned shitty. I mean *really mean and grim*. Janis Joplin and Jimi Hendrix died in 1970 from drug overdoses and it was all downhill from there."

"I know. I've been reading about it. I saw Janis here at the Fillmore West in 1970, four months before she died. She was otherworldly—pouring all of herself into her music and too much whiskey down her throat. I think she was already dying."

"Lucy and I have been living down in the West Village in a big art loft with six other people. There are deaths like Janis' and Jimi's almost every day. Ordinary people. One of my mates in the loft is sick as hell. He survived his overdose but can't remember the last three years of his life." Talley was rocking in my arms now, crying a little.

"I should have followed you to New York," I said.

"No, you shouldn't have. This feels right, the way it is now. I'm so glad you are still free. We took chances, didn't we?"

I licked my index finger and made a streak of wet on the wall by the bed.

"Why did you do that?" Talley asked.

"I'm making a mark for the chance we took."

"The mark will go away," Talley said.

"So we have to remember it, and what it means: no more chances. I won't let you go again." I held her tighter, and she wrapped her legs around me.

Talley was trying to let go of the past by telling me about it. "Last May I marched against the war with thousands of people through Times Square when America started bombing Vietnam again. We were all holding candles in our hands for the dead—not just our boys but the women and children in that poor country."

"I was there too, with you, but in San Francisco. April 24, 1971, 156,000 of us walked against the war in San Francisco."

"Lucy had gotten too big for me to carry on my shoulders like I used to when we marched, so one of the guys put her on his shoulders. There was too much loss and violence. We couldn't stay there any longer. Besides that," Talley whispered in my ear, "Lucy needs you to be her father now."

She began caressing my ear with her tongue, kissing me. I think we both tried right then to make another child—tried long and hard and tender. We were as quiet as we could be not to wake Lucy, but even so, the wait was worth more than all the gold in the world.

Deep in the night, long after we had fallen asleep, we woke up. Maybe it was the early morning fog rolling in; maybe Lucy had made a noise. As the first gray light appeared in the window and we lay listening, eyes open, I asked, "Who is Lucy's real father?"

Talley's eyes grew wider. Her lips started to move, then she turned away and didn't say anything.

From that night on, Talley and Lucy and I were a family. More children never came, even though we would have welcomed them. I had no idea if Lucy's real father was alive or dead and didn't care. From age four, Lucy was my daughter, and I was her father. Now at thirty-nine, she is married and living in LA with children of her own, designing sets at Paramount. I asked Talley a couple of more times in the years that followed who Lucy's father was, and each time she had paled and retreated. It was like Robbie not telling me for so long what had happened between him and Marilyn.

All Talley said when I asked was "I had to be with other

people to be able to create, to become the person I am now. If we had been together like I wanted so many times, being together like we are now wouldn't have happened." In addition to bringing Lucy with her, Talley brought her mail order business of tie-dyed bolts of cloth. She started with cotton and built it to bolts of silk as well, inventing new dyes, ties, and knots as her business grew.

I placed the photo of Talley and Lucy back on my desk. It was 6 p.m. Thanksgiving eve. I locked up and descended the stairs from my office to Hayes Street. On the sidewalk, I gave a parting glance at the Victorian's sunburst in the front gable, and this evening, it smiled back at me. Robbie and Madeleine were coming for Thanksgiving dinner. Our goal was to convince them to reconcile, to get her to give it a shot, and to let Robbie move back into their house. It had been tough convincing Madeleine to come. Talley had made several calls, pleading that it wouldn't be the same having Thanksgiving without her.

I told Maddie that Robbie seemed to be sinking into oblivion alone on his boat. I argued that his affair with a patient was the outcome of powerful forces from his past from way before she had met him and had nothing to do with her. Maddie finally accepted the Thanksgiving invitation.

When I pulled out of the Civic Center parking garage, streetlights were on and traffic had already eased as I drove the few blocks to Market Street. I crossed it into skid row. People were standing in lines outside the soup kitchens, huddled in small groups, or sitting alone on the sidewalk to escape their single-room-occupancy flophouses, wondering where their next meal or drink would come from.

Jack Kerouac had lived here for a time in the 1950s. It was

skid row then and it still was. Skid row never changes. It may move a block or two east or west, north or south, to make room for a new high-rise, a new parking garage, but it is still there, a state of mind and physical wasteland for the people trapped in it. Talley had the Kerouac lines that she had hummed walking in the New York City freight yards after high school tacked now on the bulletin board in her workshop at our home.

They had become my lines as well, lines that celebrated stray beauty in a world where most people saw just decay and misery. As I drove deeper into South of Market, I mouthed Kerouac's lines; I knew them by heart.

> The poor grime-bemarked Third street of lost
> Bums
> So hopeless and long left of meanings/Of
> responsibility and try
> Now it's night in Third Street/The keen little
> neons and also yellow bulblights
> Of impossible-to-believe flops with dark ruined
> Shadows.

In a way, we are all haunted by dark ruined shadows: me by people I've tried to defend in court and failed to prevent from going to jail for crimes they didn't commit, Talley by shadows I am sure were there but didn't yet know about, and Robbie by Marilyn's shadow. And now the mistake he had made with NJ, which was hanging over his life and threatening to engulf it.

I continued south on Fifth Street, past the tent camps under the freeway and past the litter of clothes-stuffed shopping carts and broken-down vehicles that served as home for people who had lost the ability, or never had it, to make a home.

Talley's bulletin board also held a passage that Robbie quoted in his valedictorian speech to our class. It was from a book by Herman Melville. "We are the pioneers of the world sent on through the wilderness to break a new path. In our youth is our strength. In our inexperience our wisdom." With his scholarly acumen and gift for making people feel special, Robbie had picked a perfect quotation for our graduation. Now he was in his own wilderness, something neither he nor Talley and I had ever imagined. He knew so much about psychiatry, supposedly about people, but didn't know enough not to sleep with a patient. Tomorrow he would be joining us for dinner, and we were going to try to help him find his way out.

In fifteen minutes, I reached Twenty-Fifth Street in the Mission District, near Garfield Square and the former printing company building we'd converted to a home and Talley's factory. She was walking back from the Pacific Mambo Café with our takeout dinner of spit-grilled meat, roast corn, and three kinds of salsa. In the kitchen, the turkey was in the refrigerator and a large bowl of tart, raw cranberries, and sweet orange segments was waiting to go into the blender. A big bag of stale baguettes leaned against the counter. The bread was hard as rocks, ready to be crushed for the turkey stuffing. That was my job. I'd wait for Talley to go to her studio to spare her the noise, fetch a mallet from my toolbox, and pound the baguettes into pieces.

Holidays were big in the Latin neighborhood. All the more reason for a party. We kept the windows open that evening and ate accompanied by the music from the band in the Mambo Café. They would play into the night, long after Talley and I were in bed, wound together in each other's arms. Her black hair was gray now with streaks of purple pizazz through it. She was rounder, softer; I was not as muscular as I had been, and now there was grey mixed into my curly red hair and beard. Almost every night, Talley ran her fingers through my beard, caught them in the knots, and tugged. "When are you going to shave this thing?" she'd say.

"I can't shave it," I'd answer. "Every good defense lawyer needs something to make the jury look at him and listen to his words. My beard, my curly hair is my thing. You'd rather I carried a gold-tipped walking stick, used a monocle, wore tattoos, cowboy boots?" It was our ritual conversation.

Tonight she said, "Okay. Make the beard do its magic for Robbie, and its work on Madeleine. Let's get them back together tomorrow."

Robbie arrived at 4 p.m. Thanksgiving afternoon. Dinner was planned for around five. He looked a bit better than he had last time I'd seen him on the boat. Talley offered him her cheek for a hello kiss. They segued it into a kiss first on one side and then the other side—French greeting style—a habit picked up by the Carossos on their trips to France when Robbie was growing up. He saw me appraising him and said, "There is a Laundromat in Half Moon Bay, you know. I finally got my act together to take my stuff there. I want to give this reunion with Madeleine a shot. There's also a liquor store."

He'd brought three bottles of dry Central Coast Chardonnay. We opened the first one. I toasted, "Cheers." I couldn't think of anything better to say. Robbie smiled wryly.

I left him sitting on the same couch he'd sat on seven months earlier when he'd told me what had happened with his patient. Now the couch was freshly decorated with Navajo

Indian Yeibichai dancers—black, red, and turquoise figures holding sheaves of corn dancing across the back of the couch. Talley had tattooed the design into the cream-colored leather with an electric ink gun. They'd told her at the local tattoo shop she couldn't get the needle into the leather shallow enough for the color show. That hadn't stopped her, and she had developed a new technique, something that involved treating the leather with a concoction of acidic redwood bark.

"What do they mean?" Robbie asked about the Indian designs.

"Pray for rain. Pray for good corn. Pray for the harvest."

"I'll drink to that," Robbie rejoined. "I guess we're praying for the future."

Talley exchanged her glass of wine for a pipe bowl of cannabis, her preferred icebreaker. The doorbell sounded, and Madeleine arrived.

She was tall like Robbie and wearing her trench coat against the chill and probable rain. Her usual big bag was slung over her shoulder, her pager attached to the cord. Inside it, we knew, was her otoscope for looking inside children's ears and her stethoscope. She was a gangly beauty with long, gray hair in a ponytail. Mostly she was gently obliging and languid in her Lauren Bacall kind of way. But we all knew that she could turn New England-stiff and Katharine Hepburn arch when it suited her. Bible church raised, she had more moral rectitude than I, or Talley, or Robbie—combined—had, and we didn't know what side of Maddie's personality would show up today: obliging or strict. She had a shopping sack with the dessert and something additional for the table.

Once restrained greetings were out of the way and Maddie's coat hung, I offered a toast. "To those who are not here." It was odd not to have children and grandchildren at this

Thanksgiving, as they had been at most previous ones. Lucy and her husband in LA were hosting Talley and me the next weekend when travel calmed down again. "What's more," Lucy had said over the phone, "I don't belong there while you and Robbie and Mom and Maddie are trying to sort things out, do I?" Neither did Maddie and Robbie's son and daughter want to have anything to do with being part of their parents' conflicts.

We sat down at a round table loaded with food—turkey, sourdough baguette stuffing with chestnuts and sausage, turkey dripping gravy, roasted root vegetables, and tart cranberry relish. Before we could fill our plates, Maddie pushed her chair back and said, "The salad. It's in my shopping bag." She came back with a grease-stained, white, takeout food carton with a red pagoda on it and spooned the oily contents onto a serving plate with a hand that started to tremble. "It's the veggie special: mung beans, bamboo shoots, garlic sauce dressing, and peppers. Hunan." Red chili peppers poured out of the carton, and the aroma of garlic took over the room.

Maddie sat back down. If she were making some kind of statement with the dish she'd brought, we couldn't tell from her face. Maybe it would taste good. Or maybe Maddie was trying to trash the dinner with a dish that might explode in our mouths. Robbie studied his wife's face for some sign that she knew what she was doing, whatever it was, but she offered no clue. Talley put her hand on Maddie's to calm the trembling.

We passed the serving platters and filled our own plates quietly except for making insipid, kind comments about the work that had gone into the dinner and giving updates on what our children were doing. Robbie replenished the wine glasses. Now, as we took our first bites, there was silence except for the clatter of utensils on china. The night before, Talley and

I had debated whether we needed a plan to coax Robbie and Madeline together again, to get Robbie out of his boat and back into his house. I favored having an agenda, talking points for things to say and arguments to throw at them during dinner. Talley wanted to improvise, to let dinner evolve and see what happened. In the end, Talley prevailed, not because we agreed but because we couldn't agree, so there was no plan. Just silence except for the sounds of eating. If Talley had listened to me, we would have scripted something for a moment like this; instead she raised her hands toward me, palms up, and opened, as if to say, "It's yours. Do something."

I decided to take the bull by the horns and took a bite of Maddie's pepper dish. At first it was deliciously garlicky and savory; sometimes, well-roasted, seeded peppers add more color than fire to a dish. Then my palate detonated with burning heat. I downed a whole glass of water and gasped for more.

"What are you trying to say, Maddie? What's your point with this dish?" Robbie asked her, clattering his fork onto his plate.

"Veggie special or midnight special?" Talley asked, handing me another glass of water.

"Midnight special!" Maddie exclaimed. "I'm sorry you got hit in the crossfire, Eli. Collateral damage. It was meant for Robbie."

Maddie and Talley were referring to the midnight special small pistol with which Frankie had shot and killed her two-timing boyfriend. A year ago, the four of us had gone to the ballet in San Francisco and seen a staging of that blues legend. I was also remembering something else. Five years ago in court, I had started cross-examining one of San Francisco's best-known citizens who lived atop Russian Hill and was lionized for his eye-grabbing, generous philanthropy. The man had given very damaging testimony against my client, a bookkeeper, who was being tried for embezzlement from the charity the prominent philanthropist headed. My client was guilty of theft but not nearly as much larceny as the man on the stand—the philanthropist—had committed.

I had buttonholed the "Mr. Big" privately the day before his scheduled testimony and told him that our firm had discovered that he was receiving hundreds of thousands of dollars in kickbacks from causes to which he directed funds. I threatened to reveal *his* corruption if he took the stand against my client. He could have refused to be a witness for the prosecution. Nonetheless, there he was on the stand, and I didn't know why. I wondered why in the world he was risking his future as I asked him my next question. "Do you know about the bank account at—" Before I could finish the question, he reached into his right dress boot, pulled out a small revolver, put it to his temple, and shot himself. The court went into shock.

Maybe he took his life because his goose would have been cooked anyway because if my office could discover what he had been doing, it would have come out sooner rather than later even if he didn't testify against my client. He must have seen that his days of shining in the social limelight were numbered. Oddly, I think the philanthropist was giving me the credit for ending his scam and departed the scene in a twisted way by killing himself on the stand as I questioned him. He had gotten past the security guards because they knew he was an important society figure and didn't want to ask him to do anything more than empty his pockets when he went through the screening. As for my client, the district attorney had no more stomach for the case, and I plea-bargained his case down to three years' probation.

"There's something else I brought to dinner," Maddie said in a hollow voice. "It's in my sack. I'll get it."

I put my mouth to Talley's ear and whispered, "What else do you think is in Maddie's sack?"

Talley looked at me queerly, not immediately remembering my midnight special witness suicide.

Maddie went to her large purse by the couch. My heart was racing, and Talley now remembered the death in court. She had put two and two together with Maddie's so-called veggie special and our jokes about a gun. Talley put her hand to her mouth and her eyes widened as Robbie's wife reached into her bag. She pulled out a sheaf of papers with a blue cover, bound together by two clips through punch holes at the top—a legal document.

She came back to the table and plopped it down hard on her husband's plate, splashing turkey giblet gravy on his shirt and face. "These are divorce papers, Robbie. It is time for us to go our separate ways." Her lips were trembling with anger or distress—or both. She stood frozen for a second as if unable to decide whether to run or stay. Talley reached for her hand and drew her down to her chair, then covered Maddie's hand with hers again.

Robbie came up with the only defense he had. Trite but what else could he say? "Maddie, I love you. This thing that happened with the patient had nothing to do with you. I promise it will never happen again." He tried flashing his sunbeam smile, but his face collapsed into sadness and remorse. I know a bit about remorse. I tell my clients that remorse will lighten their punishment. Some really feel their guilt; some fake it. Robbie was bereft.

Talley went on the offensive, "Maddie, this is about sex. It's a drive. You never know which direction it's going to point us in. Grown-ups do it all the time, even if they are not married to each other."

"I know. So what are you saying?" Madeline answered. She pulled her hand away from Talley.

"I'm saying that it's not the end of the world. Couples go through this. They get through this. Keeping your family together is more important than Robbie losing his grip with this person. It's over with her. Your children will still benefit from having the two of you together as Mom and Dad."

Talley grasped Madeline's hand again and reached across the table with her other one and took one of Robbie's hands. Would Talley be able to bring them together—keep all four of us together—the way she had once kept the three of us friends in high school when she had stopped Robbie and me from fighting? At that time, we'd fought over how Robbie dropped Talley for Marilyn. Dropped me too, in a way. Then Talley had thrown dirt in our faces to stop the fight and cleaned the dirt from our eyes afterward.

To Madeline, Robbie said, "You know it wasn't about you. It could have happened with anybody I was married to. It was about stuff from my childhood that my psychoanalysis never touched. I promise, Maddie, I'll never be unfaithful again."

Talley flinched so hard at those words that her hand came free of Robbie's and she had to take it again.

"How can I ever trust Robbie again?" Madeline said.

"You rebuild trust," Talley persisted, still holding on to the two of them. "You have to give it a chance, or you'll never know. You know what else, Maddie? No one of us is perfect. Not you, Robbie, Eli, or me. If I believed in God— which I don't, but you do, Maddie—I'd say, 'Lord knows I've done some stupid things. I hope God forgives me.' If God can forgive, we can forgive ourselves, learn from our mistakes to go forward. If we can forgive ourselves, we can forgive someone else, even Robbie for adultery. If you can't forgive Robbie for his stupidity, I guess you can't cut yourself some slack for anything. How can you live with yourself that way?"

I added, "We've been friends for almost all our grown years. Talley and I don't want to lose the two of you as a couple. You mean a lot to us. Give it a try."

"Pablum, Eli! So just because the two of you can forgive Robbie, does that mean I'm supposed to?"

"We don't forgive him; we understand him. His mistakes are part of the package," Talley replied.

"You friggin' enablers." Then Maddie closed down, moving her head up and down, maybe thinking, maybe assenting, maybe deciding we were all fools. Talley took the veggie special carton to the garbage pail.

We all took deep breaths and bites of the food that was getting cold. Maddie drained a glass of wine in a way that I'd never seen this controlled, abstemious woman do. She exhaled. "I have one more thing to say. I think part of the problem is that Robbie and I have followed a track all our lives, a track of study and achievement and never stepped away from it. When life throws us a knuckleball—excuse the baseball jargon—we don't know how to deal with its dips and twists. We swing wildly and miss. Like you, Robbie, I've been thinking it's time to do something wild, like get off my track. I'm tired of doing well-baby checkups for superhealthy babies, looking at kids' ears, and arguing with parents who don't want to vaccinate their children. I've reached my twentieth year at the Palo Alto Children's Clinic. I'm going to take a job with a religious mission in Ethiopia. I can teach at the medical school there and help kids who have never even seen a doctor." Maddie's voice had gotten far off, remote.

Momentarily spared of his wife's bitterness, Robbie perked up and tried to exert his pull on her with a boyish grin. "I can go with you, Maddie. Maybe they'd even let me teach in East Africa too, and see patients."

"No. I'm going to do this on my own."

Talley signaled me to get up. We started clearing dishes to the kitchen, where we could see our friends through the arch between the kitchen counter and dining room. They sat silently, talked out, until Maddie remembered, "The dessert. It's in my bag."

Once again, she left the table and went to the front room; once again, Talley and I looked at each other with apprehension. Maddie came back with a pumpkin pie in a white bakery box from a discount chain grocery. Always in the past she had baked the pie for Thanksgiving herself. She took it out of the box and resentfully dropped it on the table. The assembly-line-made, whipped cream rosettes around the pie's edge collapsed, and the pumpkin slid to one side.

"This pie looks like mud—or worse," Robbie said.

Then Maddie grabbed her coat and stalked out, leaving the door open to blackness. The music from the club had ended and was replaced by gusts of wind from the first winter storm.

For a few seconds, Robbie stared at the dessert, then he got his coat too and picked up the pie. "I'm going to pitch it," he said while walking out.

I watched from the window, and as he reached the sidewalk, he wound up to throw it into the street. But Talley came up behind him and grabbed his arm. Their eyes met as if searching for something in each other. "Why did you stop me, Talley?"

"I'm going to save the pie for the homeless in the park," Talley said purposefully. She took it and came back inside, leaving Robbie to walk to his car.

PART 4
THE TRIAL

CHAPTER
THIRTEEN

Not long after Thanksgiving, the San Francisco Superior Court notified us that the trial date was set for Monday, May 15, 2008. The judge who would preside over the trial hadn't yet been selected. Robbie's patient, NJ, had retained an attorney in his early forties named Jack Dietrich, whom I didn't know. He was with the high-powered San Francisco firm of Starwell, Holding, and Blumenthal—SHB for short—with offices in a sleek building on the Embarcadero. Their digs on a top floor overlooking the bay were meant to impress clients, intimidate opponents, and boost the self-esteem of their attorneys and staff in a hard knocks business. I was looking forward to meeting Dietrich when the time came, probably in a pretrial conference.

There would be many keys and key moments to Robbie's defense, and one of these was finding one or more esteemed psychiatrists who would testify on his behalf—go on record that Robbie did *not* hurt NJ and go on record that he had *helped* the patient. If the jury believed our expert witness or witnesses, half the battle would be won because without harm—if our expert testified that Robbie hadn't harmed NJ—the fraud charge might not hold water in the jury's mind. I didn't think there was a chance in hell of finding an expert to side with Robbie from the point of view of ethics. NJ's attorney would beat us up on that.

I asked Robbie for names of colleagues who might be sympathetic to him and would he make initial contact with one of them. Robbie said he couldn't do that, not because he didn't want to but because none of his colleagues would help him. They were all dismayed and disillusioned to the point of being disgusted with him. He'd seen it in their faces the last time he'd gone to the psychoanalytic society building to get his mail. They turned away, shunning him. He'd resigned from his administrative role and a day later to spare himself and the organization from further dismay he gave up his membership. This charming man with the stiff but pleasing manner and welcoming demeanor—who spoke Freud's language and ideas better than anybody in the analytic society because he had grown up hearing them on his father's lips—had let them down. He'd let Talley and me down too, of course, but we were linked to him from childhood. We didn't need or expect him to be spotless the way he had to be for the colleagues who had put him on a pedestal.

So I turned to the American Board of Forensic Specialists, shrinks who have some training in the law and like to testify in court. It takes a certain kind of doctor to do this, one who enjoys analyzing the minute legal and emotional meaning of each utterance in the doctor's office, the accuracy of any diagnosis, if the treatment fits with customary, medical practice, the appropriateness of any medication or failure to prescribe medication, and the personal conduct of the doctor who is on trial. The forensic doctor would get on the witness stand and testify if a physician was in her or his right mind. Was the treatment they provided medically sound? Were they stoned on substances? Did they respond to phone calls in a timely way and so forth? Forensic psychiatrists love the challenge of sitting in a witness chair with an audience at their feet. They get off on showing their knowledge and debating with an opposing attorney during a cross-examination.

I called two doctors I had worked with before, and they turned me down flat. Robbie didn't have a case, they said. I had offered them $600 an hour for their preparation work in reviewing records, interviewing Robbie in advance, and then sitting and testifying in court. When they said no, I jumped to $800 an hour. They still said no, but the second guy I called said he knew of a forensic doctor who might help out at $800 an hour and would take almost any case simply because he liked a contest and winning. The total fee would probably come to about $8,000 for ten hours work if we could find somebody locally, and it would come out of Robbie's pocket because his malpractice insurance company did not cover the defense and financial judgments against doctors who had sex with patients. It was a rider on his insurance contract.

We couldn't find a single local person with forensic experience willing to join our team. The guy I did find was Burl Harford, an adroit veteran of many complex cases. He was based in Malibu and said on the phone, right off the bat, that Robbie was way behind the eight ball. But Harford said, "I like being the underdog; back in the day, I was national racquetball champion. I give it everything I have, and I think I can help your case." Our arrangement with Harford was to pay him to be at our disposal for three eight-hour working days in San Francisco, which came to $19,000 and change. At least that would include his actual time in the courtroom and reviewing records and depositions and giving his own pretrial deposition if necessary. We also agreed to pay him for the gas and parking for his airplane. He was a pilot and flew himself to wherever he was testifying. We would cover his hotel on Union Square, walking distance to court, for three days. Robbie was getting poorer and poorer. At least he didn't have to pay me.

Harford, our expert, was smart. He knew from the get-go that NJ's attorney would slam Robbie for betraying NJ's hope that therapy could help her by stating that her experience with Dr. Carosso had made her afraid to ever seek psychotherapy again. He knew that Jack Dietrich would argue that victims of sexual abuse are statistically more vulnerable to depression than nonvictims. Dietrich would ask the jury, "What if Naomi Jane Morton became depressed and couldn't face going to a therapist's office because of her experience with Dr. Carosso?" Without a doctor to talk with, she might try to take her life and succeed; victims of sexual abuse had a higher incidence of suicide than nonvictims.

We began the process of gathering releases to have all the case information available for our expert. We put him on our witness list and sent the information to the courthouse and NJ's attorney. I didn't take any new clients while working on Robbie's behalf, but I was keeping an eye on the drama unfolding with Professor Aldenbrand, my client whose tenure promotion was in jeopardy because a student had accused him of blocking his advancement toward a PhD.

Julia was coming to the office to meet with me about the tenure case. She had called and cryptically said she had something to show me and wanted to do it in person. It was something of a surprise. When she arrived, I saw that it was one of her graceful dressed-up days. This time she arrived from the Cal campus wearing a green blouse unbuttoned down to the curve of her breasts and flowing pants. She had on lipstick. "I met with the university investigator this morning at her office in Thayer Hall. Aldenbrand was right when he said she is meticulous. Her book on Renaissance art is encyclopedic and makes no waves. She defends the institution, whether it's schools of art or UC Berkeley," Julia said.

"She didn't want to see me because she said that she had already met with many people, but I insisted I had something important to say about Professor Aldenbrand that was different from the rumors on campus. She consented to see me, and I spun a story for her. I told her that I took a course with Aldenbrand and he was a wonderful teacher. Some students were afraid of him because he could be a very hard grader, but I said I knew Aaron Aldenbrand had his students' best interests at heart. She listened and nodded, but she wasn't really listening. She was more interested in how my blouse was unbuttoned. Not from the point of view of decorum, but I think because it aroused her.

"A little cleavage loosens tongues as well as alcohol," I said.

"The alcohol came later. The investigator said I was too late because her report was finished. If only I'd come to her earlier, we would have had something to talk about. She said that since I was there, I might as well know that the report is not favorable to the professor. She pointed to a stack of about ten black folders on a side table. Then she said she appreciated my visit and offered me a glass of sherry."

"You accepted?"

"Eli, do you think I'm nuts? Of course I accepted. When she went to her closet to get the sherry, I got up and put one of the Aldenbrand reports in my briefcase." Julia put the purloined report on my desk. "It's completely one-sided. It slams Aldenbrand, which makes no sense because several of his students and colleagues told me they had heard rumors that he had harmed a graduate student, yet they still liked the professor and thought there must be another side. These are rumors that Lewis Hansen, Aldenbrand's adversary, is generating himself."

"It makes sense if the university is so controversy shy that the dean decided in advance to get rid of Aldenbrand and cued the investigator to go in that direction. And this case is not even about sexual harassment," I said. "I'll read the report tonight. I think I should give the professor a heads-up to soften the blow."

"What can you tell him?"

"He'll get his chance to tell *his* story in court, if it goes that far because the university withholds tenure. I don't want it to get to court. Aldenbrand gets defensive under questioning. What happened next with the investigator?"

"She offered me a second glass of sherry and started telling me how pretty I was. I said that she must find her work interesting, and, she invited me to sit in on the class she teaches on Renaissance depictions of the Madonna. She gave me her extension number if I wanted to talk with her some more. *About what?* I was thinking."

"File your visit with the investigator-professor away in your mind, Julia. We have two aces up our sleeve now."

Two days later, the dean of social sciences distributed the investigator's report to the tenure committee and the student representative on the harassment committee. Aldenbrand wasn't entitled to a copy; he could only receive whatever final report and decision the dean would issue. I immediately wrote a letter to the dean and told him that Aldenbrand had retained me as his attorney, the report I read was flawed, and that we were prepared to go to trial if necessary to protect the reputation and career of Aldenbrand if he didn't receive the tenure he deserved. The dean asked me how I had gotten a copy of the report, and I told him that was confidential. We were at a stalemate for the present, but wheels were turning and gears shifting.

Finally it was also time to meet NJ's attorney to discuss the size of the jury we wanted for the trial. A civil case doesn't require twelve jurors. It can be whatever number the two attorneys agree on. Ordinarily choosing the venue for the first meeting of opposing councils is like a pissing contest: your place, my place, or a neutral place like the Mint Café in the basement of the superior court building. I offered to go to Dietrich's office on the Embarcadero because I wanted to see what it looked like, what hint it might give about NJ's attorney that I could use in the coming litigation.

It was a crisp, clear, sunny winter day so I put on a sweater under my corduroy jacket, skipped a tie because it wasn't a day in court, and walked to California Street, where I caught the cable car and rode it to the end of the line at the Embarcadero. There I entered the lobby of a wafer-thin skyscraper where a security guard behind a big, marble desk checked my driver's license against a list of anticipated visitors. The elevator whisked me up to the top level.

Starwell, Holding, and Blumenthal occupied the bay side of the floor and another firm the opposite side. The waiting room was sumptuous and generous with comfortable couches and chairs; San Francisco, Seattle, Chicago, Atlanta, Washington, and New York newspapers; clocks with New York, London, Hong Kong, and Tokyo time; and trays of refreshments. CNN and stock market reports played on TV monitors. But I didn't have to wait; the receptionist escorted me along a hall with lawyers' offices that had glass walls on the corridor and glass walls overlooking San Francisco Bay. Each office seemed to have a personal touch: family pictures on the desk, art or photographs on the wall, bronze plaques, diplomas, and even sporting trophies on bookstands.

Jack Dietrich was at his desk when the secretary ushered me. On the wall behind him were diplomas and citations: Harvard College, University of Pennsylvania law school, member of the Bar, a certificate of honor from the US Navy Legal Corps for five years of meritorious service after law school. He neatened the papers on his desk, stood up, touched his law diploma to bring it back into a perfect horizontal, came around from his desk, pulled the curtains to the hall, and then gripped my hand firmly. He was military erect, clean-shaven, and tanned. He had on a dark suit with a faint stripe, a white shirt with silver cufflinks peeking out from his jacket, and a perfectly knotted maroon college tie with a small shield on it that said, "Veritas," truth. His hair was black, thick, and straight back with a small part on the right, remindful of how another San Franciscan, Joe DiMaggio, had combed his thick black hair more than a half century ago.

In addition to Dietrich's reputation for legal success, I wondered if Naomi Jane Morton had been drawn to the attorney because of his resemblance to Jolting Joe—the way Marilyn had been drawn to the handsome athlete. Nowadays it was common for an aggrieved woman to hire another woman to represent her in court. I would have to ask Talley what she thought about NJ's choice of attorney.

Dietrich motioned me to an armchair, and he took one opposite, a low table between us. The receptionist asked if we wanted something to drink. I shook my head, and Dietrich began. "At last we have a chance to meet. I've heard about your reputation." His face was expressionless. What did his words mean? What did his poker face mean? Was he laughing inwardly because he knew he sounded like a gunslinger in a western movie who was sizing up his opponent before he went for his gun, or was he unable to hear himself and had no sense of humor?

I said, "I haven't heard anything about you other than that you are well trained and very effective. You have to be to be brought on board by SHB. They only pick the best."

"Thank you. I believe our task for today is to agree on the size of the jury for this case. A pity what happened to our clients." He didn't sound like he had much pity.

"Dr. Carosso doesn't have an opinion on the size of the jury."

"Neither does Ms. Morton. How about cutting down the jury from twelve to eight? I think it's more efficient. The court doesn't have to have as large a pool. Deliberations are often faster." He rattled it off.

He didn't say that statistics clearly showed that a smaller jury was more likely to arrive at a guilty verdict than a jury of twelve. Holdouts for innocence were less likely, and plaintiffs in civil cases only needed three-quarters of the jurors to vote to convict. That meant six out of eight. Statistically of course Dietrich wanted a smaller jury. I didn't say what I'd researched, which was that in the two dozen personal injury cases Dietrich had tried in his seven years at SHB, Dietrich's top-notch winning record wasn't as good with smaller juries. Maybe he had never calculated it himself. Maybe he wanted to move this case along speedily because he had a bigger case waiting and small jury trials went faster with fewer conflicts. Personally, I liked the intimacy of a smaller panel. I did well playing to eight.

We chatted amiably about how long the trial might take; we agreed it would probably be about three days. I told him that for the moment I only intended to call two or three witnesses: my psychiatrist expert witness and perhaps another witness. He said that he had several expert witnesses who would testify against Robbie. He smirked a little bit when he said that he might not need to use all of his witnesses. Soon enough, we would both release the names of our experts and a summary of the points they would make on the stand to each other and the judge. The length of the trial depended a lot on how long their testimonies would take and how long our cross-examinations would take.

"Is Dr. Carosso going to testify?" Dietrich asked.

"He's planning to defend himself." What Robbie could say to defend himself wasn't clear, but he needed to show that he wasn't a monster; he needed to charm the jurors with his handsome smile.

"And Ms. Morton, will she take the stand?"

"Of course. She has a story to tell."

I wondered which Ms. Morton her lawyer would put on the stand: the timid, dowdy Naomi Jane who had first come to see Robbie; a prim, morally outraged NJ; or the Marilyn makeover he'd described at the end of therapy. Other than that, I had the information I needed: Dietrich was going to be ramrod tough and prepared. He also liked everything ordered and precise. I knew that from the way the diploma hanging slightly off-kilter on his wall had troubled him. I could probably throw his well-prepared scenario off balance with a courtroom surprise or two. I had no idea yet what I could spring on him, but in the three-odd days the trial would take something would likely come up in the course of the proceedings that I could use to shake him up.

"Next stop, the settlement conference," I said to him. We would meet in the judge's chambers about a week before the trial was scheduled to see if we could reach a financial agreement that would make it unnecessary to go to trial.

Unlikely, I thought. NJ was out for blood and Robbie had his mantra "I didn't hurt that woman."

We had finished our agenda for the day. I stood up first, went to the glass wall, and looked down at the sparkling blue waters of the bay. Far to the left was Coit Tower and North Beach, the Italian neighborhood where Joe DiMaggio had grown up. Below me on the sparkling blue waters of the bay a freighter piled high with steel shipping containers was coming in from the Golden Gate, making its way slowly toward the Bay Bridge on my right and the Port of Oakland. Ten miles across the bay, I saw the tall spire of the campanile on the Cal Berkeley campus where I had gone to school, thin as a needle in the distance. So many lives and eras were intersecting, soon to be coming to a head in a courtroom on the edge of City Hall Plaza.

Jack Dietrich had come up beside me as a magnificent yacht was coming into view on our left. "The things money can buy," he said, likely licking his lips in anticipation of his 40 percent share of the money NJ would come into if she won her case against Robbie.

CHAPTER
FOURTEEN

On Tuesday, May 9, 2018, a week before the scheduled start of the trial, Dietrich and I sat in Judge Richard Poirier's office, next to his courtroom in the San Francisco Superior Court building. The judge was old to be still working—about seventy and thin with wispy white hair—but he hadn't retired because he enjoyed his work. The color of his skin wasn't good, and his razor had left red scratches on his face. His tie was loose, and his neck creased. He was in slacks and a sport coat; his wire-rim glasses were thick, yet his eyes darted sharply back and forth between Dietrich and me, sizing up the coming contest between the two of us. I liked him and had done well in his courtroom over the years because he had a keen mind that I knew how to appeal to. He could be tough when necessary, belittling toward attorneys he felt were inflating peccadillos into tragedies and grand larceny with their rhetoric, and dryly humorous when addressing a courtroom absurdity.

There were eleven trial judges in the San Francisco Superior Court and Dietrich had tried only two cases before Poirier—a construction accident injury and a wrongful termination suit—and both times won verdicts in the seven figures.

Poirier addressed Dietrich and me wryly. "This is an unusual case, isn't it? Not many plaintiffs have gone to trial over a psychiatrist seducing them. Why hasn't this been settled out of court the way it should be?"

Dietrich and I looked at each other. He spoke first and went back and forth with Poirier. "My client believes she deserves every penny of the 8 million she is asking."

"I know. I've read the filing—a million for each episode of sexual romance. Why a million? How did you reach that figure? Why not half a million?" Poirier didn't hide his scorn.

"A million is based on the sum total of the damage Ms. Morton has suffered, incrementally over the one-month period Dr. Carosso inflicted harm on her by having sex with her in his office, twice a week."

"Your calculations seem based on assumptions drawn from a crystal ball."

"We will present concrete testimony concerning the suffering and impairment my client experienced."

"Mr. Dietrich, would your client accept an offer of 4 million for a settlement?"

"I think that is possible."

Dietrich turned to me, nodding as if weighing the likelihood that Dr. Carosso and I would accept the figure. "Mr. Meyer, are you prepared to make an offer to settle this?"

"Dr. Carosso doesn't have the resources for a reduced figure of 4 million. His home is community property with his wife and can't be touched without her consent, and she refuses. His retirement account is also community property. Otherwise, Dr. Carosso has investments and personal property worth approximately $1 million. His future earnings are very constrained because he has lost his medical license. If he settles out of court, he will be bankrupt; if he loses the suit, he will be bankrupt. If he wins, he will be able to hold on to what he has. I am defending him pro bono. He is a longtime friend."

"And your client is out for blood, isn't she?" the judge said to Dietrich.

"My client wishes to be compensated for what she has gone through and the pain she has to live with for the rest of her life. Mr. Meyer's estimate of Dr. Carosso's worth may not be accurate. There may be more—inheritance, for example."

"I see then that we have no choice other than to proceed next Tuesday. Any thoughts about what we should do if the media gets wind of this trial? It could excite them. I don't want a circus."

I didn't think Dietrich or Poirier knew about Robbie's testimony to the California Licensing Agency about his history with Marilyn Monroe and its connection to the case. I didn't know if it was going to come up in court, or how, but if it did, it might create a storm.

I kept quiet.

Dietrich said, "My client will have to expose a painful personal experience in her testimony. We hope the trial doesn't attract attention."

Judge Poirier said, "In San Francisco, murder and corruption bring the press running. Sex is third on the list. Maybe we'll get by without the reporters showing up. Let's keep our fingers crossed, gentlemen. Of course cameras and recording devices are not allowed in the courtroom."

The pace was picking up. A day later, Talley returned from Indonesia, where she had been buying supplies for making batik cloth. She planned to be at the trial. She'd also returned with spices and cooked an Indonesian rice table for the two of us for dinner. Between chopstick bites, I asked her, "Why does a woman like NJ, wronged by a man, chose a male personal injury attorney instead of a feminist attorney? There are many good women lawyers these days, hard-bitten ones, motherly, supportive ones. Why a man? This guy she chose is not even a father figure; he's more like an army officer."

She didn't answer right away, instead savoring the food and thinking. "From what you've told me, she's a man's woman."

"What do you mean by that?"

"A woman who makes herself appealing to a man. Makes herself into what a man wants her to be. She may not show it outwardly; she may not dress to kill, or she may. She's submissive to the kind of guy she thinks is tough—whatever her idea of tough is. It may be a guy with authority, some way, somehow. She has radar for this kind of man and homes in on him. You and I know that Robbie has some of it: the aristocrat in him, the authority that comes from being smart and confident. From what you told me, her lawyer Dietrich's got it. When she visited him high in his glass and steel tower, he struck a chord in NJ. I can't wait to see her in court, see him in court."

"Do I have that toughness?"

"Never. That's why I love you so much."

She dropped her chopsticks and came around behind me. "Flex your muscle," she said. I flexed my arm. She felt the knot in it. "Not bad for an old guy."

Two days, later on Friday, Dietrich and I met in Judge Poirier's courtroom for the voir dire, the see-and-say, from French jurisprudence. A panel of twenty potential jurors was there, randomly drawn from voter rolls and California ID cards. They were seated in the gallery behind the bar, which is the railing that separates the seating part of the courtroom from the working part: the defense's table, the plaintiff's table, the witness stand, the court reporter's seat, and the bailiff's post. On the wall behind the judge's dais was the California Seal—a picture of a woman wearing a dress seated on a rock in a meadow overlooking San Francisco Bay. She has a spear in her right hand, a shield on her left, a helmet on her head, and a brown bear at her feet. In the background, three-masted sailing ships plied the bay.

The woman in the seal is both protector and warrior, about right for the verbal battle soon to take place in the courtroom. The American flag was to the left, and on the right was the California flag, also adorned with the benign and mighty bear.

Judge Poirier explained to the group of twenty panelists seated in their enclosed space in front and to the right of him that the case was about a male psychiatrist who had a sexual affair during the course of treating a female patient. The female patient, the plaintiff, was suing the psychiatrist for a large sum of money on the grounds that he had committed medical malpractice, injured her emotionally, and defrauded her by charging her for treatment which he actually had not provided. In the voir dire question-and-answer that followed, Dietrich and I asked the potential jurors if they could listen to the charges against Dr. Carosso and consider his defense with a fair and open mind. Or better yet, we each were trying to find jurors who might be biased in favor of our client and get them on the panel.

Dietrich and I each had six *peremptory* challenges that we could use to excuse anybody from serving simply because we saw something that made us feel uneasy about having them on the jury. In addition, there was an unlimited number of *for cause* challenges that the attorneys and the judge could use to excuse potential jurors for whom there was good reason to believe they might not be able to make an impartial decision. For example,

I excused potential jurors who had bad experiences themselves with psychotherapists and doctors; I excused law-and-order types by asking them such questions as "Do you believe thieves should go to jail or be given probation for petty theft? Do you believe in the *three strikes and you're out law* that sends criminals to jail for life on the third conviction?" Judge Poirier excused panelists who didn't believe the court system was fair.

Dietrich excused a man who believed posttraumatic stress disorder was a sham. He wanted as many women on the jury as he could get; I played for as many men as I could get. But I wanted the two women candidates who returned my smile when I thanked them cordially for offering their time to the court. I let Dietrich think he was getting away with something by getting them seated on the jury. The selection process had taken a full day, and Robbie had made it through only the morning before he said his head was hurting so badly he couldn't stay any longer. He'd offered nothing, saying it was impossible to know anything about people this way. It took him weeks and months of exploration in his office before he could get into a patient's inner thoughts, and even then, the surprises never ended.

In the end, five women and three men had been chosen. I wouldn't know until the verdict, but I had a feeling that I had picked my share of the jurors well.

The defense team—Robbie, Talley, Julia, and me—met at 8 a.m. in Dream Fluff Donuts the morning of the trial. It was a greasy spoon on a street behind the courthouse, in the Tenderloin with its single-room occupancy hotels, cheap restaurants, sex shops, and derelicts on the street. Litter lay about because people in this neighborhood didn't complain to the government about the filth.

I liked to fuel up on Dream Fluff's jelly donuts. They had an odd scent of coriander and cumin because the family that owned and worked the place was Indian, and there were large bags of spice in the corner. The coffee wasn't quite right either. It was weak, which meant I could keep drinking it without getting too jangled. I also went there because none of the other lawyers did, so I could keep focused on the trial without having to socialize.

The donut shop refrigerator droned and dripped water on the linoleum floor. On the wall behind the cash register were large Bollywood movie posters: musicals and costume epics, swarthy men and women with long, black hair and faultless, shining smiles. Mixed in this riot of colorful images was a small, framed, black-and-white photo of Marilyn Monroe, a head and shoulders shot of her that showed the top of a short-sleeved black dress, bare neck, collarbones, and a bit of cleavage. Her lips were parted. Even through the donut-grease-misted glass, her face glowed and held one's gaze more strongly that all the Bollywood posters taken together.

Robbie noticed it and asked the slight, dark waitress, "Why do you have a picture of Marilyn Monroe up there?"

"She was so pretty."

Robbie pursued it as if he was still trying to understand what had befallen him. "You weren't even alive when she was. How do you even remember her?"

"She's a hero to us—the girl who had nothing but her dream and her beauty, who became so famous that everybody knew her when she was alive."

Talley asked her, "What does her life mean to you, personally?"

"She couldn't be happy with everything she had. It reminds me that I can be happier than her with what I have. Be careful to not want too much." She gave a self-deprecating smile.

Happiness. That was it in a nutshell: how to have it, how to hold on to it. When the counter girl served us our coffee and donuts, I gave her back a lot of extra change and bills for her thoughts. At 8:20, we walked to the Superior Court building, which was on one side of the Civic Center Plaza. City Hall was on the west side, and directly across the plaza was the Bill Graham Auditorium, named for the rock concert impresario, the guy Talley had long ago created color projections and backdrops for at the Fillmore East in New York in the days when she had wanted "to be color." At 400 McAllister Street, we pushed through the heavy art deco, steel, brass, and glass door into the courthouse lobby and went through security.

Judge Poirier's third-floor courtroom had his name on a plaque beside the door wall and a notice beneath it that read, "Case of Naomi Jane Morton vs Robert Carossso, case number GC-96Y458." Inside, the woodwork was all burnished walnut. The light was soft. The morning sun filtered through a tall window and danced on motes of dust in the air. The eight jurors and four alternates were drifting in and taking their seats. Robbie and I took our seat at the defense table, and I put the case file and writing implements on the table. Behind us ran the bar, the polished, wooden, waist-high barrier. Julia sat directly behind it, directly behind me. She was now studying for the Bar exam, but since she hadn't yet passed it, she wasn't yet allowed to join me at the table. Talley was beside her. Otherwise, the courtroom was empty except for a man and woman seated separately in back, barely awake. They were probably reporters looking for a story, close to the exit so they could leave easily if nothing worth writing about transpired.

Madeleine was absent; she said she had no intention whatsoever of being in the same room with her husband and the patient suing him.

Chameleon investigator Julia had dressed inconspicuously, purposely she said, to avoid attention. She said she'd dressed in gray the way she figured Ms. Morton had when she first came to see Dr. Carosso. Julia said she didn't want to be part of the show; it was going to be on the other side of the bar from the gallery. Talley wore a batik skirt she'd made from material she'd brought back from her trip, a blouse, and a jacket. Robbie looked okay on this day; he'd taken a studio apartment in Half Moon Bay a few blocks from the marina and didn't smell like the fishing port and his boat. His longish, fair hair was trimmed, he'd shaved, and he wore a fresh gabardine suit. For my part, I was in my trial uniform: navy blue, pin-striped suit and cinnamon-colored tie that still matched my hair and beard.

No sooner had we settled than Robbie twisted around. The door from the hall was silent, so he must have sensed Naomi Jane's entrance from her scent on a waft of air from the hall. We followed his gaze to NJ, who wasn't ceding anything with her appearance. There was no effort at pathos in it; she looked beautiful. Her blonde, fluffy hair caught the beams of sun slanting through the window, her nose was pert, and her lips bright red. It was the beauty Robbie insisted he had made possible. She was wearing a lavender suit with the skirt at her knees; matching suede, modestly high heel shoes; a silk scoop-necked blouse of a different shade of lavender; and a pearl necklace. Robbie and NJ stared at each other momentarily, their eyes widening as if stunned by seeing each other for the first time in sixteen months, and quickly broke gaze. The two reporters in back woke up.

At nine fifteen, the bailiff announced, "All rise," and the

side door from the judge's chamber opened. Poirier entered, black robed, and took his seat on his dais. He announced that court was in session and asked Dietrich to make his opening statement.

Dietrich went to a speaker's rostrum. He'd added a three-button vest to his outfit and buttoned his suit coat. He had slicked his hair back more than it had been in his office or at the voir dire, as if priming his appearance for battle. He surveyed the jurors, taking their measure—or pretending to. "Ladies and gentlemen of the jury, we shouldn't be here today. Because the harmful, wrongful actions committed by Dr. Carosso—the man sitting there at the table to my left in a tan suit—should never have happened. Fortunately they rarely do, but when they do—when a doctor goes beyond the bounds of ethics— he must be punished. A message must be sent to the medical community that doctors cannot act with impunity.

"My client, Naomi Jane Morton, is a thirty-four-year-old associate professor of English literature at Stanford University. A highly esteemed professional, she has published articles and is preparing a book on Shakespeare. She is not married and came to Dr. Carosso, a psychiatrist, for treatment of depression. Instead he seduced her and had a sexual affair with her.

"When she realized that he was not offering treatment but gratifying himself, she broke off the relationship. When she realized shortly after that Dr. Carosso's betrayal of her trust had left her profoundly wounded in ways that will impair her for the rest of her life, she filed suit against him for monetary damages to compensate the harm she had suffered. She also did this to achieve a moral victory against Robert Carosso that will lessen the sense of injustice she has experienced and provide some measure of emotional recovery."

At this point, Dietrich stepped from behind the microphone

on the rostrum and walked over to the jurors' box. He looked amiably at them and firmly, resonantly said, "You, kind jurors, will assist Ms. Morton in achieving an emotional recovery, a moral victory, and monetary restitution. You will also send a message to the psychiatric community that Dr. Carosso's kind of behavior must not be tolerated. In doing this, you will also be protecting yourself by lessening the chances that a doctor might harm you in the future. In the course of the trial, I will call expert witnesses—physicians themselves—to describe the harm Ms. Morton has suffered and the kind of emotional risk she will face in the future. Ms. Morton will also take the stand this afternoon and tell her story to you herself."

It was my turn to make an opening statement. Dietrich had delivered the first surprise. He was making Robbie an example of the whole medical community, putting it on trial as well. I skipped the microphone and went directly to stand in front of the jurors. "Dr. Carosso has admitted that he had an affair with the plaintiff; that is not in question. He doesn't deny it. However, we will show that the treatment part of his relationship with Ms. Morton had come to an end when the affair started. We will show that there was no fraud because he had stopped charging Ms. Morton when the treatment ended. Most importantly, we will show that he didn't do damage to the plaintiff. You will hear from our own expert witness about that.

"Dr. Carosso does not deny that his behavior crossed the bounds of what is ethical. He deeply regrets his poor judgment. He has already been punished by the California Medical Licensing Agency for that, and they have withdrawn his license to practice medicine."

I reached for words that would disarm Dietrich's strident legal message. "We all know the proverb 'You can't judge a book by its cover.' This case is not a simple story of a negligent doctor harming his patient, the way the plaintiff's attorney has packaged it. In the course of the trial, Dr. Carosso will testify in his own behalf. You will get to know him and understand his lapses and his strengths as well. You will also get to know the plaintiff better, and in the end, it will be your decision who has suffered most."

Jurors were nodding at me, a good sign that they had listened well and understood. I turned to my left and saw Talley and Julia smiling as I took my seat next to Robbie. He said, "Thank you," and put his hand over mine for a second. For the first time in my life, I saw a tear leave his eye.

It was time for morning break, and we went back to Dream Fluff Donuts for sandwiches. The waitress greeted me. "Mr. Meyer, how did it go?"

Julia and Talley answered, "Good. Eli did well."

I wasn't so sure. When we were seated, I said, "Dietrich is putting the medical community on trial. That resonates with juries." The mood dampened.

Julia said, "I have news about Aldenbrand's student harassment case. The tenure committee is leaning toward denying the professor tenure."

"How did you find that out? How'd you break through their wall of secrecy?" I asked playfully.

"The old three-button trick again. I pretended to be a student interested in a course and showed up at one of the committee member's office hours—in the same blouse I wore to meet with the investigator with the same third button open. I asked him whether he thought Professor Aldenbrand would be teaching next year, and he said not to count on it. He wanted to please me, give me an answer."

"I'm going to make a phone call. Play one of our aces." I

went to the back corner of the café, by the large spice and rice bags, away from the noisy refrigerator, and called an old friend, Clarence Spinkman—Cappy to me and a former teammate on our rugby team in our undergrad days. He was now the chancellor at the university. It was his personal phone, it was lunchtime, and he picked up when he saw my number on the screen. I kept it brief. "Cappy, one of your fine professors, a guy who is making a real contribution with his work, is getting shafted by some kind of faculty fear of student hysteria." I told him the facts of the case and gave him the names of the principals—my client Aldenbrand, the name of the Renaissance art professor who had conducted the investigation of the student's harassment charge, the dean who hadn't answered my letter to him stating that the investigation was a sham, and our inside news that the tenure decision looked to be going against Aldenbrand.

"How did you get the inside news?"

"Good story. I'll tell you over dinner. It's been too long."

"A promise?"

"Yes."

"Hey, Eli, I'll look into it and get back to you."

I went back to our table. Julia looked at me questioningly, and I gave her a thumbs-up sign. Then it was time to get back to the courtroom.

In the afternoon, Judge Poirier looked at his witness list and said, "Mr. Dietrich, I see you are calling your client to the stand."

"That is correct, Your Honor." Dietrich got up and offered his arm to NJ, who rose beside him, and they took the first steps to the witness box together, her attorney shielding her from the defense table before she went the last steps alone. She had exchanged her white pearl necklace for one with black beads and still wore lavender. The witness chair was to the judge's left and angled toward the jurors. When she sat down, she wiggled her hips ever so slightly, getting comfortable on the cushion, crossed her ankles one over the other, tucked her skirt under her, her knees just bare, and rested her forearms on the arms of the large chair.

At the bailiff's request, she swore to tell the whole truth and nothing but the truth. Then Dietrich walked a small circle that took in the jury, the judge, and the gallery. The number of spectators had grown to nineteen; word was getting out.

Dietrich settled himself standing in front of his client but not blocking the jury's view of her. "Ms. Morton, please tell the jury exactly what happened to you in Dr. Carosso's office." It was a provocative polite command that made everybody stir because it evoked images straight from the sex shops behind the courthouse. Judge Poirier took off his spectacles and gave Dietrich an angry look.

"The doctor promised treatment. He gave sex," NJ lashed out bitterly.

"Please start from the beginning," Dietrich coached.

"I came to Dr. Carosso for help because I was depressed. I was not doing well as an assistant professor. I was having trouble getting things done on time. I was having trouble sleeping. The dean of humanities at Stanford suggested that I get help. He said maybe medication might help and gave me the name of three psychiatrists in Palo Alto. I was up for promotion to associate professor, which would put me on track to be eligible for tenure after a year or so. You don't know how crucial getting on the tenure track is, so I had no choice but to get better. I chose Dr.

Carosso from the names the dean gave me, which I will regret for the rest of my life."

"What happened in the treatment? Did he prescribe medication?"

"No. We talked about my childhood. I had a very sad childhood. I was born in Chicago, my father abandoned me and my mother when I was a baby, and my mother died of a stroke when I was alone in the house with her when I was nine. Then I went to live with my aunt and uncle, and they were not very nice to me. I was a good student; that's all I had: my brain. I went to boarding school in Connecticut, and then the University of Michigan. After I got my PhD in English literature, Stanford offered me a job as a lecturer."

Judge Poirier was tapping his finger on his desk. "Mr. Dietrich, please help your client move along."

NJ answered, "I will do it myself, Your Honor." Her voice had gotten strong, like a teacher getting into a groove with her students. "I liked Dr. Carosso at first. Things changed when he suggested that therapy might go better if I were to lie on the couch."

Robbie scribbled quickly on the note pad in front of him, "No! *She* asked me if she could try lying on the couch."

Dietrich asked his client, "What month did your treatment with Dr. Carosso start, and when did you switch from a chair to a couch?"

"I started in October 2006. We switched to the couch in late November or early December. I think it was between Christmas and New Year's Day that Dr. Carosso first molested me. I was crying about something that I was talking about. I can't remember exactly about what, but he came over to me with a box of tissues, and when I took it, he put his hand between my legs." NJ gasped as she said that; there was an intake of breath from the audience. Robbie scribbled another note on his pad and shoved it in front of me. "No, she put my hand between her legs."

Jack Dietrich said to NJ, "Are you okay?" He rose to bring her a box of tissues.

"No, I'm fine. I can do this by myself. I have some Kleenex here if I need it."

"Please tell the jury what happened next in your so-called treatment with Dr. Carosso."

I rose swiftly, before NJ could answer. "Objection, Your Honor. Counsel is giving a hypothetical as if it were fact. He is leading the plaintiff to deny that treatment was taking place when there has been no evidence to that effect." My objection didn't make much sense; I just wanted to counter the scorn in Dietrich's voice and slow things down.

Judge Poirier looked carefully at me and said, "Objection denied. Plaintiff's counsel has a right to help Ms. Morton describe what she believes happened."

But the spell of contempt had been broken for a moment in favor of a rendition of facts as they knew them. "Ms. Morton, did you and Dr. Carosso proceed to have sexual intercourse in that visit?"

"Yes."

"When did you realize something was wrong?"

"Objection. Counsel is leading Ms. Morton to say his words as if they are hers."

"Objection sustained. Mr. Dietrich please be more careful in your choice of words."

"Okay. Ms. Morton, what were your thoughts and feelings after you had sex?"

"I knew something was wrong. I also knew something was right because it felt good, and you know the quote from the poet, John Keats. 'Beauty is pleasure taken as the quality of the thing.' It was beautiful and shitty and corrupt all at the same time. I knew it wasn't the treatment I had agreed to."

Dietrich struggled to pull his client's testimony back on course. "Why didn't you break off treatment? Why did you keep coming back for two months after he touched you sexually?"

"I had no control over what happened. You don't understand what it is like to be in treatment with a doctor, an authority. He had a big reputation. The dean of humanities had given me his name. I felt as if I had to respect him and have faith in him. In some twisted way, I believed he knew what he was doing and my role was to submit. I was paralyzed; my body was numb. The first time, I couldn't get up from the couch even if I'd wanted to. After that, it was like I was in a trance. Coming back to Dr. Carosso's office was like something I had to do, over and over until the spell was broken."

NJ's testimony was riveting the jury into full attention. It was driving Robbie into a shell. He was bent over his notepad, eyes closed, hands holding his head up, shutting out the courtroom. I made a note on my pad in capital letters. "Until the spell was broken." Robbie broke the spell when NJ asked to go away with him for President's Day weekend and Robbie told her he had plans to be with his family. That was when NJ stopped coming. That was what marked it as an affair of the heart and not treatment. I would get my chance to show this to the jury when I cross-examined NJ.

Dietrich passed it over; he said nothing about the trance. He said, "Ms. Morton, please tell the jury what has been the effect of your treatment with Dr. Carosso on you, on your life."

"I thought I was a person with a good sense of reality. Now I doubt myself. I tell myself I was a fool." NJ looked around the room, at the judge, and at the jurors haltingly and helplessly. "Are the people here real? Am I real? Is this really happening?"

"She's acting," I wrote on my notepad.

Dietrich asked, "Will you need further psychiatric treatment as a result of your experience with Dr. Carosso?"

"I don't know, but if I do, I'll never be able to speak to another psychotherapist again in my life. I'd never trust myself to be in the same room with one; I'd never trust the therapist to be honest."

"Even a woman?"

"Even a woman."

"Why?"

People shifted nervously in the courtroom.

"I'd have to tell whomever I went to for help what had happened with Dr. Carosso. I'd have to go over the whole thing again. It would be too shameful, too painful exposing myself, not just my body but my stupidity that I could have let that man lead me along like that." NJ pointed her finger at Robbie head bent over the defense table, elbows on the table, pressing his hands tighter around his head.

"I'm not going to be able to cry in another therapist's office; I'm not going to be able to lie down on a couch in an office. I'm never again going to be able to let myself be vulnerable." NJ made her right hand—a shapely hand with delicate fingers and red-painted nails—into a fist and brought it down firmly onto the arm of her chair. She turned to Judge Poirier and said, "Please, Your Honor, I want to stop talking. I want to take a recess."

Poirier gave NJ a look of fatherly tolerance. "Ms. Morton, your wish is granted. Court will recess for the day and continue tomorrow morning at nine sharp."

I'd never seen a witness so in charge of her own testimony

as Robbie's nemesis. Dietrich himself looked out of sorts. He evidently was used to being in charge, and he'd let his client run away from his guidance with her testimony—some of it to her benefit and some of it which he and I knew I could use later to her detriment.

Robbie and I reconnoitered with Talley and Julia at their seats just behind the bar in the gallery. It was getting toward 4 p.m. so Julia separated from us to go her way. Disconsolately, Robbie said he wanted to beat the traffic and spend the night alone in Half Moon Bay. But first we had to negotiate a small gaggle of reporters and photographers waiting on the sidewalk. Marilyn's role in the drama had not come out, but Naomi Jane's appearance was newsworthy and so was the story of the fall of a prominent psychiatrist seduced by his patient's beauty. I could see a headline of an article in next morning's paper. "Lavender Lady Accuses Prominent Psychiatrist of Sexual Transgression."

Jack Dietrich, his junior attorney, and NJ had already left. Robbie, Talley, and I walked quickly, Robbie between us, Talley to his left and me on his right. The newspeople snapped their pictures and flung questions at us. "Mr. Meyer, do you have a comment? What is your strategy for tomorrow?" "Dr. Carosso, do you have any hope that the jury will rule in your favor?" And at Talley. "Could you tell us who you are? What is your role in the case?" I had coached Robbie and Talley to smile but not respond to the questions, just keep smiling, and I flung back at the reporters, "Tomorrow I hope to have a good discussion with the plaintiff on the witness stand. Then we will move on to expert witnesses."

"Will Dr. Carosso testify?"

"Yes, he will tell his side of the story. There are two sides to every story."

When we cleared our way through the reporters, Robbie

headed for his car, and Talley and I walked to Hayes Street, where I found in my office that NJ's Stanford personnel file had finally arrived—just in time. After NJ and her attorney had finally agreed to sign the release, the university resisted and we had to file a motion to compel them to send us the records. The motion eased the way. Without the personnel files, we only had Robbie's statement that his treatment had benefitted NJ. She would probably agree during my cross-examination with the fact that since her treatment with Robbie she had been promoted up the assistant professor track and was in line for advancement to associate professor and tenure, but she would likely clam up about anything more. We finally had the details we needed from the university.

I opened the large envelope with Talley standing at my side, and copies of annual performance reviews and two-and-a-half-inch by three-inch personnel photographs spilled out. I skimmed the department chair's notes on NJ and her annual performance reviews. The reviews were basically checklist ratings of performance categories from one (deficient) to five (excellent). They confirmed what Robbie had told me. Starting with the beginning of her treatment with Robbie in October 2006, NJ's reviews had gone from deficient to threes (improvement desirable) to all fives. The department chairman's notes elaborated on the checklists. From being absent in her office hours, tardy grading papers, lackluster in her lectures, and nearly fired, she had grown markedly as a professor. I wondered what Dietrich was making of the university file.

The pictures told the story. "Eli, look at these." Talley had Professor Morton's yearly head and shoulders university photographs in her hand. "You have to use them." There were seven photos, one for each year NJ had been at Stanford. From a fresh-faced, intense-looking twenty-eight-year-old with a frown in 2000, Naomi Jane's appearance gradually declined into sadness, eye avoidance, and neglect of her clothes as the years went on. Until the fall 2007 photograph—the one after she came to Robbie's office in October 2006. She smiled for the camera for the first time. A year later in her fall 2008 photograph, her hair was fluffy, blonde, and curled below her ears; she wore a black jersey that bared her slim neck, a pearl necklace, and gave a sweet, luminous smile that welcomed the camera.

Marylyn immortalized the look in a famous 1960 photograph in which she was dressed in the same clothes and necklace that Naomi Jane Morton was wearing in her photograph. Robbie and I knew that Marilyn photograph; we had talked about how the face of the Marilyn in it looked like the way she was the night Robbie took her to the prom. In her 2008 university photo, NJ's hair and Marilyn's were the same. So was the shape of their face, neck, and shoulders. In the photograph, Marilyn Monroe was holding a birthday cake with one candle, pursing her lips to blow it out. The crew of the film *Let's Make Love* had given the cake to her to celebrate her thirty-fourth birthday. The Cannes Film Festival had also used that photo or one just like it for its fiftieth anniversary poster. Thirty-four years old too, Naomi Jane had modeled herself into the actress's look-alike—elegant, happy, sedate, and appealing.

Talley said, "The truth is in the pictures. That's where the therapy is. That wasn't Naomi Jane improving her performance because she had to hold on to her job; that was her responding to Robbie."

I asked my secretary to scan the photographs and yearly performance reviews into a PowerPoint file for my computer and to let Judge Poirier's secretary know that we needed a projector in court tomorrow. I also asked her to do an internet search to retrieve the famous Marilyn photo and add it to the file. Marilyn would probably make her appearance in Robbie's case tomorrow, in court and on his side.

CHAPTER
FIFTEEN

The next morning—Tuesday, May 16, 2008—when Robbie, Talley, Julia, and I gathered at Dream Fluff Donuts, the newspaper in the paper box outside greeted us with the biggest, boldest headlines since 9/11/2001: "California Supreme Court Overturns Gay Marriage Ban." Love was in the air. But on page three, a headline spelled out love gone wrong. "Prominent Psychiatrist and Ex-Patient in Salacious Courtroom Confrontation." The two-column, quarter-page article on the upper left-hand side of the page had small pictures of Robbie and NJ taken as they left the courthouse. The story, summarizing the plaintiff's complaint and the first day's testimony, was meant to draw readers for the story's next installment. Robbie and NJ looked handsome enough in the newspaper to compete with the story about the legalization of gay marriage for the readers' attention.

As we placed our orders, the waitress, Asmita, said, "You're the doctor in that picture, aren't you?" Robbie nodded. "I wish I could be there to hear what you say when you answer that lady. You have a nice face."

"Read the newspaper tomorrow morning, Asmita," I said.

"The trial may be on the front page. The story will probably indicate when Dr. Carosso is going to testify." Anticipating that sooner or later Robbie or NJ would bring Marilyn Monroe's name into the trial, I pointed up to the actress's faded picture on the wall behind the waitress and added, "She may be in tomorrow's story."

Asmita's eyes widened with surprise, trying to put the past and present together and imagine why and how the deceased star would be included. Judge Poirier would probably have a similar reaction, although more likely he would also be angry because when Marilyn arrived in court, so to speak, some chaos would likely follow. But he couldn't prevent her appearance because he wouldn't know in advance what I was going to spring later that morning. I figured chaos was good—anything to throw NJ's lawyer off balance.

On this morning, a slightly larger gaggle of reporters gathered outside the 400 McAllister Street courthouse door, mostly eagerly waiting for Naomi Jane Morton, with a passing interest in seeing if Robbie looked any different. He didn't, except for wearing a fresh white shirt. We walked right through queries like "How do you feel about Ms. Morton's testimony?" and requests for personal interviews after court.

Moments after we took our places in the courtroom—Robbie and me at the defense table and Talley and Julia just behind the bar in the spectator section—Naomi Jane arrived just as she had the day before. She was carrying a shoe-size, white, plastic bag with a drawstring she slid under her chair at the defense table. Today she was wearing a clinging black dress with a V-neckline and a lavender silk neckerchief. She'd changed to shiny, leather, lavender shoes. Her heels had become higher and thinner. I got up, went to the railing, and whispered to Talley, "Why lavender? What is that about?"

"It's got blue in it—blue for sad, blue for abused. And there's red in it—red for 'Look at me,' red to show off. She's perfect; she knows what she's doing."

"To a point," I whispered back.

By the time the bailiff announced that court was in session and Judge Poirier had taken his seat, the courtroom had a few more reporters than yesterday. They had taken seats near the rear, and there were now almost fifteen spectators.

Some procedural minutes later, I had NJ on the witness stand.

"Ms. Morton, my name is Eli Meyer, Dr. Carosso's attorney. I'm pleased to meet you, though I wish it wasn't under these circumstances."

She almost smiled at me before she frowned and said, "Yes."

"We all know that you have been through a very difficult time, and I am happy to see that you are looking well. There are just a few points I would like to clarify, as gently as possible." I nodded at her, running my hand pensively through my beard, turning to the jury to also draw them into cooperation with me.

"My first question is this: did Dr. Carosso continue to bill you for sessions after the sexual affair began?"

Dietrich was on his feet. "Objection, Your Honor. The defendant's attorney is using words to manipulate the witness—the plaintiff. It was not an affair. It was fraudulent therapy and sexual battery."

"Objection sustained. Mr. Meyer, please refrain from the term 'affair.'"

"Yes, Your Honor. Let me rephrase. Did Dr. Carosso continue to bill you after the sexual relationship began?"

Before Dietrich could object again, NJ said, "No, he did not."

"Then would it be fair to say that the relationship came after the treatment had ended?"

Dietrich was on his feet to demand Poirier censure me for using the word "relationship," but NJ cut him off. "Before, during, or after? Why is it important? It was an affair, in his fucking office. It was his idea of treatment, whatever you want to call it, not mine. The affair is all that counts."

Judge Poirier glared angrily at NJ. "Ms. Morton, control your language. This is a courtroom."

"I'm sorry, Your Honor. You don't know how angry what he did makes me." She threw a glance toward Robbie.

Dietrich was on his feet. "Your Honor, Mr. Meyer is baiting the witness with his questions. He is trying to get her to muddy what happened in the doctor's office. He is trying to get her upset so her testimony will look flawed to the jury."

"Mr. Meyer, the plaintiff's lawyer is correct. Bring this line of questioning to a quick conclusion, or I will have it struck from the record."

Admonishment or no admonishment, the jury had heard Ms. Morton's confusion about whether the affair was part of treatment or not. What remained was to get into the therapy itself, the first two months of her visits to Robbie's office. I continued. "Ms. Morton, I apologize for upsetting you; however, the question is important because you are suing Dr. Carosso for fraudulent treatment, malpractice, and theft of service. If treatment had concluded and the affair followed, there is no theft of service. As for fraudulent treatment and malpractice, we have to look at the treatment itself, don't we?"

I rubbed my beard again, pulling judge, jury, NJ, and even the gallery into my next question. "Ms. Morton, we know from your testimony yesterday that your work at the university improved greatly after you began treatment with

Dr. Carosso. I admire you. Depression is very painful, very personally destructive. It is very difficult to recover from it, and you did, without the help of antidepressants. Can we credit at least some of your recovery to your work with Dr. Carosso?"

"Mr. Meyer, I testified earlier that I pulled myself together after my department chairman warned me that my contract might not be renewed."

"I understand. I think he also referred you to Dr. Carosso?"

"Yes."

I turned to the judge. "Your Honor, I would like to introduce exhibit one into the trial now."

"What is it?"

"Yesterday I received delivery of the plaintiff's personnel files from her university. I would like to project relevant materials onto the screen."

Judge Poirier nodded, waiting for Dietrich's inevitable eruption. The lawyer was on his feet and immediately objecting. "Your Honor, this exhibit should be inadmissible. It should have been released to the court during pretrial discovery."

"Mr. Meyer, what do you have to say?"

"It is not my fault, not any of our faults that the files only reached our offices after the trial began. If the court and Mr. Dietrich check the mail, both will probably find the same mailing. Or it may be stuck in mailrooms and not made it to your offices yet. Ms. Morton and her attorney sent a signed release to Stanford to send us her personnel files some months ago. Apparently the wheels turned slowly, yet just in time for us all to see information that has an important bearing on this case. This is new material evidence that flows directly from the testimonies given in court yesterday and this morning."

Poirier had two alternatives now. He could let me project my PowerPoint slides of the personnel files or he could recess court for the day while he and the plaintiff looked over the personnel files. Recessing court for the day would extend the trial, ultimately probably into the next week, which nobody wanted to happen. Everybody was eager to let the drama unfold uninterrupted.

Dietrich put his hands in his pockets, and Poirier said, "Okay, Mr. Meyer, proceed." He nodded to the bailiff to dim the lights. NJ's lawyer sat down.

I left my position at the rostrum near Ms. Morton and went to my computer on the defense table. I started with the most recent one-page performance checklists for 2006, 2007, and 2008 and duly used my pointer to show the jury the progress from deficient to excellent. I didn't dwell on them because I knew the pictures would override words and numbers. The emotional action was in the photographs. I moved the mouse on my computer and started clicking the yearly personnel photographs all the way from 2000 to 2007. I did it slowly from one to the next, taking my time, letting everybody in the courtroom study them fully as they appeared on the screen behind the judge's dais. When the 2007 photo appeared, the one in which NJ smiles for the first time, there was a big sigh of relief in the courtroom. Everybody felt released from Naomi Jane's depression. I snuck a look at her in the witness stand. She was smiling too, almost wearing a look of triumph as if she'd won an award for her on-screen appearance.

I clicked the 2008 school photograph onto the screen, the Marilyn look-alike photo. There was a lot of rustling in the courtroom—bodies moving in their seats, feet scraping the floor, the rear door opening and closing as two reporters quickly left. There were quick intakes of breath. People seemed uncomfortable, unsure of themselves, and uncertain about how to respond. The jury was staring intently from NJ's projected image back to her and back again at the screen. Two or three people in the room may have consciously realized that NJ's appearance in the 2008 photograph was strikingly similar to Marilyn's in her birthday cake photo. Many others were probably dimly aware of the resemblance between NJ and the actress.

Finally Judge Poirier rapped his gavel, the room quieted, and he said, "Are you finished with your exhibit, counsel?"

"Yes, Your Honor."

"Please proceed with your cross."

I returned to the rostrum and faced Naomi Jane. She was beaming at me with a look of self-admiration, almost with a look of gratitude for how I had let everyone see the beauty she had achieved since she'd met Robbie. Robbie for his part looked amazed.

"Ms. Morton, could you describe how this review of your personnel photographs has made your feel?"

She pointed at Robbie. "That man, Dr. Carosso, had a fixation on Marilyn Monroe. After he began sexually molesting me, he brought a big, coffee-table book of the actress's photographs into the office, sittings for fashion photographers and stills from her movies. He'd move the side table over, put the book on it, and we'd sit on the couch looking at the pictures. He'd point to one and say, 'You can look like that.'" Or he'd ask me what I thought of a photograph, and I'd tell him which ones pleased me. Then he'd say, 'You can become that one.' Sometimes I brought a dress in a style similar to one from the photographs and changed into it in front of him. Then we'd make love.

"I want to show you something else. Don't think I didn't come prepared." NJ left the witness chair, amid a rustling from the courtroom and a look of consternation on the judge's face, but she moved so quickly and purposely that nobody including me or her attorney intervened. She retrieved the white sack she had brought in earlier from under her chair at the plaintiff's table and, grimacing, dumped a pair of fancy shoes on it, then waved them at the jury, judge, and Robbie. They were red satin with open toes and back with spike heels, almost the same as the ones Marilyn had worn to the prom years ago. "Dr. Carosso gave these shoes to me and asked me to wear them. Apparently his actress fixation wore them once. You know what these shoes are? They are fuck-me shoes! That was his perverted therapy. I can't believe I listened to him and wore them."

The judged rapped the courtroom to order and directed NJ to take her seat at the witness box and behave herself. He wielded the threat of contempt of court if the plaintiff and her attorney didn't respect the rules of testimony and evidence.

Now the word *Marilyn* was out in court for everyone to hear, and there were more quick exits from the courtroom by people eager to make use of the news. Poirier frowned. He knew court the next day would be standing room only. Dietrich looked like an attorney who didn't know whether his client had just blown or won the case for herself and for him with her behavior. Whether he was looking at enough money to buy the yacht we'd seen from his office sailing on the bay or whether he'd just have to chalk this case up to a learning experience.

"Do you have any more questions for the plaintiff, Mr. Meyer?"

"No. I've concluded." I couldn't predict what would come next from the plaintiff if I asked anything more so I followed the cardinal courtroom rule: don't ask a question if you don't know how the witness is going to answer in advance. I stayed silent.

"Then we can recess for the day."

"No!" Naomi Jane said. "I have something more to say."

"Ms. Morton, proper procedure during cross-examination is for the plaintiff to respond to specific questions the defense puts to you. You presented your complaint yesterday," the judge said.

"This is my case. I have a right to tell my story." She nailed Poirier with her eyes and Dietrich seemed to shrink in size into his suit.

A courtroom is like a big circus tent, and the judge is the ringmaster. He has to follow a procedural book of rules and snap his whip so that everybody does the same. At the same time, he has a lot of freedom in how he can interpret the rules and when to snap the whip or pound his gavel. Everyone was looking at Poirier. All he did was nod to NJ that it was okay to continue. What the heck? He was going to retire soon. He was enjoying listening to her and looking at her clinging black dress. When it comes time to vote for the defendant or the plaintiff, jurors also give a nod to the one who takes the most pride in how they dress. They all wanted NJ to continue.

She picked up her story. "When I came to see Dr. Carosso, my body needed to grow into my mind. I've got an overblown mind. All my life, it was all I had while the rest of me was gradually disappearing. Pretty soon I would have become a speck of dust if Dr. Carosso hadn't seen something in me and brought it to life."

Naomi Jane ran her hands down her dress from her hips to her knees, caressing herself and showing herself off to the court at the same time. Then she balled her right hand into a fist and brought it down hard on the wooden arm of the chair she was sitting in. "Yes, I fell in love with Dr. Carosso. He was a smart, beautiful, caring man unlike any other man I had known. That's what made it possible for me to change. But a psychiatrist is supposed to understand transference love and manage it. He didn't."

She looked at the jury and said to them, "Transference love is a connection a patient feels for her therapist that comes from loving somebody long ago—in my case my mother, before she died when I was nine. The people who raised me after that scarcely cared about me. They abused me. I was a chore to them. And Dr. Carosso abused me. He was supposed to use the transference to help me, not have sex with me to please himself. When I suggested, I mean *he* suggested, that I lie on the couch rather than sit in a chair, he was supposed to know that the couch had to be a safe refuge where I could learn how to think about things and feel things. He was supposed to know that the couch wasn't a place to act out his own pitiful psychological drama with me.

"That's it in a nutshell. I'm not going to surrender what I've gained from my so-called 'doctor.' But I'm going to have to carry with me the shame I feel that that I could have fallen for a man who acted like that."

I looked at Robbie. He was cringing. I looked at the jurors, and they were exchanging perplexed, mouth-open glances with each other. Judge Poirier tapped his gavel. "Are you finished, Ms. Morton?" She said yes. He rapped his gavel. "Court is in recess until nine o'clock tomorrow morning."

Robbie, Julia, Talley, and I waited in our places until the courtroom had emptied and then Robbie and I reconnoitered with Julia and Talley where they were sitting just behind the bar. They all looked at me. "What do you think? How do you think it's going?" Julia asked me.

"I think I understand how you fell for her, Robbie," I said.

Talley gave one of her kicks at my foot. "I think Robbie is going to lose this trial," she said.

Robbie said meekly, "Did you hear how she admitted that she suggested using the couch? Yesterday she said it was my idea."

"Bad idea either way," I said.

Talley said, "I think we have to come up with something fast to help you, Robbie."

"Tomorrow morning we hear from the expert witnesses. That's like playing roulette. You never know in advance where the wheel will stop and which expert the jury will believe. Dietrich and I may give our final arguments tomorrow afternoon. The judge will probably give his instructions to the jury on Friday morning. It will all hinge on what he tells them constitutes fraud."

Talley had leaned back in her seat and closed her eyes, thinking hard and fast. In moments she announced, "I have an idea. You guys can go. I want to tell it to Julia, in private."

"Why in private?" I pushed.

"It's confidential because you'd never approve. You know the lingo; it's *extrajudicial*." Talley was grinning at me. I never said no when she was grinning at me. It was the same grin she had back in high school when she told Robbie and me that the three of us needed some adventure. That was the day she came up with the idea to go pool-hopping, the night she lost her virginity to Robbie.

Robbie and I left the courtroom together while Talley and Julia stayed behind to scheme. At the door to the corridor, I cast a look back at the two women, and Julia was tapping intently at her smartphone. Her new accessory was brand new with a soft golden band around it. The first iPhone had come out just months earlier in 2007, and Julia was the first in our office to get one—the only one so far. We exited the courthouse onto McAllister. A big crowd of reporters pressed toward us, triple the number from the day before. If some of them left to trail NJ and her attorneys, enough remained to make it hard for Robbie and me to leave.

Robbie shrunk back. "I don't want to do this."

"You have to do this unless you want to sleep in the hallway. Put a smile on your face. Don't say anything. Let me do the talking."

It was as if I were telling him not to be Robbie, not to talk. He shot me a scared look and pasted a grin on his face. My smile was cordial, tolerant, and patient because I knew the media had a job to do. Why not help? If I didn't, they could turn on Robbie and me, and although Judge Poirier had told the jurors not to read about the trial or watch TV news reports about it, some jurors would inevitably catch headlines and some would ignore the judge. The media slant on the trial would influence them. I paused a moment to take questions.

"How do you think the trial is going, Dr. Carosso?"

I answered for Robbie. "It's very painful. Clearly, both Dr. Carosso and the plaintiff have suffered. The question is: who is responsible for the suffering? It will become clearer tomorrow."

"How many experts will you call?"

"One."

"What did you think of Ms. Morton's testimony today?"

"She is a very articulate young woman." With that, I put my arm around Robbie's back, moved him through the knot of media people, and we crossed the street. "Do you want to stay overnight with us?" I asked him.

"No. I want to go back to Half Moon Bay. I want to be alone." He had wounds to lick. We walked to the stairs that descended to the garage under the Civic Center. A nasty miasma of disinfectant and urine rose up from the stairwell, and Robbie descended into it to retrieve his Mustang.

That night at home, I asked Talley what idea she had come up with, what she and Julia had cooked up. She repeated that she couldn't tell me and added that she and Julia would miss next morning's court session. She said they would be back in court in the afternoon. I couldn't wait to see what they would bring with them because I loved Talley's surprises most of the time, yet at the same time, we were involved in a regimented legal process in Superior Court. I didn't want hijinks in the courtroom that could lead Judge Poirier to sanction our defense with contempt of court. If Poirier cited me for contempt because of something that Talley or Julia did, it would be contagious. Whatever sympathy the jurors may feel for Robbie would be lost.

CHAPTER
SIXTEEN

At eight o'clock on Thursday morning, Julia arrived at our home in her car, a little, red, generic Asian import. She and Talley were both wearing blue jeans, dark sweatshirts with hoods, and jogging shoes. Just before they got into my wife's van, Talley pulled off the magnetized logos for her business, Furthur Cloth, from the side panels. Then the plain, faded-yellow, dented, unmarked van headed up Twenty-Fifth Street and turned left on Van Ness Avenue. For a moment I wondered if they were going to rob the same bank Patty Hearst had in 1974 and return with enough loot so Robbie could pay off his debt to Naomi Jane and keep the *Impulse*.

An idle thought, but you never know.

What I learned when they told me later that day in my office was they had turned left at Cesar Chavez, south on 101, and taken the 280 Freeway south out of the City. Julia had found NJ's address on the internet, and Talley's plan was leading them to NJ's home in La Honda, a tiny community in the coast hills twelve miles west of the Stanford Campus. If I'd known in advance, I would have said, "No, don't go there," not that Talley would necessarily have listened.

Julia should have known better herself, but Talley was old enough to be her mother—a persuasive, colorful mother. With Julia using her smartphone to navigate, they were in NJ's village in an hour and a half or so. The highway ran along the eastern flank of the coastal hills, past Crystal Springs reservoir, and through parkland and pastures. Talley and Julia couldn't see the actual university campus but knew they were abreast Stanford when they saw a cluster of high-tech electronic towers and satellite dishes on a hillside to their left. That's where the narrow two-lane road to La Honda veered off on the right. They took it west to the crest of the hills and descended tight switchback curves at a snail's pace into a deep, narrow valley. That was how La Honda got its name from early Spanish settlers—deep and dark.

In the 1960s and 1970s, rumors of mysterious goings-on rose from the valley. Writers, philosophers, hallucinogenic drug experimenters, and their hangers-on had lived and played there. The hamlet is at the bottom of the valley in a redwood forest that keeps it shadowed and moist. There is a general store with a post office, a bar, a fire station, a mechanic's shop, and a school. They told me how on the morning they were there, a man and a woman ambled down Main Street on horses. People live in mostly hand-built houses scattered up little lanes in hillside clearings that let sun in.

There was no wireless connection so Talley and Julia stopped at the general store and got directions to the lane on which NJ lived. Up to then, Julia only knew that Talley wanted to find NJ's house. "Willful ignorance," Julia later said. After they got the directions at the store, Julia told me how Talley revealed her plan, which ran something like this:

Talley: We find an open door or window or break in if we

have to. We don't have to worry. She lives alone, I think. She's in court. She'll be there all day.

Julia: Are you nuts? We can't break in. Maybe if I had a private investigator's license I could. But I don't, and I don't know if I could do it even with a p.i.'s license.

Talley: You're not an attorney yet, so you're not breaking any oath if we do go inside. Come on, Julia. Nobody will know. It's an adventure. If you won't come with me, I'll do it myself.

Julia (getting into the excitement as Talley started the van): What do we do when we get inside?

Talley: We look for something that will get Robbie off. Something that will turn the jury against NJ. That's where you come in, Julia. Tell me when you see it. You're the investigator. You'll know what Eli can use in court.

Julia: Yes, newly discovered material evidence to the case, like how Eli got NJ's personnel photos admitted. Okay, I'm on board.

It didn't take them more than five minutes to locate the address, but the house seemed too large to belong to NJ. Made from wooden planks, it had a long front deck, large picture windows, and a slanting roof. A shiny, new, four-wheel-drive pickup truck with oversize tires sat in front. The curtains were pulled.

Talley: There's a path that curves around the side of the house. I can see a little cottage up the hill in back. That must be it.

Julia: Why would NJ live way out here?

Then Talley hit Julia with her historical romance, the way she lived life as if it were one picaresque episode to the next.

Talley: I guess you're too young to know about this valley. Counterculture types from the Stanford English department used to live here back in the old days. It was part of the back-to-the-earth movement—teach a course or two at the university during the day then go home to the country, get stoned, garden, and write the rest of the time. Or at least imagine writing a great book.

Julia: You've got a really faraway look in your eyes.

Talley: I'm not dreaming about writing. That's not my thing. I was thinking about the back-to-the-earth times and the sculpture and painting that went on here. I was dreaming about Ken Kesey. He lived in La Honda. He was really creative. I never had a chance to work in the country. I was in New York City those years.

Julia: I think I've heard about him.

Talley: Kesey's gang was called the Merry Pranksters. He ran the acid tests at his place.

Julia: You mean LSD?

Talley: Yes. It wasn't really a test but a group chemical séance. The idea was to have visions, learn from them, paint them, enact them. They had an old school bus called Furthur that they painted in bright, wild colors and drove across the country. That's where I got the name Furthur for my fabric business. When I heard about that bus, I wanted to decorate it. They invited me to come to the valley because they knew I did the color slides for the rock shows at the Fillmore East, but I stayed in New York instead.

Julia (beguiled): I wish I had known you then, but I wasn't even born yet.

Talley: We're not in La Honda just to get some kind of

exonerating information for Robbie. I've never been here before, and I want to imagine what it may have been like when I was young. Maybe the past has something to do with why NJ is living here now. Finding that out could help Robbie.

They drove the van farther up the hillside lane until the two dwellings were downhill and then got out. The front house and NJ's place in the rear were now below them, barely visible through a copse of scruffy tan oaks stunted by taller redwoods blocking the sun. Talley led the way through the copse into a sunny field.

Talley: We're in a large marijuana garden. This explains the expensive pickup truck in front of the big house. Let's take a few buds.

Julia: No, thanks. It isn't legal yet. I can't have anything on my record.

Talley (pocketing cannabis buds): Smart for you not to, I guess.

After a few minutes of walking, they were just above NJ's place, a cozy cabin with a front deck hanging out over the slope and a rear door. The hill down to the cabin was short and steep on ground that was still slick from the winter rains. They lost their footing and slid down.

Talley (laughing): We've got dirt and pine needles all over our butts.

Julia: Shut up. You're making too much noise. Let's check the doors and windows.

After finding nothing open, Julia opened a puny back door

lock into the kitchen by slipping a credit card between the jamb and the bolt.

Julia: We have to take off our shoes. You take the bedroom and I'll take the other room. Let's see what we find.

The main room had a bit of furniture, a bookshelf packed with Shakespeare's works, English literature anthologies, literary criticism, a worn copy of Ken Kesey's *One Flew over the Cuckoo's Nest,* a file cabinet, and NJ's desk and computer. Manuscript pages with the header "Ophelia's Reflection by Naomi Jane Morton" littered the desk and filled a wastebasket. Gaudy, bodice-ripper, paperback romance novels with covers of half-dressed women and impossibly handsome men lay strewn on the floor.

On the bedroom dresser, Talley found an eight-and-a-half-by-eleven-inch enlargement of NJ's 2008 university personnel photograph under glass in a gold filigree frame, the picture in which she was wearing a dress just like Marilyn wore in her photo holding the birthday cake. NJ had placed it so she could look at her beautiful self every day when she stood in front of her the mirror on the wall in back of the dresser. With lipstick she had written over the photo, "Dear Dr. C., thank you for everything," and left an impression of her lips on the glass. It could have been mistaken for a kiss Marilyn might have left on a photo of herself for Abel Carosso forty-six years ago, except the lipstick was too fresh. Julia came into the bedroom and took close-up photos with her phone.

Julia then returned to the main room and continued quickly skimming through folders in NJ's file cabinet with an investigator's skill. She extracted a desiccated manila folder and pulled pictures from it. She found a series of snapshots of a brown-haired adolescent in pin-up girl poses—shot nude from behind, looking coyly over her shoulder, mugging and teasing for the camera, and frontal shots of her in lingerie. Unmistakably NJ, they were taken in a studio elegantly furnished in an older man's style with art deco period pieces. NJ looked very young, fifteen or sixteen, when she posed for the photographer.

There was a letter in the folder with the letterhead Vista Modeling Agency, Chicago, Illinois. They laid the yellowing paper on NJ's desk, and Talley read aloud.

> January 25, 1981
>
> My Dearest Naomi Jane,
>
> I love you with love beyond all feeling and am losing you. I miss you with a pain beyond all tears. As long as I live, you will be missed. Remembered. I will forever hold you in my heart. When your despicable aunt and uncle banish you to Connecticut, you will take me with you and forever hold my heart inside of you. You were the finest thing in my life, and I will miss you forever. As your aunt and uncle requested, here are the photos and negatives of the pictures, and the check for $3,000 made out to them that they demanded in return for not reporting me to the police for being much older than you. What does age matter! You are so much smarter than me. You are the best lover and model I have ever had. You are so beautiful and intelligent. You will have a great future.
>
> I will love you forever,
>
> Your Harold

Julia (slapping her hand down on NJ's desk): That woman is *not* an innocent. She's not a naive victim.

Talley: She's been a mistress before.

Julia: NJ may have set Robbie up in order to extort money from him, the way her aunt and uncle may have used her to extort Harold. I'm going to photograph it and send it to Eli's office right now.

But with no wireless connection, Julia failed. They did succeed in transmitting from the general store on Main Street, and Julia texted my secretary to print everything in color and make a computer file that I could project in court that afternoon. It was just past ten thirty when they started back to San Francisco, just enough time to get to my office by noon.

When we all reconnoitered in my office during the midday court recess, Julia said, "Eli, if you had a smartphone, I could have sent everything directly to you. You need one."

"He's a stick in the mud. He thinks they're just gadgets," said Talley.

A lunch buffet sat at the end of our conference table, hand delivered by Asmita from Dream Fluff: Indian nan with pizza toppings and samosas. Our secretary had printed multiple color copies of the photos and the farewell letter to NJ from the man named Harold at the Vista Modeling Agency. I spread the evidence out on the table.

It dumbfounded Robbie. When he found his voice, he said, "I never imagined."

"Don't you have to imagine things like this in your business?" Talley asked.

Robbie said, "I know that the meek young professor who came to my office wasn't putting on an act at first. That's the way NJ really was then. She was hiding from the world in shapeless clothes. I think it was her aunt and uncle who made her ashamed of herself. First they shamed her by not loving her, and then they shamed her for having sex with the photographer. Then they degraded her by making money off her photographs. Maybe her uncle did molest her the way she thinks he may have in middle school. Maybe that triggered her into sex when she was so young.

"Maybe Harold would have helped Naomi Jane feel good about herself in the long run, the way I did in the short run. I think nowadays NJ is living in La Honda because she wants to write a famous book and hopes the aura there will help her write. Then her book's success will make up for all that's been bad in her life."

The old Hollywood syndrome, people wanting to be close to other people's fame to get some glow in their own lives, here in Northern California, probably everywhere. But I didn't say that because it was too close to what happened in Robbie's family, his parents wanting to be close to the movie crowd.

Julia offered, "What about her past history of the aunt and uncle getting money from her affair with the photographer? Could NJ have seduced you in order to end up with a payday in court?"

"She was their victim. She wouldn't do to me what they did to the photographer, extort me. I don't believe she would have put her career at the university into a nose-dive in order to have an excuse to go into therapy with me."

"You're a pretty magnetic guy, Dr. Carosso. Maybe it was after she met you that she got the idea," Julia persisted.

"I don't believe it." Robbie wasn't as hard-nosed as Julia, who had a point. Still, he was getting his psychological chops back and was thinking about NJ's gritty and confusing life in a way he hadn't during the treatment or the affair. He started to turn green, and it was not the kind of green that came from the Indian food we were eating—or seasickness or the flu. It was the stomach-turning green of shame and defeat I had seen on the face of people who were recognizing their own self-delusion for the first time. He was realizing how little he had really known NJ and how his being married had doomed the intense affection they had for each other from the start. He crumpled into his chair, leaving us staring at the material on the table.

Time was passing and we needed to get down to the brass tacks of what to do with the evidence in the afternoon court session. Finally I released the anger I had been holding in about the whole sortie to NJ's house. "You two had to be out of your minds breaking into the plaintiff's home."

Julia shuffled her feet and looked sheepish. Talley didn't back down. "Look at what we found, Eli. When the jury sees this stuff, they're going to think that Naomi Jane is just playing a charade to get money."

"The jury is *not* going to see it!"

"Why not?" Talley was offended.

"Because if it appears in court, NJ will know somebody connected with us broke into her house to get the material. Dietrich will get his guys to trace it back to you two. Look at you. You're dropping crumbs of dirt from your shoes and jeans on my office floor every step you take. Think of what you left behind at NJ's house: footprints, mud, tire tracks, fingerprints. Julia, look at the images you took of NJ's framed photograph. Your face is reflected in the glass. You know what will happen if Dietrich loses his case?" They shook their heads not sure where I was going. "He will file a report on Julia with the ethics committee of the California Bar. When Julia passes her Bar exam, they will never in a million years give her a license to practice law because what you two did today is a fucking felony."

"That can't happen," Talley said.

Julia said, "Thank you, Eli, for thinking about me, but

don't lawyers go around the law all the time to get information for their clients?"

"Yes, until they get caught. Me, I don't care what happens to me. It wasn't my idea; I didn't know about it. The evidence just fell into my lap, so to speak. Maybe I can use it and get away with it. If I lose my license, I can just travel the world with Talley while she looks for new fabrics. You'll get caught, Julia, if we use this evidence, and I'm not going to be responsible for that. And ultimately Dietrich could just file for a retrial and get it as easily as lifting his finger."

"Poor Robbie," Talley said. She went to his chair and from behind momentarily put her head on his shoulder.

I softened my tone. "Honey," I said to Talley, "we know so much more now about NJ, thanks to you. We can use what we know in our thinking even if we can't produce the photos and letter in court."

Talley relaxed and Robbie murmured, "I don't know *anything* anymore. I don't think NJ did anything on purpose."

Talley continued, "I bet she looks in her mirror over the dresser every morning and doesn't know who she is seeing. I bet she turns her head to her photo on the dresser and sees herself dressed like Marilyn and thinks maybe she is the actress. I looked at some of the pages on her floor from the book she's writing and NJ's obsessed with reflections. She's obsessed with Ophelia, who was Hamlet's lover. She wants to know what Ophelia saw when she looked into the river. She wants to know what went through her mind before she threw herself into the water because she thought she'd lost Hamlet."

"Maybe she was looking so hard she just fell in and drowned," Julia offered.

Robbie mumbled, "Does anybody ever know who they really are without a mirror? Marilyn kept searching for herself;

NJ is searching. Aren't we all just the reflection of what other people see in us—our parents first and everybody else from then on?"

The trial had gotten out of my control, the opposite of my hope that NJ's attorney, trained in military regimentation and a maven for predictability, would be the one thrown for a loop by the unexpected. I looked at my watch. I pulled Robbie out of his reverie. "Robbie, it's time to leave for the courtroom now."

"What are you going to do?"

"Recall Dietrich's experts and cross-examine them. They smeared you this morning, and I'm going to try to soften the impression they left with the jury. It's our last chance before we get to closing arguments tomorrow."

"You've got no chance, Eli. Everything they spoke was true," Robbie said, biting his lip strongly enough to draw blood.

"So?" I threw the word out like a referee in a rugby match rolling the ball into a scrum, offering it up to see who would come out with it.

"Don't recall them. Recall me," Robbie answered. "I'll talk to the jury. I'm the only one left who has anything worth saying, that nobody has heard before, including you, Eli." His hair was flopped over his forehead, hiding his eyes, but the firmness in his chin was obvious. "Yes, I'll try to use what we learned about NJ to let the jury understand how it all happened, and no, I won't put Julia in danger. Maybe those eight men and women will sympathize with me after I tell them what I have to tell them. I mean they know about what happened between me and my patient, but they haven't heard the whole story of what happened between me and Marilyn. That's the real why of this lawsuit. Maybe they'll see me as more than just a doctor gone astray."

Talley concluded. "Be yourself, Robbie. We love you. Show the jury why."

CHAPTER
SEVENTEEN

As we walked toward Superior Court, I filled Julia and Talley in on the testimonies the expert witnesses had given in court that morning. Jack Dietrich had called two experts, and we had one. Dietrich had taken his time letting his experts recite their impeccable professional credentials to the courtroom. Then he had asked them to tell the court their opinion of Dr. Carosso's admitted affair with his patient in his office. Clearly Dietrich had framed the direction he wanted his experts' testimonies to go in order to complement each other. They needed very little prompting from the attorney. His first expert was the president of the Northern California Society of Board-Certified Forensic Psychiatrists. A relaxed man in a tweed suit, he quoted a sheaf of statistics, the most telling of which was that if a patient has been seduced by a therapist, there was a 37 percent greater risk of suicide than if a sexual boundary violation had not occurred. Those were his words: "seduced by a therapist and sexual boundary violation." The jurors had listened, but many wrinkled their brows uncertainly. From what they had seen of NJ on the stand, they probably couldn't imagine her desperate enough to hurt herself. More likely, they'd seen that the target of her anger was Robbie—get him to pay her restitution, shame him, punish him, not herself.

However the expert's next point was more telling. "If a patient has been sexually molested by her therapist, there is a 68 percent greater risk of depression in the future." This time, all the jurors nodded in sympathy with the expert's information, some with full up and down movements of their heads, some with just a slight inclination. He continued. "Dr. Carosso is a board-certified psychiatrist. The examination he once took to receive his certification includes questions about what kind of touching is permissible in a psychiatrist's office. It is okay for a doctor to touch a patient to offer reassurance, to give physical support, and to offer sympathy over bad news. Sexual touching is *not* okay; it is forbidden. Dr. Carosso passed his examination years ago. He knew that. There is a body of knowledge all psychiatrists receive in their training that makes it clear that sexual contact in a treatment setting constitutes medical malpractice."

Dietrich asked his witness if it was ever okay for a psychiatrist to date a patient after the treatment had ended or to marry a former patient. The president of the Northern California Society of Board-Certified Forensic Psychiatrists said, "That is an excellent question which has been asked many times by doctors and patients alike because deep feelings can grow between patients and therapists. Deep feelings, even erotic ones, are normal. Sometimes they can and should be engaged in words, the patient speaking of them, the therapist listening and understanding. But they should never be acted on during therapy. Some professional writers on the subject say that it is permissible for a doctor and a patient to have a personal relationship three years after therapy is finished; some suggest two years. Most say never. There have been a few successful marriages reported between therapists and former patients, but these rare successes have usually happened only when the patients are therapists themselves. There are far more reports of disastrous marriages of this sort, some ending tragically with the death of the former patient or the former therapist. However, to say that Dr. Carosso and his patient had concluded therapy before their affair began, let alone waited for a period of time, is a travesty, a twisting of facts that is unsupportable."

Jack Dietrich had picked his expert well. He gave his testimony in a soft, knowledgeable, dispassionate, even regretful voice. Dietrich's next expert was an emerita professor of psychiatry from the University of California medical school in Sacramento, a woman who specialized in treating psychologically sexually traumatized women and men. An older woman with gray hair and reading glasses hanging from a beaded cord over her chest, she had been a court-appointed evaluator for over two hundred adults who had been molested by clergy as children, not just priests molesting altar boys but also ministers molesting choir girls. Her statistics closely matched Dietrich's first expert, but her manner was different. She wasn't calm, and she didn't need to use her reading glasses. All she did was talk angrily, passionately, and definitively. She rapped the rostrum in time with each or her words. "Sex in treatment is an unspeakable sin and breach of trust." The jurors seemed stunned by her strength.

Then she turned from the jurors to focus on Naomi Jane. "I feel so sorry for what you have been through, Ms. Morton. It will affect you for the rest of your life. You should never have been exposed to this. You are not a child; you are an adult. You had mature psychological defenses with which to deal with the sexual approach of your doctor. But you didn't push him away and terminate treatment immediately, which means that, as Dr.

Carosso's own chart notes of his so-called treatment say, you were probably molested as a child. You were probably trying to master a childhood trauma."

The professor turned to the jury. "Now Ms. Morton has two traumas. She is coping well. My congratulations to her. But research shows that psychological trauma is like an iceberg. Only the tip shows. The rest of the emotional injury is covered over with psychological defense mechanisms like denial and repression. The immensity of the trauma is looming unseen with potential to destroy as assuredly as the iceberg that brought down the *Titanic*. All it takes is for Ms. Morton to encounter an event that triggers memories of the way in which Dr. Carosso misused her, and repressed rage can erupt. With one hand—that's all it takes, one hand—she can pick up a razor blade, slash herself, and bleed to death. In my work as a sexual molestation evaluator, I have seen this too many times."

I watched NJ listen to the doctor's testimony. She looked angry at the way she was being depicted. When I finished describing the expert's testimony to Julia and Talley, Julia shook her head with disgust. Talley said, "That doctor from Sacramento sounds like an opera singer taking too long to die."

"That may be the way you and I feel, but I also watched the jurors. The doctor had them in the palm of her hand. They were riveted on her. When her lips curled in anger at Robbie, the jurors looked angry too; when the doctor became horrified while describing how poor Ms. Morton would pick up a razor and slash her wrists someday, the jurors were horrified too."

When Dietrich's two experts had finished their testimonies, I'd decided that I didn't want to cross-examine them at that time. I wanted to be rid of them, move on to my own expert, Burl Harford, and use him to rebut the previous testimonies. I could also recall Dietrich's experts for cross-examination in the afternoon and take a swing at them in my closing arguments.

Harford was eager to take the stand, eager to deliver his testimony and fly away in his airplane to his next gig in Phoenix. He took his place on the witness stand like a self-assured performer in the spotlight. Cocky, foppish, and round, he wore a gray, three-piece suit with a gold chain looped from a button on his vest into a watch pocket. He was only testifying for us because he liked being the center of attention, he liked to earn a lot of money in a short time, and he liked to show how smart he was. His academic credentials were limited. Unlike Dietrich's two witnesses who believed in what they said, Harford wasn't with us because he had any convictions about Robbie's case. He was all I could get: a hired gun to side with Robbie.

Still, Harford could make himself believe in what he was saying. "Let's look at the statistics," he'd said to the jurors. "You have heard that when a sexual relationship occurs between doctor and patient, the patient has a 37 percent greater risk of suicide than if there is no sex. What the doctor didn't tell you is that 63 percent of patients have *no* greater risk. No greater risk. You heard that patients who are sexually involved with their doctors have a 68 percent greater risk of depression. What the doctor didn't tell you is that 32 percent of sexually involved patients have no greater risk of depression. You have seen the plaintiff for yourselves; you have heard of her stellar accomplishments. You can trust your impressions more than numbers. Does this woman look like she falls into the at-risk of suicide and depression group? Of course not.

"Further, the so-called experts' numbers lie. Most of the very same patients who came for treatment were already depressed, and many already were having suicidal ideation.

That means they were already thinking of taking their lives. Their later depressions and the rare deaths were not caused by having sex with their doctors. They were preexisting conditions. A preexisting condition is a prior illness that has interfered with their life, for which they had been treated or for which they should have been treated. Sex was just a blip on the radar screens of their lives."

To prep Burl Harford for his testimony, I had shared with him the story of the two famous women who had affairs with their therapists whom Robbie had told me about a few months earlier on his boat. Assuming a confidential tone, Harford said to the jury, "There are two notable women I want you to know about who had affairs with their therapists. The first was Sabina Spielrun with Carl Jung in 1909; the second was Anais Nin with Otto Rank in 1934. Both men were pioneering psychoanalysts. They did not wait for a period of time to elapse between the end of treatment and the start of the personal relationships. There was mutual agreement between the women and their doctors that it was time to deepen their relationships by consummating it with intercourse."

Then Harford challenged the jurors "What if you fell in love with your doctor? Would you want him to tell you that you had to wait two or three years before you could be lovers? Would you want the law to tell you how long to wait, or the law to forbid you to ever consummate your relationship?"

Harford finished up by saying, "Neither patient married their doctors. Spielrein went on to become a successful physician, psychoanalyst, and author of important professional papers. Anais Nin became a best-selling diarist, a role model for many young women in the 1960s and 1970s for her sexual independence. She celebrated her relationship with Dr. Rank, and like Sabina Spielrein, she had many successes in her life.

You should read her books. Sex with their therapists," he repeated, "was a blip in their lives."

I looked to the jurors to see their reaction to Harford's performance. A couple of women snickered; the three men winced; the three others frowned. I had not told Harford that Anais Nin had an incestuous relationship with her father before she had an affair with her shrink or that both Jung and Spielrein had nervous breakdowns during their affairs and went into sanitariums for a time. If the jurors knew that, it would just muddy my expert witness's point that sex between patient and doctor could just be an innocent fling. I was betting that nobody else in the courtroom except maybe Judge Poirier knew those details. Harford's testimony had left me unsettled. He had sounded flippant and glib. If a jury feels an expert is condescending to them, they can turn around and bite you.

We were walking through Civic Center Plaza now, almost at the courthouse, and it was a beautiful day. Couples were picnicking on the grass; many same-sex couples were in each other's arms celebrating the ruling allowing them to get married. In thirty days when the new law became effective, they would be lined up on the steps of City Hall and around the block to get married inside. Today, instead of the smell of disinfectant and waste rising from the stairwells as it had yesterday, neatly cropped jasmine bushes perfumed the air.

I stopped and took Robbie by the arm. "When I recall you to the stand, please do what you offered to do in the office a few minutes ago. Tell the jury everything about your night with Marilyn, even the part that you haven't told me yet. Look. I'm a lawyer, Robbie, and I can feel it when somebody is hiding something. You've been holding out on me, even after all you've told me on our river trips and on the *Impulse*. Let the jury know you and win this case for yourself."

We reached the edge of the plaza. Crossing the street to 400 McAllister, Talley took Robbie's hand. He straightened his slumped shoulders, regaining his old, erect, confident demeanor. Just as we reached the courthouse steps, Dietrich, his junior attorney, and Naomi Jane rounded the corner from Polk Street. It was the first time we arrived at the same time. For an instant, we took their measure—Naomi Jane, back in her lavender lady outfit from day one, walking in lockstep with her two serious-faced attorneys, swaying her hips slightly. And they took ours—glancing curiously at Julia's and Talley's dirt-streaked jeans and jogging shoes and appraising Robbie, who looked almost self-assured for the first time in the trial. Startled by having all of us in the same place at the same time, the reporters cleared a path. Julia pushed Robbie quickly through security, and Dietrich shielded NJ with his body.

Inside the courtroom, just before Robbie and I went through the bar to take our seats at the defense table, Talley held Robbie back and took my comb out of my back pocket. She stood on tiptoe, tenderly took Robbie's cheek in her left hand, and combed his fair hair back from where it was still falling over his forehead and eyes. She straightened the knot of his tie into the collar of his white shirt and neatened the lapels of his handsome, beige suit. Now he looked really good.

A few minutes later I rose before a packed courtroom and announced to Judge Poirier that I intended to recall Robbie to the stand to testify. Dietrich looked surprised. Poirier said, "I thought we were going to closing arguments this afternoon."

"We were, but Dr. Carosso wants to tell the court something he held back when he made his statement on Tuesday. It is important. It has a direct bearing on what transpired in his office with the plaintiff."

"Please be brief."

With that, Robbie was sworn in again, and I said from the rostrum, "Dr. Carosso, I understand that you would like to explain to the court why your treatment of Ms. Morton took such an unorthodox turn."

"May I stand?" Robbie asked me.

I looked at Poirier, and he nodded. "You may stand."

Robbie rose from his chair and stepped out of the witness box. His left hand rested casually on the shiny wood side of the compartment. He scanned the gallery, NJ, and her lawyers, before resting his eyes on the jurors. For the first time in a year, I saw his face soften into his easy smile, which he offered to the jury as if he was delighting in their presence. "Ladies and gentlemen, I appreciate this moment to share more with you, and thank the court for giving me the opportunity." As he spoke, he gestured with his right arm and hand up with an open palm to the jurors as if to say, "I am defenseless. I beg you to be generous to me. I am an open book." Then with his arms flung wide open, his mellifluous voice returned and Robbie welcomed the jury into his embrace.

"I want to help you understand my sin, for surely what happened in my office with Ms. Morton was a mistake. A mistake that had its roots many years ago when my father, a psychiatrist like me, was treating Marilyn Monroe in the last two years of her life before she died accidentally from an overdose of sleeping medicines. She came to my father's home office for sessions several times a week. She often had dinner with our family. Sometimes she sat next to my father, my mother on his other side, sometimes next to me. Sometimes she stayed overnight in the cabana that was like a studio by the swimming pool. She swam in our pool for exercise regularly. I liked to watch her swim.   "Forty-seven years ago, my father was trying to rescue her and didn't succeed. Forty-seven years ago, he didn't realize that it was wrong to bring Marilyn into our home with his teenage son—me—living there. He didn't understand how it could affect me. He was a good father and a good doctor, but I think he was seduced by celebrity and wanted to be one himself. He couldn't resist the idea of having a famous person like Marilyn in his life, nor could my mother. I loved it too.

"My father was trying to rescue his patient, and that's what I was trying to do: rescue Ms. Morton." Robbie extended his arm gently toward NJ, offering her a warm, glowing smile as if he were inviting her to come and take his hand. "Ms. Morton came to me as forlorn as Marilyn was when she came to my father, and now Ms. Morton looks as beautiful as that tragic figure from the past." Robbie's face was glowing so beatifically that Naomi Jane smiled back at him and reached her hand forward across the table, only to have it clasped back in place by Dietrich.

Robbie's expression was self-contented and self-confident. It was filled with self-love, which spilled over onto those who basked in it. It was the smile that made me and Talley fall in love with him when we were kids. He bathed the courtroom in it, and they returned his sunlike embrace. Talley was grinning at him like a cheerleader flirting with a high school sports star, smiling because she loved him when he was like that and because she sensed he was going to win his case right then and there.

In a calm, modulated voice with lots of hand gestures rounding his words, Robbie controlled his audience. "My father wanted us to be a real family for Marilyn, to give her a normal family life for the first time. He suggested that Marilyn and I go together to my senior prom at Hollywood High School; we would go like brother and sister. I was just seventeen and she was thirty-five, but she looked like seventeen when she was happy, and she jumped at the idea. I did too."

At that moment, many in the courtroom fully understood for the first time that the plaintiff not only resembled Marilyn Monroe but that the trial actually intersected with the movie star's life. The gallery erupted in a cacophony of body movement. When the judged rapped his gavel, they fell back into rapt silence.

Robbie continued, speaking calmly and intimately like a teacher sharing history with his favorite students. "It was impossible for me to just feel like a brother to Marilyn. She was too beautiful and so needy for love that she was asking me for it too. After the prom, she had me drive her around to all the places she had lived when she was growing up, then she wanted to go back to my house. My parents were away and Marilyn said we should go into my father's office. It had a locked outside entrance and a door from inside the house that wasn't locked."

Robbie clasped his hands tightly together in front of his chest and shook them three times in a measured way, holding his audience. He nodded at them ruefully. "I shouldn't have listened to her, but I couldn't say no. I could not help but listen to her. Once we were in the office, Marilyn lay down on the couch and asked me to take my father's chair just behind her. Up to a point, she was reenacting a therapy session with my father. Then she shifted into a fantasy of having sex with him. I didn't get this at the time. Maybe she didn't either. I just went along with it, excited as hell with what was happening. She lay back, then she asked me to loosen the zipper in the back of her

strapless ball gown and let it slip down from her breasts when
she lay back.

"I remember her exact words. 'Do you know about sex yet,
Robbie?' I said, 'Yes, a little.'"

He knew about sex with Talley, of course; Robbie, Talley,
and I each knew this as we heard him answer Marilyn's question,
but this wasn't about us. It was about him and the movie star.
Robbie continued. "She said, 'Ask me a question, Robbie,
honey, the way your father does,' and all I could think of saying
was, 'Doesn't it make you feel wonderful being so beautiful?'
And she said, 'You don't know anything yet, Robbie.' We were
both quiet for a moment, waiting for what would come next.
Then she said, 'Come here and make love to me, honey.'

"I was thrilled and scared at the same time. I began realizing
it wasn't just me she wanted to make love to; it was also my
father. I didn't care; I was so excited that my leg was trembling.
And then I couldn't do it; I couldn't keep an erection. Marilyn
was very tender to me. The last thing she said that night before
she went to the cabana was 'Be careful, son of my shrink.' She
was giving me some kind of a warning."

This was the first time Robbie had told anyone. Feeling
shame over a failure when you are having sex when you are
just finding your way into your sexual life lasts a long time. It
happened with Talley and me, but she protected me when she
said it would be better next time.

Robbie seemed liberated by his admission to the jury.
He let his breath out, and the audience let theirs out as well.
Gathering himself up again and smiling with relief, he said
to the eight men and women, "There. You know my story.
The last part took place when Ms. Morton came to me as
a patient. It was my chance to consummate what I couldn't
with Marilyn. I think that was what Marilyn was warning me

about—not to keep thinking about her and to be careful if I did. I consummated my teenage relationship with my father's patient with my patient, Ms. Morton. She and I were willing partners. It was wrong for both of us; it was right for both of us. That is what I have to say."

Robbie had been masterful, and nobody wanted to break the spell. I had no questions for him.

Dietrich rose and said fiercely to the judge, "I object to Mr. Carosso's whole testimony today. It is entirely irrelevant to the facts of the encounter we are litigating. I move that it be stricken from the record."

Poirier said, "We will let the jury decide if it is relevant or not. Stricken or not, they have heard it." Dietrich would of course take his cracks at Robbie during his closing argument.

Robbie stayed over with Talley and me that night. He got the space in our garage for his Mustang, a car you don't leave out on the street at night in San Francisco, even as worn as his current model was getting. Robbie's glow from his testimony had also faded. He had retreated from us, silently going into himself, and scarcely touched the empanadas and roast chicken Talley brought over from the Pacific Mambo Club. That night, the band's trumpet and trombone fanfares sounded like a call to a bullfight in Spain or Mexico: half call to action and half dirge for the death of the bull—or the bullfighter.

When Talley and I were alone in bed, she said, "Robbie gave a great speech in court today, didn't he?"

"Yes, I think he really touched the jury. And for the first time, he showed me the cost of being so special that he's carried all these years, the need to always be at the top of his game."

"Yes, I get it," Talley said. "When he couldn't perform on

his dad's psychoanalytic couch, the hurt never left him. Some guys are so sensitive about that. It came down to this sad story of him and that NJ. I think we're losing him, Eli. Or he's losing himself." Talley hugged in closer to me as she felt Robbie growing smaller and fading away.

"You know that story Robbie told me about the young woman who had an affair with Karl Jung when she was in treatment with him, the affair that sent them both into psych hospitals?" I asked. "Years later she wrote a famous essay, 'Destruction as the Cause of Coming into Being.' Who knows how Robbie will come out of this after the jury gives its verdict? Maybe a rebirth into a better Robbie. A rebirth for NJ too?"

Talley's cheek was moist against mine. "We have to let go of Robbie, don't we? We have to let him slip away if that's what he needs to do. It feels like saying goodbye to our past, to high school, to all the excitement over everything we would discover when we left home. We have to let him slip away," she murmured falling asleep.

CHAPTER
EIGHTEEN

We assembled at Dream Fluff Donuts the next morning for the last time. The headline story on top left of the front page of the paper in the newsstand was "Courtroom Couple Grapple." Right beneath came photos of Robbie, NJ, Marilyn, and an old file photo of his father. When the waitress brought Robbie his coffee and roll, she hugged him. "You're innocent. You're both innocent, and you're both guilty, you and that lady. Sometimes things happen and nobody is to blame. It's karma."

Robbie gave Asmita a wan smile. "Fate. Yes, you're right."

My old flip phone buzzed. I looked at the screen. Chancellor Clarence Spinkman. I went into the corner by the leaking refrigerator and answered. "Hey, Cappy. What's up?" It was my other ongoing case.

"Your boy Professor Aldenbrand is going to get his tenure. You're right. I looked into it. Anger management problem or not, he deserves it. I made the final decision."

"Now for our lunch."

"Call my secretary. I've got time next week. I want the backstory on the case you're arguing in San Francisco. Fascinating. Give them hell."

I went back to our table and told Julia. "Aldenbrand's going to be okay, thanks to you." She smiled over that little triumph. Maybe we would win two cases in one day.

When we were all in our seats in court and the bailiff declared court in session, Maddie came down the aisle and squeezed in beside Talley and Julia, her first appearance at the trial. She looked severe as hell, with a brimmed hat low over her forehead. NJ had chosen, or taken Dietrich's advice, to dress down and look like a victim. A gray dress hid her figure and came below her knees, but it was not so full that her shapely shoulders didn't show. In place of high heels, she had chosen short, stacked heels. She'd accentuated the hollow of her cheek with makeup in a way that might arouse pity and a wish to kiss it. And she couldn't resist a touch of adornment; she had ceramic lavender studs in her ears. Maybe they were a talisman of power for herself, a message of thanks to Robbie, a seductive gesture toward her attorney. Anything was possible.

Dietrich rose and stood in front of the jury. With his first words, he drew blood, like a picador planting the first pick into Robbie's side. "Dr. Carosso is a predatory narcissist. You have heard all the testimonies. He unmistakably groomed his patient slowly but surely to be the object of his perverse desire. He brought an album of sexually suggestive photographs into the office and proceeded to lead his patient to model herself on his fantasies. He used photographs to sexually arouse and seduce his patient and then control her for his personal profit. This was not therapy; it was sexual self-gratification. He planned it each step of the way."

How much had NJ also planned it, I was beginning to wonder. But before I could finish my thought, Robbie, like a lanced bull in the ring, leaped up and yelled at NJ ten feet away, "Why are you so angry at me? When you first came to see me, you were hiding from the world like Marilyn hid when she didn't want to be recognized! Look at you now! You are so attractive and successful! Why are you so angry?"

Before Judge Poirier could bring his gavel down, NJ stood up and yelled at Robbie, "This treatment was your crooked dream of having sex with Marilyn's ghost! You projected everything onto me! Who am I now but your projection?"

The bailiff was ready to step in, but whom to grab first: Robbie or NJ?

The judge had his gavel in the air yet also a twinkle in his eye.

Robbie shouted, "The treatment was a fantasy we shared! You came with it! You planted it in me! We created it together!"

"Bullshit," NJ replied. "Who planted it? You are supposed to know your unconscious and not spin it out on me, Doctor." She wrapped the word *Doctor* in sarcasm and scorn. "When it suited you, your fairy tale was over. You would just go home to your wife."

Poirier held his gavel in the air and motioned the bailiff to stay put.

NJ continued yelling at Robbie. "Do you think I'm still naïve and innocent?"

"You were never innocent," Robbie stabbed back.

I knew he was thinking of the pictures, the letter from the photographer, the evidence that NJ had been the victim of pedophilia when she was a teenager. One more word from Robbie and Julia's future could go down the drain. I grabbed him back into his chair and spit, "Shut up," into his ear.

Dietrich pulled NJ back into her chair.

Poirier brought his gavel down and said, "Enough!"

Almost in unison, Dietrich and I answered that we wouldn't let it happen again. I didn't want Robbie led out of the courtroom for being disruptive. That would be a huge black mark against him.

Maddie got up and left the courtroom, crying. She'd seen more passion between NJ and Robbie than there had ever been in their marriage, and NJ wanted her husband now more than she did. It shamed her.

"Are you finished with your closing argument, Mr. Dietrich?"

Standing in front of the jurors, Dietrich lanced Robbie again. "Dr. Carosso is an arrogant man. You have seen his disregard for rules in front of your very eyes, his disregard for rules of procedure in this very courtroom. You have just witnessed the pain he inflicted on Ms. Morton, and you saw him continue to inflict it before your eyes. The psychiatrist abandoned his duty to the patient, and this dereliction was the direct cause of Ms. Morton's emotional distress. It was fraud and malpractice because under the guise of treatment, he charged his patient good money. He used his training to set her up psychologically to the point that she couldn't protect herself and submitted to him sexually. We ask for a verdict of guilty to send a message to doctors that behavior like Dr. Carosso's won't be tolerated in this community. We ask the jury to return a verdict of guilty to compensate the patient for the fraud and pain and suffering he has inflicted on her in a manner that will make it impossible for her to trust a psychiatrist or psychotherapist in the future."

Dietrich clasped his hands together, signaling closure, then raised them for an instant. It looked as if he were praying to the jury or applauding them—or both. It was a split-second subliminal gesture that would nonetheless rest in the jurors' minds. He turned to the judge and with a slight bow said, "We rest our case."

It was my turn. Dietrich had been skillful in using Robbie's outburst to his benefit. Yet he could have been better because part of his closing argument had also been pabulum, standard courtroom rhetoric. I had been right after our first meeting in his office: the trial surprises—the photos I projected and NJ's and Robbie's eruptions at each other—had thrown him off his game. Actually I enjoyed the chaos and the blunt speaking. Trials generally are too buttoned down by rules that stifle everybody. NJ had also given me a huge opening with her passionate outburst.

Thinking on my feet, nodding to the jurors as if we were longtime allies, I said, "Love! This case is about love. Disappointed love. Sometimes when circumstances force lovers apart, one or the other tries to replace affection with money, and money becomes the currency through which the relationship can continue—at least for a while. Sometimes people try to make money off doomed love." That was my nod to the information Talley and Julia had discovered in NJ's house about how her aunt and uncle had extorted $3,000 from the photographer who had been the teenage girl's lover, in return for not reporting him to the police. Perhaps that had taught NJ how to try to get something from Robbie now.

NJ was looking at me wide-eyed from her chair with an expression half of anger and half fear like a deer caught in the headlights of a car on a dark night. I couldn't go any further without opening the door to the break-in. I returned to the facts at hand. "Ms. Morton continued to meet with Dr. Carosso of her own free will because she believed he would leave his wife for her. When he scorned her by not breaking up his marriage, she embarked on a course of revenge. She is a Shakespeare scholar who, like Shylock, wants her pound of flesh, and the only way she can extract it is by winning a settlement in court.

"Are we to bring every case of love gone wrong into court for a financial settlement? Have we reached the point in our society where everything is measured in its monetary value? Are we willing to allow every person who has been disappointed in love to seek reimbursement through a judicial proceeding? That used to be called a suit for alienation of affection. We haven't seen suits like that for over half a century, with good reason.

"Who here has not hurt somebody unintentionally? I have. We try to learn to live with pain we have caused others, make amends for it, learn from it, not do it again, not go to court over it." I said that gently to the jurors. I quoted Asmita's wisdom to them with a touch of my own. "Both parties in this trial are innocent. Both parties are guilty. When bad things happen, we want to point our finger at somebody, but sometimes it is fate and there is nobody to blame." I paused to let my words sink in.

"The real issue before you today is whether Dr. Carosso has damaged Ms. Morton. Certainly he has hurt her pride and her feelings. But has her ability to teach at the university been diminished by her contact with her psychiatrist? No. The evidence is clear that she is professionally more capable than she has ever been. Is her future mental health at risk? That we don't know, but her mental health at present is more robust than it has ever been."

Then I used NJ's actual behavior in the courtroom a few minutes earlier when she stood up and yelled at Robbie, as Dietrich had used her outburst to say she was in pain. I said to the jurors, "You have seen how strong she is. Who else here would be able to stand and face their accuser as effectively as

Ms. Morton did? Would you? She is resilient and able, perhaps more so than any of us. There has been no *evidence* offered that her future emotional health is in jeopardy, only a few statistics that *some* patients who have had sex with their therapists suffer psychiatric symptoms later. There is no indication, let alone *evidence,* that Ms. Morton will be one of those."

I paused again and looked at the eight jurors, the five women and three men, some of whom I had wanted on the panel, some of whom Dietrich had favored. Two of the women had severe frowns on their faces and might hate Robbie by now, but the three other women's faces had softened and might be feeling sympathy for my friend. The three men had knit brows and could be thinking anything from *The woman asked for it* to *Give the guy a break* and *String him up.* One, a retired grocer, had said during the voir dire that laws were the only thing that kept people civilized. I didn't have much hope in him.

One of the lady jurors wore clothes that were very tight, heavy eye makeup, and ran a beauty salon. She'd said during the voir dire that women were created to be pleasing to the eye and should do whatever they could to enhance what God gave them. Where did she stand now that Robbie had helped NJ morph into a beauty? Would she see NJ as a victim or a success? That juror's face had softened over the course of the trial. A frowning woman juror had answered Dietrich's question about how she felt about adultery by stammering that she didn't know because it was complicated. She could go either way.

My favorite juror, the junior high school teacher, still smiled at me. She'd said during the voir dire that teaching kids about right and wrong was the most important thing she did. Sometimes she taught that right or wrong wasn't always clear, so *trying* to do right was more important than knowing exactly. I figured the jurors would probably pick her to be the jury forewoman. It was going to be a crapshoot. I took a deep breath and rolled my dice for the last time. "Ladies and gentlemen, there can be no fraud if the patient gets better. We can even say Dr. Carosso's treatment was successful even though unethical and not in accordance with accepted psychiatric practice. Ethical missteps are not the same as medical malpractice, and this is a trial about legality not morality. For his ethical lapses, Dr. Carosso has lost his license and can no longer practice his profession. He has suffered *more* than his former patient and will continue to suffer for the rest of his life for having lost his ability to practice the profession he loved and earn a living. He does not need to be punished further."

I looked at Talley and Julia sitting behind the bar. They were nodding yes to me. NJ glowered. Robbie was staring at his notepad. I sat down.

A few people slid out of their seats and exited the courtroom to relay updates. Judge Poirier looked at his watch. It was 11:10 a.m. He pulled the microphone closer to him. "Thank you, counsels, for being brief this morning. Let's take a fifteen-minute break to stretch, and then I will give the jury their instructions. You can begin deliberations over lunch. Please keep your eyes off newspaper headlines and TV screens, if that is possible. Perhaps we will have a verdict before the end of the day."

Robbie and I stretched in place, walked over to the bar, and huddled with Talley and Julia, but there was nothing to say. NJ and her attorney disappeared from view. Poirier exited through the side door into his private office. Then, as if in the blink of an eye, the fifteen-minute break was over and Judge Poirier was rapping us to attention with his gavel. Poirier shifted papers on his dais, brought his notes in front of him, and tapped his microphone to hear if it was on.

"Ladies and gentlemen of the jury, thank you for your patience. The task is at hand for you to render your judgment. You will be considering two counts: medical malpractice and fraud. In order to find the defendant guilty of malpractice, you have to consider whether as a physician specializing in psychiatry Dr. Carosso did *not* show a high degree of skill in his treatment of the plaintiff; whether the treatment he provided was inappropriate for her condition; and whether he breached his duty to conform to the accepted standard of care in his profession. If you decide that he breached his duty, you will also have to decide whether this caused injury to the patient. Injury may be emotional, physical, or loss of money. If there is no injury, there are no grounds for a claim. You can also consider if the defendant adequately informed his patient of the risks of the treatment.

"Now for the suit of fraud. You will have to decide whether Dr. Carosso intentionally misrepresented the purpose and method of his treatment to induce Ms. Morton to act in a way that resulted in her being damaged emotionally and/or physically or to lose money. You will also have to determine whether he falsely described his treatment to her intentionally, not because he did it by mistake or by accident. If Ms. Morton suffered injury because of Dr. Carosso's misrepresentation, she is entitled to recover money to compensate for the injury, pain, and suffering. If you decide that Dr. Carosso's actions were harmful and intentional, the sum of money Ms. Morton receives may include punitive damages—that is punishment—for the defendant, as well as to make a public example of him to the medical community."

The jurors looked perplexed. Poirier nodded at them. "I understand that these are complicated instructions. The bailiff will give you a printout of them to take with you into your deliberations. This is a civil case; you don't have to come to a unanimous decision. All you have to do is decide whether the preponderance of the evidence for one or both counts shows that the defendant is guilty, and that at least six of the eight of you agree to that."

With that, the judge took off his glasses and rubbed his eyes. He undoubtedly knew what I did, and Dietrich was probably too young to know, that the jurors weren't going to use logic to make up their minds in this case. In spite of Poirier's instructions, they weren't going to decide that *this happened because that happened, which caused that to occur and therefore guilt or innocence is the consequence.* It was going to be about the hopes and hurts in *their* lives and how they affected their feelings about Robbie, Naomi Jane, and even Marilyn. Then Poirier put his glasses back on and recessed court for the jury to come up with a verdict.

It didn't take long. The call from the judge's clerk came in three hours later, at three thirty. Apparently the jurors wanted to finish with the trial, not spend time arguing about fine points and make it go into a fifth day on Monday. We reassembled— me from my office, Talley from the Asian Art Museum on the south side of the Civic Center, Julia from the law school library two blocks down McAllister, and Robbie from resting in our guest room on Twenty-Fifth Street.

After the judge announced that court was back in session, there was a pause as most people readjusted themselves in their seats and the message got through to the jury room. Then they filed in like a chorus at a symphony, solemn and orderly. Most of the jurors turned their heads in an arc right to left, taking in the gallery, the defense, the plaintiffs, and lastly the judge.

One or two looked at the floor. I was interested in the junior high school teacher because I knew she had in fact been selected as the forewoman of the jury. I wanted to catch her gaze as it swept toward me. But she wouldn't let me. Just as her eyes went across the room and came to the point that they would have met mine, she looked down at the floor. I knew then that Robbie had lost his case.

The bailiff took the envelope from her hands and passed it to Poirier, who sliced it open with a blade and announced that "the jury finds Robert Carosso liable for medical malpractice and fraud by a vote of six in favor and two opposed on both counts." The judge added that the jury awarded the plaintiff $8 million, the sum requested in the suit. Poirier then said to the jurors, "Do you say one and all that this is your verdict?" They answered yes in unison.

Robbie shook his head back and forth three or four times and shuddered, wounded to the core. He stiffened and stretched out his whole length in his chair, from the tips of his shoes pushing hard against the back leg of the table to his head thrown back as he stared at the ceiling. NJ hugged Dietrich, who shook hands with his junior attorney, then they gathered up their papers and left.

While we waited for court to clear, I told Robbie that I didn't see any legal ground on which we could appeal. By contrast, if the jury vote had gone for Robbie, Dietrich would have had plenty of legal points on which to appeal for the way I had introduced evidence and Poirier had denied some of his objections. Furthermore, Robbie would incur a lot of court costs in an appeal, and there was no sure way that we could do any better than finding two jurors sympathetic to our arguments in a second trial. I told Robbie that Poirier might reduce the amount of the award a little, perhaps by one-third to 5 million, but that would be about the best Robbie could hope for.

We waited so long that by the time we left, only three reporters and one cameraman remained on the courthouse steps. We knew better than answer their questions of "Dr. Carosso, how do you feel about the verdict? Are you going to appeal?" One reporter managed to get Robbie's attention long enough to hand him his card and say, "Call me up if you want to tell me your story." Robbie crumpled the card into his pocket and, looking into the distance, said, "I've told my story."

Robbie told us that he was going to his harbor at Half Moon Bay. He didn't give us a chance to exchange goodbyes or make tentative plans to be in touch. He didn't even wait for me to tell him how the financial damages against him would be garnered and how he would have to make arrangements to liquidate everything that was his to begin to pay an impossible debt. He just strode across McAllister and disappeared into the underground garage.

Talley called Maddie and got her voicemail. She left the message that Robbie had been found guilty and liable for damages. There was no point in holding it back. Talley would have left a long message with news if Robbie had won the case, though she wasn't even sure if Maddie wanted him to win.

EPILOGUE

An eerie calm settled in for two days, as if the worst of a storm has passed but clouds were still lingering and could come together again. On the evening of the third day, Monday night, when he knew Talley and I would be winding up dinner, Robbie called.

"I'm on the *Impulse.*"

"At sea?" I was teasing him; I knew he couldn't call from his local phone number from sea. He'd been at sea emotionally for weeks and I was hoping with the trial over he would get his feet back on the ground.

He didn't laugh. "Where do you think I am?"

"I know."

"Yes, in the fucking harbor." His speech was slurred. "You know what, Eli? She's a vamp."

"Who, NJ?" I was thinking about her seductiveness.

"No. Marilyn. She's a vampire. Vamp means vampire—evil. She sucks the blood out of you. A witch." Robbie was loopy. I put the phone on speaker so Talley could hear. "Marilyn sent that woman to me—NJ. She cast a spell on the fucking jury. Why didn't they like me?"

He was back into the vampire thing again. I cut him off. "One man and one woman voted for you. Two people liked you. You knew what the odds were going into court. How many psychiatrists have ever gotten away with having sex with their patients?"

"A lot. Why not me?"

"I mean gotten off in court, in a lawsuit? Never."

"NJ came to me damaged goods. I didn't hurt her."

I'd heard that "didn't hurt her" refrain too many times from him and coming out of my own mouth. "Move on, Robbie."

A loud popping noise came over the phone line. I asked him what it was and he said, "I popped another Champagne cork."

I said, "Scotch is your drink and Cuban beer on the boat."

"Champagne was Marilyn's. Dom Perignon."

"You're pretending to be Marilyn now?"

"No, I'm just sitting here sipping Champagne with her. I think I'll just sit here and wait for the curtain to fall."

"What curtain?"

"The tax man, the bill collector, the repo man, whatever you call it. They're not going to get the *Impulse*. It's a piece of me, you know."

I knew. I had a picture of him in my mind—in the cockpit of his boat with his long-billed Hemingway cap and his metal-rimmed sunglasses staring at the sea, his right hand resting lightly on the wheel, his left hand on the throttle. Robbie at his fullest, his most relaxed, the way he was when he was in command, the way he had been almost all his life.

The sound of a crash of glass coming over the phone made Talley grimace. "Shit. I broke a glass," we heard Robbie say. "Doesn't matter. I have more, and a whole case of her Champagne. Do you know that Marilyn's ghost walked into my fucking office? That's what NJ was: a ghost pretending to be a patient."

Talley leaned in to say something, then pulled back and put

her hand over the phone and said to me, "There's something more going on than alcohol. He's really loose."

For a moment, there was silence until Robbie said, "Say something, man."

"Get some professional help, Robbie. Give me the name of someone, and I'll call him or her right now."

"Come down here and join me," he answered. "Remember how we were going to sail across the ocean? Thor Heyerdahl, *Kon Tiki,* Sterling Hayden, and all that?"

"Sure."

"We can still do it, Eli. Come and join me. Bring Talley."

"This is not the time, Robbie." There had been a time; this was not it. He didn't say anything, and the line went dead.

The next morning, I called Robbie, but he didn't answer. He reached us in the evening. "I pumped two hundred gallons of diesel into the *Impulse,"* he said. "Do you know how far I can go on that?"

"How far?"

"All the way to Mexico. I talked to Maddie yesterday. I asked her if I could come home."

"What did she say?" Talley asked.

"She said there is no home anymore. NJ's lawyer will put a lien on the house and take it, or half of it, when it is sold. Those fucking vigilantes on the jury might as well have hung a noose around my neck. Anyway, Maddie's going to work in a clinic in Ethiopia." There was a long pause. At least we didn't hear any more breaking glass or popping corks. "I can't sleep, Eli. Should I take a sleeping pill or drink till I fall asleep?"

"Stop thinking about Marilyn, Robbie," said Talley. "You're not her, she's not there, and this is 2008, not 1962."

"If I take one pill and it doesn't work, should I take a second?"

"That's probably what Marilyn used to ask your father, Robbie. I'm not your doctor; I'm your lawyer, your friend. What are you up to?"

"Should I take another sleeping pill, Eli?"

"People start over, Robbie," I said.

"I gave NJ a future. She gets a life and I get nothing. Marilyn left them all in the lurch in the middle of her last movie. She just up and left to go on a date with Bobby Kennedy. Did you know that, *kemosabe?*"

"Yes. She was just a kid with stars in her eyes. You're a grownup. You're educated. You're not Marilyn."

"I need you, Meyer. Come on down here and go on this trip with me. You know, count up the old risk-benefit thing. Shit, we'll have a blast. Shit, I love Talley. I should have stuck with her. Bring her along, the three of us will go out together."

He was really rambling. He didn't know who or where he was or when it was.

"Should I call NJ?" he asked.

That stunned me. "Dietrich could charge you with harassment."

Talley poked me. "Maybe she wouldn't tell Dietrich."

"I think I'll sail the *Impulse* to—" Robbie's voice broke off. We could hear him saying a name with *p* in it, but he couldn't get the word out.

"Where, Robbie?"

"Marilyn went there."

"Where?"

Something was blocking his words or his thoughts. Finally he got words out, clipped utterances and unfinished sentences. "Acapulco. She went on a date ... a Mexican businessman."

"I remember."

"My dad said."

I filled it in. "He told you her Mexican friend offered to produce her next movie. He told her to take it slowly with this new guy. Get some sleep, Robbie. I'll call you tomorrow."

"Thanks, Eli. Don't forget to call me."

The next day, Wednesday, Clarence Spinkman and I had lunch at the UC faculty club. It was a long lunch. He commiserated with me over the outcome of Robbie's case and told me that my client Aldenbrand's Signs of Love Scale was going great guns. The hassle over his tenure had died down and researchers at other universities were replicating the scale, hunting for the numerical alchemy that would predict how relationships would turn out.

I told him I didn't think there would ever be such an alchemy. That a rating scale for love was a farce. Love was too amorphous, too ambiguous. Robbie and his patient had been in love, but Aldenbrand's scale would have been clueless to what lay hidden beneath the ease with which they settled into the therapy from the very beginning.

"But then trying to measure things is what the social sciences try to do, isn't it?" I ribbed Cappy.

We segued into memories of rugby matches we had won and lost, mostly won. Spinkman was smaller and faster than most of us on the team. He played scrum halfback and would grab the ball out of the melee of bodies and pass it free. Nowadays he needed to do the same with the governor and the university board of regents—dart into their board meetings and come out with a ball of funding for the school.

It was 3 p.m. when lunch was over and I called Robbie. His voicemail said to leave a message. I told him I would call when I got home. I was driving in traffic on the Bay Bridge when I felt my cell phone buzzing in my pocket. Robbie was calling me back, but I couldn't answer. When I got home, Talley and I sat down to eat. I called Robbie at 8 p.m., but he didn't answer, and his phone didn't pick up. It just rang and rang until it cut off.

The next day, it still rang and rang until it cut off. I drove down to Half Moon Bay and walked out on the Pillar Point dock to the *Impulse's* berth. The storm had blown back into shore from the ocean and the dock was pitching, spray flying, and the boats were straining against their leashes. The slip where Robbie kept his boat was empty. I checked with the harbormaster. He showed me the log of boats coming and going. The *Impulse* had cleared the harbor at 4 p.m. the previous afternoon, a few minutes after he had called me back while I was crossing the Bay Bridge. He hadn't logged a destination and was heading into the teeth of the storm. He had a good boat and knew it well, but still he was a doctor first and a seaman second.

Days passed and there was no word from Robbie. I called the ports between San Francisco and Acapulco, places Robbie may have stopped for fuel and supplies—San Luis Obispo, Long Beach, San Diego, Cabo, Mazatlan, Puerto Vallarta, and others. Lastly Acapulco. None had logged the *Impulse*.

Julia came up for air from studying case law for her Bar exam and tracked down NJ's unlisted telephone number. I called her intending to ask if she had heard from Robbie. When NJ realized who I was, she slammed the phone down on me. A few minutes later, she called back. She let me tell her that we didn't know where Robbie was, or even if he was alive, and we were worried about him. This time, she put the phone down quietly without saying anything.

Talley and I planned to take a long trip to look for any sign that Robbie had survived the ocean and reached one of the ports along the coast, but that wouldn't be possible for a while.

The summer passed and one October full-sun, no-fog late afternoon, we took the city bus from Market Street eighty-two slow blocks out Geary Boulevard to the ocean. It was like a trip traveling around the world, past Chinese, Japanese, Irish, Italian, Jewish, Russian, and Indian shops and restaurants and more, to where the bus stopped at Land's End. From the high bluff, we scanned the water—Ocean Beach stretching south to the horizon and off to our right the foundation of a giant saltwater swimming pool abandoned a half century ago. A trail descended between the bluff and the remains of the pool to a small cove where very few people came because the trail was steep and the ruins reeked with the scent of loss. The cove was our favorite place to listen to the sound of the waves roll in. This afternoon, it was a gentle, rhythmic lapping at the sand.

The lowering sun turned the world golden—the mist, sand, the boulders on each side of the cove, and the cliffs. Talley got up from where we were sitting and walked the hundred-odd yards to one end of the beach. After a few minutes, I saw her sitting on a large, flat rock. I walked down the beach to her, picked up a handful of throwing stones, and skipped a few across a tidal pool. I counted the skips, wishing that Robbie and I were taking turns flinging, counting, and competing like we always did when we were on the edge of water, knowing the *Impulse* had probably gone down and that he was dead.

"Come up here," Talley said to me. She was frowning.

I joined her. The rock we were sitting on was granite, and she was rubbing her fingers across its pebbly surface and seams of quartz and crystal the way she always felt the texture of a fabric she was interested in but rubbing so hard that her skin was raw. "I've never told you who Lucy's father is, have I?" she said.

"No. The two times I asked, you seemed scared. So I stopped asking."

"Robbie and I got together once in New York, in 1968. He was a junior in medical school thinking about going into psychiatry like his dad, so he decided to attend the annual meeting of the American Psychoanalytic Society to see what it was like. It was at the Waldorf Astoria Hotel and he called me up. He and Maddie were already engaged but he'd come to the meeting alone. He asked me to meet him in the lobby, by the hanging tapestry. You know what I did?" Her infectious grin appeared.

"I haven't a clue."

"I wore my painter's bibs to see him. I walked into that gleaming, marble lobby with big, leather couches everywhere, thick carpets, guests in suits and designer dresses, staff in uniforms, and me in my paint-splattered bibs. It was my way of saying, "I don't care what people think of me. I don't care if meeting him is a good idea or a bad idea but I want to. I'm just going to do what I'm going to do." Talley laughed at the memory.

"Dressed how I was, and him in his beautiful, brown, herringbone Harris tweed jacket, white shirt, and tie, there was no way Robbie was going to take me into one of the lobby bars to hang out. We just went right up the elevator to his room, and of course we made love."

"Is Robbie Lucy's father?"

"The truth is I can't tell you." Her face shadowed the way it had when I'd asked before. She put her hand over mine on the rock. "I'm not ashamed of anything I've ever done, Eli, except one thing. I don't know who Lucy's father is and that's why I never told you. Robbie could be. There were too many other men that week, that month, that year. Good-looking men tripping on colors and sensations just like me. And I didn't care enough about any of them, except Robbie, to want to know who the father was even if I could." Her voice trailed off.

"You could, with DNA."

Talley studied our rock some more. "I know, and I don't want to know because then you would have to share being her father with someone else. I don't want you to have to share her. Are you okay with that, Eli?

I nodded. Of course I was.

She looked at the veins and pebbles of crystal and quartz that were catching the orange, lilac and purple shades of the sun as it settled into the water. "I need to make a cloth like this," she said.

NJ's hanging up the phone on me wasn't the end of our contact. One day several months later, I was walking along the Embarcadero for my lunch break and saw her leaning on the railing, looking at ships on the bay: two fishing boats heading toward their anchorage, a splendid sloop under full sail, and a container ship angling toward the Port of Oakland. NJ had on a Giants baseball cap and fancy, tight-fitting jogging gear that showed off her beauty. Her hair was brown now, the color it was when she was a teenager. She had grown it into a long ponytail that came down from the back of her cap. Her face was serene.

I couldn't resist leaning on the rail next to her, staring with her at the ships. After a time, I said, "How are you?"

She turned and studied my face before she said, "I'm fine. Have you heard from Robbie?"

"No. Have you?"

She shook her head. "I come here a lot and look at the

boats. I wonder if this boat or that boat is his, but I don't know what his looks like. He never took me out on it. Everything between us was in his office."

"There was more to it than that."

"I don't blame him anymore. He couldn't help how his parents brought Marilyn into the home. He had no say in it. Maybe one of these days I'll see him on one of the passing boats." She brought her hand up from the railing and gestured out at the bay. "Except he's probably dead."

"Yes. We all miss him. You look good."

"Thank you. I left Stanford and moved to the city. I live over there." She pointed to a row of new apartments down the quay on the right. "I'm teaching at City College now. It's a junior college, and I like it better. There is less pressure; the students are eager to learn. I don't have to prove anything. I don't have to publish. I'm not going to write anything that will make me famous. I gave that idea up." She gazed into the water.

I took a chance. "Are you looking at your reflection?"

She snapped her head back at me. "You know, don't you? You saw everything."

"I know."

"I don't look at my reflection anymore. I know who I am. I trashed my book on Ophelia and I threw away the photo I had of myself on my dresser in front of the mirror. I threw away the other photos."

I doubted that. She had probably buried them somewhere deep in her apartment to be taken out and savored if she wanted to someday.

"His wife left him, you know."

"He left me," she said. "I have to run now."

"Please call me if you hear anything," I said.

"I will."

I turned and started walking back along the quay in the direction I had come. The Bay Bridge loomed high ahead, a freighter emerging from under it, a lower deck of cars heading east, and an upper one heading west. I was on the upper deck near the San Francisco anchorage when Robbie made his last call to me. What if I'd reached into my pocket for my phone and answered? Could I have saved him? Could he or his dad have saved Marilyn if they had been home to take her last calls?

How do you rewrite history? Had Marilyn lived, Robbie might have worked out his painful memory with her in person rather than with NJ. There would have been no NJ story to tell. Without that story, NJ might not be who she had become. If Robbie hadn't disappeared, Talley might never have told me who my daughter's father might be.

I craned my head higher and saw the bridge's silver towers with their lacy crossbeams rising into the sky, the suspension cables gracefully swooping down to the roadways. The towers, the cables, the moving cars fractured the one o'clock sun into shards of light and color. They made my head spin with the old delirium and pleasure Robbie and I felt hanging from the oak limb in the rainbow mist over Charybdis's swirling waters and Talley felt trying to be color in her psychedelic days. We were youngsters testing and shaping ourselves. The prismed light played tricks. I saw Dr. and Mrs. Carosso's house that Robbie grew up in, the pool, and the circle of movie stars who swam in it, strutted, and relaxed around it. I saw the ancient Hollywood sign Robbie and I had sat under when we were kids, listening to the moan of wind and steel, heard again Peg's ghost warning us not to lose our way.

ACKNOWLEDGMENTS

My fine editor, Linda Watanabe McFerrin, time and again rescued me when my words and story became plodding. Bridget Connelly, my wife, a writer herself, was as always my final, deepest reader. My daughter Kate Massie, an attorney and investigator, was always there to decipher legal procedure. Several friends—Cheryl Colopy, Kathryn Hughes, Larry Michalak, Bruce Stegner, Ray Poirier, Anne Poirier, Jean Marie Apostolides, Roger Rapoport, and Karen Trocki—read early drafts of the manuscript and kept me going with their advice and encouragement.

I read widely to obtain the background for *The Boy Who Took Marilyn to the Prom*. The excellent book *Marilyn Monroe: Fragments*, edited by Stanley Buchtal and Bernard Comment, brought together and annotated the actress's poems, intimate notes, and letters, which provided invaluable insights into her inner emotional life that differed so greatly from her public, glamorous personal. Gloria Steinem's *Marilyn: Norma Jeane* eschewed all clichés about the actress and catches her essence and the sociocultural context in which she lived better than anything else I read. Arthur Miller's autobiography *Time Bends: A Life* reveals the hopes and pain of his and Marilyn's marriage. Other very useful titles were *The Many Lives of Marilyn Monroe*

(Sarah Churchwell), *The Secret Life of Marilyn Monroe* (J. Randy Taraborrelli), *Norma Jean* (Ted Jordan), *Hollywood on the Couch: A Candid Look at the Overheated Love Affair between Psychiatrists and Moviemakers* (Stephen Farber and Mark Green), and *Who the Hell's in It* (Peter Bogdanovich). I also greatly appreciated my conversations with Hollywood biographer John Brady, which offered a trove of information. In addition, the Wikipedia provided the lines from Jack Kerouac's *Railroad Earth,* and has been an exceptional source of biographical data and movie history. Herman Melville's words quoted in Robbie's valedictorian speech are from his novel *White Jacket.*

The irrepressible San Francisco courtroom innovator and disrupter Melvin Belli provided fine clues for the courtroom scenes with his memoir *Melvin Belli: My Life on Trial,* written with Robert Blair Kaiser. Michael Connelly's legal thriller *The Gods of Guilt* was especially helpful. To the unknown author of the unsigned message of loss that I found tacked to a tree by the Russian River, you express longing better than I possibly can. Your words evoke the feeling NJ inspired in the novel, and I have used some of them. Thank you. Finally I want to thank Josie McGraw and the team at Archway Publications who managed the production of the novel from manuscript to release with expertise and efficiency.

If I have left anyone or any source out, please excuse me. It was inadvertent.

ABOUT THE AUTHOR

Henry Massie is a writer and psychiatrist who lives in Berkeley, California. He is the author of the biography *Art of a Jewish Woman: Felice's Worlds*, and coauthor of *Lives Across Time*, a study of emotional health and illness. He is also coauthor of "My Life is a Longing," the classic 2006 International Journal of Psychoanalysis article on child abuse, and author of many other articles in professional journals. This is his second novel.